HOMELAND

Barbara Kingsolver was trained as a biologist before becoming a writer. Her books include poetry, non-fiction and three award-winning novels. She lives with her husband and daughter in southern Arizona and in the mountains of southern Appalachia.

"Kingsolver's humanity sounds the clearest note . . . telling us about characters in the middle of their days, who live as we really do, from one small incident of awareness to the next."
—*Los Angeles Times*

"Kingsolver understands in an uncanny way the significance of the ordinary, the fleeting moment that may become lost or become catharsis. She writes with refreshing clarity, humor and honesty." —*Detroit Free Press*

"Kingsolver's voice has remarkable range. . . . Her stories are sharply defined and deftly constructed." —*Kirkus Reviews*

"Delightful." —*New York Woman*

"Every [story] supports Kingsolver's newly won reputation. . . . Her perceptions are touching, her phrases felicitous, her characters memorable." —*Arizona Daily Star*

"Kingsolver's voice is sure and her narrative skill accomplished. Highly recommended." —*Library Journal*

"These 12 beautifully imagined stories are funny, flip, sagacious . . . [and] carry all the pain and surprise of real life."
—*7 Days*

by the same author

fiction

HIGH TIDE IN TUCSON

PIGS IN HEAVEN

ANIMAL DREAMS

THE BEAN TREES

poetry

ANOTHER AMERICA

non-fiction

HOLDING THE LINE:

WOMEN IN THE GREAT ARIZONA MINE STRIKE OF 1983

BARBARA KINGSOLVER

Homeland

and other stories

faber and faber

LONDON · BOSTON

First published in the USA in 1989
by Harper & Row, Publishers
This paperback edition published in Great Britain in 1996
Faber and Faber Limited
3 Queen Square London WC1N 3AU

Printed and bound in Great Britain by
Mackays of Chatham PLC, Chatham, Kent

Some of the stories in this collection first appeared in other publications, as follows: 'Blueprints', under a different title, in *Mademoiselle*; 'Quality Time' in *Redbook*; 'Bereaved Apartments' in *Tucson Guide Quarterly*; 'Rose-Johnny' in *The Virginia Quarterly Review* and *New Stories From the South: The Year's Best, 1988*; 'Why I Am a Danger to the Public', in somewhat different form, in *New Times*

A CIP record for this book is available from the British Library

ISBN 0–571–17957–6

2 4 6 8 10 9 7 5 3 1

for my family

CONTENTS

HOMELAND

I

My great-grandmother belonged to the Bird Clan. Hers was one of the fugitive bands of Cherokee who resisted capture in the year that General Winfield Scott was in charge of prodding the forest people from their beds and removing them westward. Those few who escaped his notice moved like wildcat families through the Carolina mountains, leaving the ferns unbroken where they passed, eating wild grapes and chestnuts, drinking when they found streams. The ones who could not travel, the aged and the infirm and the very young, were hidden in deep cane thickets where they would remain undiscovered until they were bones. When the people's hearts could not bear any more, they laid their deerskin packs on the ground and settled again.

General Scott had moved on to other endeavors by this time, and he allowed them to thrive or perish as they would. They built clay houses with thin, bent poles for spines, and in autumn they went down to the streams where the sycamore trees had let their year's work fall, the water steeped brown as leaf tea, and the people cleansed themselves of the sins of the scattered-bone time. They called their refugee years The Time When We Were Not, and they were forgiven, because they had carried the truth of themselves in a sheltered place inside the flesh, exactly the way a fruit that has gone soft still carries inside itself the clean, hard stone of its future.

II

My name is Gloria St. Clair, but like most people I've been called many things. My maiden name was Murray. My grown children have at one time or another hailed me by nearly anything pronounceable. When I was a child myself, my great-grandmother called me by the odd name of Waterbug. I asked her many times why this was, until she said once, to quiet me, "I'll tell you that story."

We were on the front-porch swing, in summer, in darkness. I waited while she drew tobacco smoke in and out of her mouth, but she said nothing. "Well," I said.

Moonlight caught the fronts of her steel-framed spectacles and she looked at me from her invisible place in the dark. "I said I'd tell you that story. I didn't say I would tell it right now."

We lived in Morning Glory, a coal town hacked with sharp blades out of a forest that threatened always to take it back. The hickories encroached on the town, springing up unbidden in the middle of dog pens and front yards and the cemetery. The creeping vines for which the town was named drew themselves along wire fences and up the sides of houses with the persistence of the displaced. I have heard it said that if a man stood still in Morning Glory, he would be tied down by vines and not found until first frost. Even the earth underneath us sometimes moved to repossess its losses: the long, deep shafts that men opened to rob the coal veins would close themselves up again, as quietly as flesh wounds.

My great-grandmother lived with us for her last two

years. When she came to us we were instructed to call her Great Grandmother, but that proved impossible and so we called her Great Mam. My knowledge of her life follows an oddly obscured pattern, like a mountain road where much of the scenery is blocked by high laurel bushes, not because they were planted there, but because no one thought to cut them down.

I know that her maternal lineage was distinguished. Her mother's mother's father was said to have gone to England, where he dined with King George and contracted smallpox. When he returned home his family plunged him into an icy stream, which was the curative custom, and he died. Also, her mother was one of the Bird Clan's Beloved Women. When I asked what made her a Beloved Woman, Great Mam said that it was because she kept track of things.

But of Great Mam's own life, before she came to us, I know only a little. She rarely spoke of personal things, favoring instead the legendary and the historic, and so what I did discover came from my mother, who exercised over all matters a form of reverse censorship: she spoke loudly and often of events of which she disapproved, and rarely of those that might have been ordinary or redemptive. She told us, for instance, that Great-Grandfather Murray brought Great Mam from her tribal home in the Hiwassee Valley to live in Kentucky, without Christian sanction, as his common-law wife. According to Mother, he accomplished all of this on a stolen horse. From that time forward Great Mam went by the name of Ruth.

It was my mother's opinion that Great-Grandfather Murray was unfit for respectable work. He died after taking up the honest vocation of coal mining, which also killed their four sons, all on the same day, in a collapsed shaft. Their daughter perished of fever after producing a single illegitimate boy, who turned out to be my father, John Murray. Great Mam was thus returned to refugee ways, raising her grandson alone in hard circumstances, moving from place to place where she could find the odd bit of work. She was quite remarkably old when she came to us.

I know, also, that her true name was Green Leaf, although there is no earthly record of this. The gravesite is marked Ruth. Mother felt we ought to bury her under her Christian name in the hope that God in His infinite mercy would forget about the heathen marriage and stolen horses and call her home. It is likely, however, that He might have passed over the headstone altogether in his search for her, since virtually all the information written there is counterfeit. We even had to invent a date and year of birth for her since these things were unknown. This, especially, was unthinkable to my brothers and me. But we were children, of course, and believed our own birthdays began and ended the calendar.

To look at her, you would not have thought her an Indian. She wore blue and lavender flowered dresses with hand-tatted collars, and brown lace-up shoes with sturdy high heels, and she smoked a regular pipe. She was tall, with bowed calves and a faintly bent-forward posture, spine straight and elbows out and palms forward, giving the impression that she was at any moment prepared to stoop and lift a burden of great bulk or weight. She spoke with a soft hill accent, and spoke properly. My great-grandfather had been an educated man, more prone in his lifetime to errors of judgment than errors of grammar.

Great Mam smoked her pipe mainly in the evenings, and always on the front porch. For a time I believed this was because my mother so vigorously objected to the smell, but Great Mam told me otherwise. A pipe had to be smoked outdoors, she said, where the smoke could return to the Beloved Old Father who gave us tobacco. When I asked her what she meant, she said she meant nothing special at all. It was just the simplest thing, like a bread-and-butter note you send to an aunt after she has fed you a meal.

I often sat with Great Mam in the evenings on our porch swing, which was suspended by four thin, painted chains that squeaked. The air at night smelled of oil and dust, and faintly of livestock, for the man at the end of our lane kept hogs. Great Mam would strike a match and suck the flame into her pipe, lighting her creased face in brief orange bursts.

"The small people are not very bright tonight," she would say, meaning the stars. She held surprising convictions, such as that in the daytime the small people walked among us. I could not begin to picture it.

"You mean down here in the world, or do you mean right here in Morning Glory?" I asked repeatedly. "Would they walk along with Jack and Nathan and me to school?"

She nodded. "They would."

"But why would they come *here?*" I asked.

"Well, why wouldn't they?" she said.

I thought about this for a while, entirely unconvinced.

"You don't ever have to be lonesome," she said. "That's one thing you never need be."

"But mightn't I step on one of them, if it got in my way and I didn't see it?"

Great Mam said, "No. They aren't that small."

She had particular names for many things, including the months. February she called "Hungry Month." She spoke of certain animals as if they were relatives our parents had neglected to tell us about. The cowering white dog that begged at our kitchen door she called "the sad little cousin." If she felt like it, on these evenings, she would tell me stories about the animals, their personalities and kindnesses and trickery, and the permanent physical markings they invariably earned by doing something they ought not to have done. "Remember that story," she often commanded at the end, and I would be stunned with guilt because my mind had wandered onto crickets and pencil erasers and Black Beauty.

"I might not remember," I told her. "It's too hard."

Great Mam allowed that I might *think* I had forgotten. "But you haven't. You'll keep it stored away," she said. "If it's important, your heart remembers."

I had known that hearts could break and sometimes even be attacked, with disastrous result, but I had not heard of hearts remembering. I was eleven years old. I did not trust any of my internal parts with the capacity of memory.

When the seasons changed, it never occurred to us to think to ourselves, "This will be Great Mam's last spring. Her last June apples. Her last fresh roasting ears from the garden." She was like an old pine, whose accumulated years cause one to ponder how long it has stood, not how soon it will fall. Of all of us, I think Papa was the only one who believed she could die. He planned the trip to Tennessee. We children simply thought it was a great lark.

This was in June, following a bad spring during which the whole southern spine of the Appalachians had broken out in a rash of wildcat strikes. Papa was back to work at last, no longer home taking up kitchen-table space, but still Mother complained of having to make soups of neckbones and cut our school shoes open to bare our too-long toes to summer's dust, for the whole darn town to see. Papa pointed out that the whole darn town had been on the picket lines, and wouldn't pass judgment on the Murray kids if they ran their bare bottoms down Main Street. And what's more, he said, it wasn't his fault if John L. Lewis had sold him down the river.

My brothers and I thrilled to imagine ourselves racing naked past the Post Office and the women shopping at Herman Ritchie's Market, but we did not laugh out loud. We didn't know exactly who Mr. John L. Lewis was, or what river Papa meant, but we knew not to expect much. The last thing we expected was a trip.

My brother Jack, because of his nature and superior age, was suspicious from the outset. While Papa explained his plan, Jack made a point of pushing lima beans around his plate in single file to illustrate his boredom. It was 1955. Patti Page and Elvis were on the radio and high school boys were fighting their mothers over ducktails. Jack had a year to go before high school, but already the future was plainly evident.

He asked where in Tennessee we would be going, if we did go. The three of us had not seen the far side of a county line.

"The Hiwassee Valley, where Great Mam was born," Papa said.

My brother Nathan grew interested when Jack laid down his fork. Nathan was only eight, but he watched grownups. If there were no men around, he watched Jack.

"Eat your beans, Jack," Mother said. "I didn't put up these limas last fall so you could torment them."

Jack stated, "I'm not eating no beans with guts in them."

Mother took a swat at Jack's arm. "Young man, you watch your mouth. That's the insides of a hog, and a hog's a perfectly respectable animal to eat." Nathan was making noises with his throat. I tried not to make any face one way or the other.

Great Mam told Mother it would have been enough just to have the limas, without the meat. "A person can live on green corn and beans, Florence Ann," she said. "There's no shame in vegetables."

We knew what would happen next, and watched with interest. "If I have to go out myself and throw a rock at a songbird," Mother said, having deepened to the color of beetroot, "nobody is going to say this family goes without meat!"

Mother was a tiny woman who wore stockings and shirtwaists even to hoe the garden. She had yellow hair pinned in a tight bun, with curly bangs in front. We waited with our chins cupped in our palms for Papa's opinion of her plan to make a soup of Robin Redbreast, but he got up from the table and rummaged in the bureau drawer for the gas-station map. Great Mam ate her beans in a careful way, as though each one had its own private importance.

"Are we going to see Injuns?" Nathan asked, but no one answered. Mother began making a great deal of noise clearing up the dishes. We could hear her out in the kitchen, scrubbing.

Papa unfolded the Texaco map on the table and found where Tennessee and North Carolina and Georgia came together in three different pastel colors. Great Mam looked down at the colored lines and squinted, holding the sides of her glasses. "Is this the Hiwassee River?" she wanted to know.

"No, now those lines are highways," he said. "Red is interstate. Blue is river."

"Well, what's this?"

He looked. "That's the state line."

"Now why would they put that on the map? You can't see it."

Papa flattened the creases of the map with his broad hands, which were crisscrossed with fine black lines of coal dust, like a map themselves, no matter how clean. "The Hiwassee Valley's got a town in it now, it says 'Cherokee.' Right here."

"Well, those lines make my eyes smart," Great Mam said. "I'm not going to look anymore."

The boys started to snicker, but Papa gave us a look that said he meant business and sent us off to bed before it went any farther.

"Great Mam's blind as a post hole," Jack said once we were in bed. "She don't know a road from a river."

"She don't know beans from taters," said Nathan.

"You boys hush up, I'm tired," I said. Jack and Nathan slept lengthwise in the bed, and I slept across the top with my own blanket.

"Here's Great Mam," Nathan said. He sucked in his cheeks and crossed his eyes and keeled over backward, bouncing us all on the bedsprings. Jack punched him in the ribs, and Nathan started to cry louder than he had to. I got up and sat by the bedroom door hugging my knees, listening to Papa and Mother. I could hear them in the kitchen.

"As if I hadn't put up with enough, John. It's not enough that Murrays have populated God's earth without the benefit of marriage," Mother said. This was her usual starting point. She was legally married to my father in a Baptist Church, a fact she could work into any conversation.

"Well, I don't see why," she said, "if we never had the money to take the kids anyplace before."

Papa's voice was quieter, and I couldn't hear his answers.

"Was this her idea, John, or yours?"

When Nathan and Jack were asleep I went to the window and slipped over the sill. My feet landed where they always did, in the cool mud of Mother's gladiolus patch alongside the house. Great Mam did not believe in flower patches. Why take a hoe and kill all the growing things in a piece of ground, and then plant others that have been uprooted from somewhere else? This was what she asked me. She thought Mother spent a fearful amount of time moving things needlessly from one place to another.

"I see you, Waterbug," said Great Mam in the darkness, though what she probably meant was that she heard me. All I could see was the glow of her pipe bowl moving above the porch swing.

"Tell me the waterbug story tonight," I said, settling onto the swing. The fireflies were blinking on and off in the black air above the front yard.

"No, I won't," she said. The orange glow moved to her

lap, and faded from bright to dim. "I'll tell you another time."

The swing squeaked its sad song, and I thought about Tennessee. It had never occurred to me that the place where Great Mam had been a child was still on this earth. "Why'd you go away from home?" I asked her.

"You have to marry outside your clan," she said. "That's law. And all the people we knew were Bird Clan. All the others were gone. So when Stewart Murray came and made baby eyes at me, I had to go with him." She laughed. "I liked his horse."

I imagined the two of them on a frisking, strong horse, crossing the mountains to Kentucky. Great Mam with black hair. "Weren't you afraid to go?" I asked.

"Oh, yes I was. The canebrakes were high as a house. I was afraid we'd get lost."

We were to leave on Saturday after Papa got off work. He worked days then, after many graveyard-shift years during which we rarely saw him except asleep, snoring and waking throughout the afternoon, with Mother forever forced to shush us; it was too easy to forget someone was trying to sleep in daylight. My father was a soft-spoken man who sometimes drank but was never mean. He had thick black hair, no beard stubble at all nor hair on his chest, and a nose he called his Cherokee nose. Mother said she thanked the Lord that at least He had seen fit not to put that nose on her children. She also claimed he wore his hair long to flout her, although it wasn't truly long, in our opinion. His nickname in the mine was "Indian John."

There wasn't much to get ready for the trip. All we had to do in the morning was wait for afternoon. Mother was in the house scrubbing so it would be clean when we came back. The primary business of Mother's life was scrubbing things, and she herself looked scrubbed. Her skin was the color of a clean boiled potato. We didn't get in her way.

My brothers were playing a ferocious game of cowboys and Indians in the backyard, but I soon defected to my own amusements along the yard's weedy borders, picking morning glories, pretending to be a June bride. I grew tired of trying to weave the flowers into my coarse hair and decided to give them to Great Mam. I went around to the front and came up the three porch steps in one jump, just exactly the way Mother said a lady wouldn't do.

"Surprise," I announced. "These are for you." The flowers were already wilting in my hand.

"You shouldn't have picked those," she said.

"They were a present." I sat down, feeling stung.

"Those are not mine to have and not yours to pick," she said, looking at me, not with anger but with intensity. Her brown pupils were as dark as two pits in the earth. "A flower is alive, just as much as you are. A flower is your cousin. Didn't you know that?"

I said, No ma'am, that I didn't.

"Well, I'm telling you now, so you will know. Sometimes a person has got to take a life, like a chicken's or a hog's when you need it. If you're hungry, then they're happy to give their flesh up to you because they're your relatives. But nobody is so hungry they need to kill a flower."

I said nothing.

"They ought to be left where they stand, Waterbug. You need to leave them for the small people to see. When they die they'll fall where they are, and make a seed for next year."

"Nobody cared about these," I contended. "They weren't but just weeds."

"It doesn't matter what they were or were not. It's a bad thing to take for yourself something beautiful that belongs to everybody. Do you understand? To take it is a sin."

I didn't, and I did. I could sense something of wasted life in the sticky leaves, translucent with death, and the purple flowers turning wrinkled and limp. I'd once brought home a balloon from a Ritchie child's birthday party, and it had shriveled and shrunk with just such a slow blue agony.

"I'm sorry," I said.

"It's all right." She patted my hands. "Just throw them over the porch rail there, give them back to the ground. The small people will come and take them back."

I threw the flowers over the railing in a clump, and came back, trying to rub the purple and green juices off my hands onto my dress. In my mother's eyes, this would have been the first sin of my afternoon. I understood the difference between Great Mam's rules and the Sunday-school variety, and that you could read Mother's Bible forward and backward and never find where it said it's a sin to pick flowers because they are our cousins.

"I'll try to remember," I said.

"I want you to," said Great Mam. "I want you to tell your children."

"I'm not going to have any children," I said. "No boy's going to marry me. I'm too tall. I've got knob knees."

"Don't ever say you hate what you are." She tucked a loose sheaf of black hair behind my ear. "It's an unkindness to those that made you. That's like a red flower saying it's too red, do you see what I mean?"

"I guess," I said.

"You will have children. And you'll remember about the flowers," she said, and I felt the weight of these promises fall like a deerskin pack between my shoulder blades.

By four o'clock we were waiting so hard we heard the truck crackle up the gravel road. Papa's truck was a rust-colored Ford with complicated cracks hanging like spiderwebs in the corners of the windshield. He jumped out with his long, blue-jean strides and patted the round front fender.

"Old Paint's had her oats," he said. "She's raring to go." This was a game he played with Great Mam. Sometimes she would say, "John Murray, you couldn't ride a mule with a saddle on it," and she'd laugh, and we would for a moment see the woman who raised Papa. Her bewilderment and pleasure, to have ended up with this broad-shouldered boy.

Today she said nothing, and Papa went in for Mother. There was only room for three in the cab, so Jack and Nathan and I climbed into the back with the old quilt Mother gave us and a tarpaulin in case of rain.

"What's she waiting for, her own funeral?" Jack asked me.

I looked at Great Mam, sitting still on the porch like a funny old doll. The whole house was crooked, the stoop sagged almost to the ground, and there sat Great Mam as straight as a schoolteacher's ruler. Seeing her there, I fiercely wished to defend my feeling that I knew her better than others did.

"She doesn't want to go," I said. I knew as soon as I'd spoken that it was the absolute truth.

"That's stupid. She's the whole reason we're going. Why wouldn't she want to go see her people?"

"I don't know, Jack," I said.

Papa and Mother eventually came out of the house, Papa in a clean shirt already darkening under the arms, and Mother with her Sunday purse, the scuff marks freshly covered with white shoe polish. She came down the front steps in the bent-over way she walked when she wore high heels. Papa put his hand under Great Mam's elbow and she silently climbed into the cab.

When he came around to the other side I asked him, "Are you sure Great Mam wants to go?"

"Sure she does," he said. "She wants to see the place where she grew up. Like what Morning Glory is to you."

"When I grow up I'm not never coming back to Morning Glory," Jack said.

"Me neither." Nathan spat over the side of the truck, the way he'd seen men do.

"Don't spit, Nathan," Papa said.

"Shut up," Nathan said, after Papa had gotten in the truck and shut the door.

The houses we passed had peeled paint and slumped porches like our own, and they all wore coats of morning-glory vines, deliciously textured and fat as fur coats. We pointed out to each other the company men's houses, which had bright white paint and were known to have indoor bathrooms. The deep ditches along the road, filled with blackberry brambles and early goldenrod, ran past us like rivers. On our walks to school we put these ditches to daily use practicing Duck and Cover, which was what our teachers felt we ought to do when the Communists dropped the H-bomb.

"We'll see Indians in Tennessee," Jack said. I knew we would. Great Mam had told me how it was.

"Great Mam don't look like an Indian," Nathan said.

"Shut up, Nathan," Jack said. "How do you know what an Indian looks like? You ever seen one?"

"She does so look like an Indian," I informed my brothers. "She is one."

According to Papa we all looked like little Indians, I especially. Mother hounded me continually to stay out of the sun, but by each summer's end I was so dark-skinned my schoolmates teased me, saying I ought to be sent over to the Negro school.

"Are we going to be Indians when we grow up?" Nathan asked.

"No, stupid," said Jack. "We'll just be the same as we are now."

We soon ran out of anything productive to do. We played White Horse Zit many times over, until Nathan won, and we tried to play Alphabet but there weren't enough signs. The only public evidence of literacy in that part of the country was the Beech Nut Tobacco signs on barn roofs, and every so often, nailed to a tree trunk, a clapboard on which someone had painted "PREPARE TO MEET GOD."

Papa's old truck didn't go as fast as other cars. Jack and Nathan slapped the fenders like jockeys as we were passed on the uphill slopes, but their coaxing amounted to nought. By the time we went over Jellico Mountain, it was dark.

An enormous amount of sky glittered down at us on the mountain pass, and even though it was June we were cold. Nathan had taken the quilt for himself and gone to sleep. Jack said he ought to punch him one to teach him to be nice, but truthfully, nothing in this world could have taught Nathan to share. Jack and I huddled together under the tarp, which stank of coal oil, and sat against the back of the cab where the engine rendered up through the truck's metal body a faint warmth.

"Jack?" I said.

"What."

"Do you reckon Great Mam's asleep?"

He turned around and cupped his hands to see into the cab. "Nope," he said. "She's sitting up there in between 'em, stiff as a broom handle."

"I'm worried about her," I said.

"Why? If we were home she'd be sitting up just the same, only out front on the porch."

"I know."

"Glorie, you know what?" he asked me.

"What?"

A trailer truck loomed up behind us, decked with rows

of red and amber lights like a Christmas tree. We could see the driver inside the cab. A faint blue light on his face made him seem ghostly and entirely alone. He passed us by, staring ahead, as though only he were real on this cold night and we were among all the many things that were not. I shivered, and felt an identical chill run across Jack's shoulders.

"What?" I asked again.

"What, what?"

"You were going to tell me something."

"Oh. I forgot what it was."

"Great Mam says the way to remember something you forgot is to turn your back on it. Say, 'The small people came dancing. They ran through the woods today.' Talk about what they did, and then whatever it was you forgot, they'll bring it back to you."

"That's dumb," Jack said. "That's Great Mam's hobbledy-gobbledy."

For a while we played See Who Can Go to Sleep First, which we knew to be a game that can't consciously be won. He never remembered what he'd meant to say.

When Papa woke us the next morning we were at a truck stop in Knoxville. He took a nap in the truck with his boots sticking out the door while the rest of us went in for breakfast. Inside the restaurant was a long glass counter containing packs of Kools and Mars Bars lined up on cotton batting, objects of great value to be protected from dust and children. The waitress who brought us our eggs had a red wig perched like a bird on her head, and red eyebrows painted on over the real ones.

When it was time to get back in the truck we dragged and pulled on Mother's tired, bread-dough arms, like little babies, asking her how much farther.

"Oh, it's not far. I expect we'll be in Cherokee by lunchtime," she said, but her mouth was set and we knew she was as tired of this trip as any of us.

It was high noon before we saw a sign that indicated we were approaching Cherokee. Jack pummeled the cab window with his fists to make sure they all saw it, but Papa and Mother were absorbed in some kind of argument. There were more signs after that, with pictures of cartoon Indian boys urging us to buy souvenirs or stay in so-and-so's motor lodge. The signs were shaped like log cabins and teepees. Then we saw a real teepee. It was made of aluminum and taller than a house. Inside, it was a souvenir store.

We drove around the streets of Cherokee and saw that the town was all the same, as single-minded in its offerings as a corn patch or an orchard, so that it made no difference where we stopped. We parked in front of Sitting Bull's Genuine Indian Made Souvenirs, and Mother crossed the street to get groceries for our lunch. I had a sense of something gone badly wrong, like a lie told in my past and then forgotten, and now about to catch up with me.

A man in a feather war bonnet danced across from us in the parking lot. His outfit was bright orange, with white fringe trembling along the seams of the pants and sleeves, and a woman in the same clothes sat cross-legged on the pavement playing a tom-tom while he danced. People with cameras gathered and side-stepped around one another to snap their shots. The woman told them that she and her husband Chief Many Feathers were genuine Cherokees, and that this was their welcoming dance. Papa sat with his hands frozen on the steering wheel for a very long time. Then suddenly, without saying anything, he got out of the truck and took Jack and Nathan and me into Sitting Bull's. Nathan wanted a tomahawk.

The store was full of items crowded on shelves, so bright-colored it hurt my eyes to look at them all. I lagged behind the boys. There were some Indian dolls with real feathers on them, red and green, and I would like to have stroked the soft feathers but the dolls were wrapped in cellophane. Among all those bright things, I grew fearfully uncertain about what I ought to want. I went back out to the truck and found Great Mam still sitting in the cab.

"Don't you want to get out?" I asked.

The man in the parking lot was dancing again, and she was watching. "I don't know what they think they're doing. Cherokee don't wear feather bonnets like that," she said.

They looked like Indians to me. I couldn't imagine Indians without feathers. I climbed up onto the seat and closed the door and we sat for a while. I felt a great sadness and embarrassment, as though it were I who had forced her to come here, and I tried to cover it up by pretending to be foolishly cheerful.

"Where's the pole houses, where everybody lives, I wonder," I said. "Do you think maybe they're out of town a ways?"

She didn't answer. Chief Many Feathers hopped around his circle, forward on one leg and backward on the other. Then the dance was over. The woman beating the tom-tom turned it upside down and passed it around for money.

"I guess things have changed pretty much since you moved away, huh, Great Mam?" I asked.

She said, "I've never been here before."

Mother made bologna sandwiches and we ate lunch in a place called Cherokee Park. It was a shaded spot along the river, where the dry banks were worn bald of their grass. Sycamore trees grew at the water's edge, with colorful, waterlogged trash floating in circles in the eddies around their roots. The park's principal attraction was an old buffalo in a pen, identified by a sign as the Last Remaining Buffalo East of the Mississippi. I pitied the beast, thinking it must be lonely without a buffalo wife or buffalo husband, whichever it needed. One of its eyes was put out.

I tried to feed it some dead grass through the cage, while Nathan pelted it with gravel. He said he wanted to see it get mad and charge the fence down, but naturally it did not do that. It simply stood and stared and blinked with its one good eye, and flicked its tail. There were flies all over it, and shiny bald patches on its back, which Papa said were caused by the mange. Mother said we'd better get away from it or we would have the mange too. Great Mam sat at the picnic table with her shoes together, and looked at her sandwich.

We had to go back that same night. It seemed an impossible thing, to come such a distance only to turn right around, but Mother reminded us all that Papa had laid off from work without pay. Where money was concerned we did not argue. The trip home was quiet except for Nathan, who pretended at great length to scalp me with his tomahawk, until the rubber head came loose from its painted stick and fell with a clunk.

III

Before there was a world, there was only the sea, and the high, bright sky arched above it like an overturned bowl.

For as many years as anyone can imagine, the people in the stars looked down at the ocean's glittering face without giving a thought to what it was, or what might lie beneath it. They had their own concerns. But as more time passed, as is natural, they began to grow curious. Eventually it was the waterbug who volunteered to go exploring. She flew down and landed on top of the water, which was beautiful, but not firm as it had appeared. She skated in every direction but could not find a place to stop and rest, so she dived underneath.

She was gone for days and the star people thought she must have drowned, but she hadn't. When she joyfully broke the surface again she had the answer: on the bottom of the sea, there was mud. She had brought a piece of it back with her, and she held up her sodden bit of proof to the bright light.

There, before the crowd of skeptical star eyes, the ball of mud began to grow, and dry up, and grow some more, and out of it came all the voices and life that now dwell on this island that is the earth. The star people fastened it to the sky with four long grape vines so it wouldn't be lost again.

"In school," I told Great Mam, "they said the world's round."

"I didn't say it wasn't round," she said. "It's whatever shape they say it is. But that's how it started. Remember that."

These last words terrified me, always, with their impossible weight. I have had dreams of trying to hold a mountain of water in my arms. "What if I forget?" I asked.

"We already talked about that. I told you how to remember."

"Well, all right," I said. "But if that's how the world started, then what about Adam and Eve?"

She thought about that. "They were the waterbug's children," she said. "Adam and Eve, and the others."

"But they started all the trouble," I pointed out. "Adam and Eve started sin."

"Sometimes that happens. Children can be your heartache. But that doesn't matter, you have to go on and have them," she said. "It works out."

IV

Morning Glory looked no different after we had seen the world and returned to it. Summer settled in, with heat in the air and coal dust thick on the vines. Nearly every night I slipped out and sat with Great Mam where there was the tangible hope of a cool breeze. I felt pleased to be up while my brothers breathed and tossed without consciousness on the hot mattress. During those secret hours, Great Mam and I lived in our own place, a world apart from the arguments and the tired, yellowish light bulbs burning away inside, seeping faintly out the windows, getting used up. Mother's voice in the kitchen was as distant as heat lightning, and as unthreatening. But we could make out words, and I realized once, with a shock, that they were discussing Great Mam's burial.

"Well, it surely can't do her any harm once she's dead and gone, John, for heaven's sakes," Mother said.

Papa spoke more softly and we could never make out his answer.

Great Mam seemed untroubled. "In the old days," she said, "whoever spoke the quietest would win the argument."

She died in October, the Harvest Month. It was my mother who organized the burial and the Bible verses and had her say even about the name that went on the gravestone, but Great Mam secretly prevailed in the question of flowers. Very few would ever have their beauty wasted upon her grave. Only one time for the burial service, and never again after that, did Mother trouble herself to bring up flowers. It was half a dozen white gladioli cut hastily from her garden with a bread knife, and she carried them from home in a jar of water, attempting to trick them into believing they were still alive.

My father's shoes were restless in the grass and hickory saplings at the edge of the cemetery. Mother knelt down in her navy dress and nylon stockings and with her white-gloved hands thumped the flower stems impatiently against the jar bottom to get them to stand up straight. Already the petals were shriveling from thirst.

As soon as we turned our backs, the small people would come dancing and pick up the flowers. They would kick over the jar and run through the forest, swinging the hollow stems above their heads, scattering them like bones.

BLUEPRINTS

The soup bowls slam against the sink, she's being careless, and Lydia wonders how it would feel to break something important on purpose. The crockery set would qualify. It has matching parts: the bowls, a large tureen, and a ladle in the elongated shape of a water fowl, all handmade by a woman in Sacramento named Earth, who gave it to Whitman last year as a solstice present. Lydia likes the crockery well enough. That isn't the problem.

"You sleep in the bathtub," she says to Whitman. "I'm sorry the light keeps you awake. But I'm not going to do my lesson plans in the bathroom."

The bathroom is the only part of the cabin that is actually a separate room, with a door. Lydia is standing at the kitchen sink and Whitman is still at the dining table and they are not very far apart at all.

"Last night you were up till eleven forty-five," he says.

"So sleep with the blanket over your head," she tells him in a reasonable voice. "For God's sake, Whitman, give me a break. It's not like you have to get up early to milk cows."

"I don't have to get up for any reason, you mean. And you do."

"That's not what I mean." She's about to say, "I respect

your work," but instead decides she will just stop talking. Men do it all the time, she reasons, and men run the world.

What they told themselves last summer, when they moved from Sacramento to Blind Gap, was that the cabin would be romantic. Her mother pointed out that it's hard moving from a larger to a smaller place, that she and Hank did it once early in their marriage and the storage-space problem drove her insane. Lydia smiles into the dishwater, imagining her mother wild-haired and bug-eyed, stalking the house for a place to stash the punch bowl. Can this marriage be saved? Why, yes! By storage space. It's true, the Sacramento house had had plenty of it, closets gone to waste in fact, and bedrooms enough for an Indian tribe. But Whitman and Lydia had been living under the same roof for nine years and had reason to believe they were infinitely compatible. They figured they'd make it without closets.

They aren't making it, though. The couple they were then seems impossible to Lydia now, a sort of hippie Barbie and Ken sharing a life of household chores in that big, run-down house. Her memories from Sacramento smell like salt-rising bread—they used to do such wholesome, complicated cooking: Whitman with his sleeves rolled up, gregarious in a way that never came easily to Lydia, kneading dough and giving his kindest advice on copper plumbing and boyfriend problems to the people who gravitated endlessly to their kitchen. But when the Whitman-doll was removed from that warm, crowded place he'd hardened like a rock. Lydia would give her teeth right now to know why. She dries her hands and spreads papers over the table to prepare her lessons for the next day. Whitman hasn't surrendered his corner of the table. He leans on his elbows and works a spoon in his hands as if preparing to bend it double, and it occurs to Lydia that she can't predict whether or not he'll destroy the spoon. Certainly he is capable of it. Whitman is large and bearded and given to lumberjack flannel, and people often say of him that he has capable hands. The kitchen table is one of his pieces. He builds furniture without the use of power tools, using wooden pegs instead of nails. People in Sacramento were crazy about this furniture, and Lydia expected it would sell well up here too, but she was wrong. In Blind Gap, people's tastes run more along the lines of velveteen and easy-care Formica. They drive the hour to Sacramento to make their purchases in places like the Bargain Heaven Direct-2-U Warehouse. Whitman has to pile his pieces onto the truck and make the same drive, to show them on consignment in the Country Home Gallery.

David, the retriever, is pacing between the kitchen and bedroom areas. The click of his toenails on the wood floor is interrupted when he crosses the braided rug.

"Pantry," Whitman says, and David flops down in the corner behind the wood stove, sounding like a bag of elbows hitting the floor. David responds to eleven different commands regarding places to lie down. The house in Sacramento had eleven usable rooms, and the dog would go to any one of them on command. He was nervous after the move, circling and sniffing the walls, until Whitman and Lydia reassigned the names to eleven different areas of the new place. Now he's happy. Dogs like to know exactly what's expected of them.

Whitman is spinning the spoon on the table, some unconscious derivative of Spin the Bottle maybe. Or just annoyance. "We could just not talk to each other, that's always a good idea," says Lydia. "I heard about these two guys who lived in the same cabin and didn't talk to each other for fifty years. They painted a line down the middle."

"It was sixty-three years," he says. "You got that out of the *Guinness Book of Records*. The guys were brothers."

Whitman has an astonishing memory for details. Often he will draw out the plans for something he's building and then complete the whole piece without referring again to the blueprints. This talent once made Lydia go weak with admiration, but at this moment it doesn't. She looks up from her book, called *Hands-On Learning*, which is about teaching science to kids.

"Sometimes I think you try not to hear what I'm saying."

Whitman gets up and goes outside, leaving the spoon spinning on the table. When it stops, it's pointing at Lydia.

The best part of her day is the walk home from school. From Blind Gap Junior High she takes a dirt road that passes through town, winds through a tunnel of hemlocks, and then follows Blind Creek up the mountain to their six acres. She could have used this in Sacramento—a time to clear her mind of the day's frustrations.

Even at the stoplight, the dead center of Blind Gap, Lydia can hear birds. She inhales deeply. A daily hike like this would be a good tonic for some of her students too, most of whom are obliged to spend a couple of hours a day behaving like maniacs on the school bus. The area served by the school is large; there are probably no more than a dozen kids of junior-high age in Blind Gap itself. The town's main claim to fame is a Shell station and a grocery store with a front porch.

She leaves town and walks through the hemlock forest, content to be among the mosses and beetles. "Bugs are our friends," Whitman says, mocking her, but Lydia feels this friendship in a more serious way than he imagines. The bugs, and the plants too, are all related to her in a complicated family tree that Lydia can describe in convincing detail. Back in college her friends were very concerned about the Existential Dilemma, and in the cafeteria would demand while forking up potatoes and peas, "Why are we here?" Lydia would say, "Because we're adapted for survival." The way she explained it, whatever ancestors were more dexterous and quick would live longer and reproduce more. Each generation got to be more like us, until here we were. "It's still going on," she would point out. "We're not the end of the line, you know." It all started with the blue-green algae, and if humans blew themselves off the map it would start all over again. Blue-green algae had been found growing on the inside of the nuclear reactors at San Onofre.

When she told this to her ninth grade class they just stared at her. None of them had ever been to San Onofre. They were waiting for the part about apes turning into men, so that according to their parents' instructions they could stop listening. Lydia thinks this is a shame. Evolution is just a way of making sense of the world, which is something she figures most ninth graders could use.

If they tell her to stop teaching evolution, she decides, she'll just call it something else. No one will be the wiser if she leaves out the part about ape-to-man. They couldn't seem to understand, ape-to-man was the least important part.

On her way up the last hill Lydia stops at Verna Delmar's. Verna is a sturdy woman of indeterminate age who owns the farm next to theirs. She has chickens and gives Lydia a good price on eggs because, she says, she had this same arrangement with the couple who owned the six-acre place before Whitman and Lydia bought it. Lydia is curious about how those people got along in the little cabin, and is tempted to ask, but doesn't, because she's afraid of hearing something akin to a ghost story.

Today Verna details a problem she's having with chicken mites, and then asks after Lydia's garden and her husband's furniture business. Lydia tactfully doesn't correct Verna, but expects that eventually her neighbor will find out they aren't husband and wife. She has perpetuated this deception since their first conversation, when Verna asked how long they'd been married and Lydia, fearing the disapproval of her first acquaintance in Blind Gap, didn't lie outright but said they had "been together" for almost ten years, which was true. "We both turned thirty this year," she said.

"Lots of kids been married and divorced two or three times before they're your age," Verna had said, and Lydia agreed that ten years was longer than most people they knew. In Sacramento their friends referred to Lydia and Whitman as an institution. Now the word makes Lydia think of a many-windowed building with deranged faces pressing at the glass.

Whitman is building a bridge over Blind Creek, and she stops to watch him work. Their house is near the road, but the creek bank cuts steeply down from the shoulder, cutting off access to all the land on the left side of the road. Verna's farm has a front entrance bridge, but theirs doesn't; they have to continue on for a quarter mile to where the road passes over an old concrete bridge, then circle back by way of the orchard road at the back of their property. The new bridge will create a front entrance to their farm. Whitman is absorbed and doesn't see her. The design of the bridge is unusual, incorporating a big old sycamore. Lydia likes the tree, with its knotty white roots clutching at the creek boulders like giant, arthritic hands. He's left a square hole in the bridge for the tree trunk to pass through, with just enough room on the side for the truck to get by. She watches his hands and arms and feels he's someone she's never talked with or made love to. She has no idea how this happened.

Whitman looks up. Possibly he did know she was watching. "Your friend Miss Busybody Delmar was up here earlier," he says.

"I know, she mentioned it. She doesn't think it's a good idea to build the bridge that way. She says that old tree is due to come down."

Whitman drives a nail too close to the end of a board and curses when it splits. Unlike his furniture construction, this project requires nails and a gasoline-powered table saw.

"You tell her I admire her expertise in bridge building," he says. "Tell her I'd appreciate it if she would come up here and tell me how to build an end table."

Lydia can feel her bones dissolving, a skeleton soaking in acid. "It's a real nice bridge, Whitman. I like the design."

For the rest of the afternoon she tries to work on lesson plans so she won't keep him up late, but she can't concentrate on the families of the animal kingdom. She finishes the dishes she abandoned the night before. Whitman has gradually stopped doing housework, and Lydia has lost the energy to complain about it. For some reason she thinks of Whitman's mother. Lydia never met her, she has been dead a long time, but she wishes she could ask her what kind of little boy Whitman was. She used to imagine light brown curls, a woman's child, but now she pictures a tight-lipped boy waiting for his mother to guess where the hurt is and kiss it away. Whitman's story on his mother is that she was mistreated by his father, a Coast Guard man who eventually stopped coming home on leave. The martyred wife, the absent husband. Lydia's own mother is alive and well but equally martyred, in her way: the overly efficient, do-it-all-and-don't-complain type. Back when things were going well, when everybody was telling Whitman how evolved he was, the cliché of their parents' lives seemed like a quaint old photograph you'd hang on the wall. Now it's not so charming. Now it looks like one of those carnival take-your-picture setups with Lydia and Whitman's faces looking out through the holes. She realizes this with a physical shock, as if she's laid hands on a badly wired appliance. This is what's happened to them. They struck out so boldly as a couple, but the minute they lost their bearings they'd homed in on terra firma. It's frightening, she thinks, how when the going gets rough you fall back on whatever awful thing you grew up with:

The mail brings in the usual odd assortment of catalogues: one with clever household items and one called "Ultimate Forester," which sells chainsaws and splitting mauls and handmade axes as expensive as diamond jewelry. Lydia hates the people who lived here before and calls them "Betty and Paul," for Betty Crocker and Paul Bunyan. There's also a catalogue for Lydia—Carolina Biological Supply—and some legal forms for Whitman. Of all things, he's changing his name: it's Walter Whitman Smith, and he's legally dropping the Walter, which he doesn't use anyway.

Lydia can't relate. People often find Bogtree—her own last name—humorous, but growing up with it has planted in her imagination a wonderful cypress tree spreading its foliage over a swamp at the dawn of the world. She believes now she got this image from a James Weldon Johnson poem containing the line "Blacker than a hundred midnights down in a cypress swamp." Lydia was the kind of child who knew "bog" meant swamp. The poem was about the creation of the earth. "I've always been a Bogtree and always will, don't blame me," she says, whenever her mother hints about Lydia and Whitman getting married. She knows, of course, that she could keep her own name, but even so, being married would sooner or later make her Mrs. Smith, she suspects.

Their old friends in Sacramento had gone through names like Kleenex. A woman she considered to be mainly Whitman's friend had christened herself Tofu, and actually named her children Maize, Amaranth, and Bean. In Lydia's opinion this was a bit much. "Aren't you kind of putting your own expectations on them?" she'd asked. "What if when they grow up they don't want to be vegetarians? What if your mother had named you Pot Roast?"

Lydia remembers this conversation, she realizes, with

unusual bitterness. Tofu had what was called an open marriage, which became so open that it more or less lost its clasp. Her husband Bernard, as far as anyone knew, was still up in Washington picking apples. One of Tofu's numerous affairs was with Whitman during their brief experiment with non-monogamy. There was much talk about the complexity of human nature and satisfying different needs, but in the end Lydia sat on the bed and downed nearly a bottle of peppermint schnapps, and when Whitman came home she met him at the door demanding to know how he could have sex with a person named after a vegetable product. Lydia thinks of this as the low point of their relationship, before now.

Over dinner they argue about whether to drive into Sacramento for the weekend. They should be thinking about firewood, but Whitman complains that they never see their friends anymore.

"Who'd have thought we'd *survive* without them," Lydia says, distressed at how much they sound like ninth graders. After so many years together it's as if they've suddenly used up all their words, like paper plates and cups, and are now using the last set over and over.

"If you didn't like my friends why didn't you say so? Why didn't you have your own friends?" Whitman swallows his dinner without comment. It's a type of chili Lydia invented, based on garbanzo beans, and it hasn't turned out too well.

"I don't know." She hesitates. "I don't think you ever understood how hard it was for me. All those people so absolutely sure they're right."

"That's your interpretation."

She tries salting her chili to see if this will help. Once Lydia was given a lecture on salt, the most insidious kind of poison, by a friend who'd come over for dinner. He would rather put Drano on his food, he said. She'd had half a mind to tell him to help himself, there was some under the sink.

"Whitman, I'm just trying to tell you how I feel," she says.

"Well you should have said how you felt back then."

"And you should have told me you didn't want to move here. Before I applied for the job. You sure seemed hot on the idea at the time."

Whitman scrapes his bowl. "It's only an hour. I didn't know we were going into seclusion."

Lydia goes to check the refrigerator, coming back with some carrots she harvested that morning. "I don't make the rules," she says. "The way your pals glorify the backwoods life, don't you think it's interesting they've never come up here for a visit?"

He picks up one of the carrots, its wilted tassel of leaves still attached, and bites off the tip. He looks like Bugs Bunny and she wishes to God he would say, "What's up, Doc?" Instead he says, "We don't have room for them to stay with us here. They're just being considerate."

Lydia laughs. As big as it was, the house in the city never seemed big enough for all the people passing through. Once for two months they put up a man named Father John and his "family," four women with seven children among them. They parked their school bus, in which they normally lived, in the backyard. The women did everything for Father John except drive the bus: they washed his clothes, bore his children, and cooked his meals in the bus on a wood stove with a blue mandala painted on it. They had to use their own stove because Lydia and Whitman couldn't guarantee the Karmic purity of their kitchen. At one time, in fact, Whitman and Lydia had been quite the carnivores, but Whitman didn't go into that. The people were friends of a friend and he didn't have the heart to throw them out until they got their bus fixed, which promised to be never.

Lydia pitied the bedraggled women and tried to strike up cheery conversations about how pleasant it was that Whitman shared all the cooking and cleaning up. One night at dinner Lydia explained that she'd first fallen in love with Whitman because of his Beef Mongolian. Several members of Father John's family had to be excused.

But it was true. Whitman had been a rarity in their circle, the jewel in the crown, and Lydia understands now that most of the women they knew were in love with him for more or less the same reason. Really, she thinks, they ought to see him now. The water-fowl crockery set, handmade by Earth, she's left sitting in the sink unwashed for days, as a sort of test. Not unexpectedly, Whitman failed. Without an audience the performance is pointless.

On Saturday Lydia goes to see Verna. She carries two empty cartons which she'll bring back full of eggs. Verna's hens lay beautiful eggs: brown with maroon speckles and a red spot inside, where, as Verna puts it, the rooster leaves his John Henry. The food co-op in Sacramento sold eggs like these for $2.50 a dozen, a price Lydia thought preposterous and still does. She once had a huge argument with one of their friends, a woman named Randy, who acted like fertile eggs were everything short of a cure for cancer. "The only difference between a dozen fertile eggs and a dozen regular ones is twelve sperms," Lydia had explained to her. "That's what you're paying the extra dollar-fifty for. It comes to around twelve cents per sperm."

Later that same evening Randy had been in the kitchen helping Whitman make spaghetti, and Lydia overheard her complaining that she, Lydia, lacked imagination. Whitman had come to her defense, sort of. "Well, she's a science teacher," he said. "She probably knows what she's talking about."

"Don't I know *that*," Randy said. "She even dresses like a schoolteacher."

The next day Lydia had gone to the Salvation Army and bought some fashionably non-new clothes.

She's surprised to find herself confiding in Verna about her problems with Whitman. Verna's kitchen has an extra refrigerator dedicated entirely to eggs, stacked carefully in boxes of straw. She listens to Lydia while she places eggs gently in cartons.

"I guess we're just getting on each other's nerves," she says. "The house we had before was a lot bigger."

Verna nods. They both know that isn't the problem. "Once you've got used to having more, it's hard to get by on less," she says.

Lydia is amazed that Verna can handle so many eggs without getting nervous.

On the way back she stops by the stone outbuilding Whitman has converted into his shop. It's lucky that his special kind of woodworking doesn't require electricity, although if the building were wired she could read out here at night without disturbing him. This strikes her as a provident idea, which she'll suggest when he's in a better mood.

She stands well out of his way and watches him plane the surface of a walnut board. She loves the dark, rippled surface of the wood and the way it becomes something under his hands. He's working on a coffee table that's a replica of an Early American cobbler's bench. In the niches where shoemakers used to keep their tools and leather, people can put magazines and ashtrays. These tables are popular in the city, and Whitman has sold six or seven. As a rule he makes each one of his pieces a little different, but he no longer changes this design, explaining that you can't beat success.

"I was talking to Verna this morning," Lydia says uneasily. "She thinks it's understandable that we'd have trouble living in such a small place." Whitman doesn't respond, but she continues. "She says we ought to forget the past, and pretend we're just starting out."

"So Verna's a psychologist, on top of being a civil engineer."

"She's my friend, Whitman. The only one I've got at the moment."

"These country people are amazing, all experts on the human condition." His back is to Lydia, and as he pushes the plane over the board in steady, long strokes, she watches the definition of the muscles through his damp T-shirt. It's as if the muscles are slipping from one compartment to another in his back.

"They don't knife each other in study hall," she says quietly. "Or take their neighbors hostage."

Whitman speaks rhythmically as his body moves forward and back. "With enough space between them anybody can get along. We ought to know that."

"There's more to it than that. They know what to expect from each other. It's not like that for our generation, that's our whole trouble. We've got to start from scratch."

The plane continues to bite at the wood, spitting out little brown curls. Whitman makes no sound other than this.

"I know it's not easy for you up here, Whitman. That everybody doesn't love you the way they did in Sacramento, but . . ." She intended to say, "I still do." But these are less than words, they're just sounds she's uttered probably three thousand times in their years together, and now they hang flat in the air before she's even completely thought them. It's going to take more than this, she thinks, more than talk, but she doesn't know what.

"But this is where we are now," she says finally. "That's all. We're committed to the place, so we have to figure out a way to go on from here."

"Fine, Lydia, forge ahead. It's easy for you, you always know exactly where you're headed." Every time he shoves the plane forward, a slice of wood curls out and drops to the floor, and she wonders if he's going to plane the board right down to nothing.

The rain starts on Sunday night and doesn't let up all week. The old people in Blind Gap are saying it's because of those bomb tests, the weather is changing. It's too warm. If it were colder it would have been snow, rather than rain, and would come to no harm.

After Tuesday, school is shut down for the week. So many bridges are out, the buses can't run. One of the bridges washed away in the flood is the new one Whitman built on their farm. Lydia sees now that Verna was right, the design was a mistake. The flood loosened the ground under the roots of the sycamore and pulled it down, taking the bridge with it. Whitman blames the tree, saying that if it had been smaller or more flexible it wouldn't have taken out the whole bridge. Lydia can see that his pride is badly damaged. He's trapped inside the house now, despondent, like a prisoner long past the memory of fresh air. The rain makes a constant noise on the roof, making even the sounds inside her skull seem to go dead.

She wonders if everything would be all right if they could just scream at each other. Or cry. The first time she saw him cry was when David had parvo virus as a puppy and they expected him not to make it. Whitman sat up all night beside David's box on the kitchen floor, and when she found him the next morning asleep against the doorsill she told herself that, regardless of the fate of the puppy, this was the man she would be living with in her seventies. Forty years to go, she says aloud into the strange, sound-dead air. She can't begin to imagine it. Now Whitman doesn't even notice if David has food or water.

As she pads around the cabin in wool socks and skirt and down vest, Lydia develops a bizarre fantasy that they are part of some severe religious order gone into mourning, observing the silence of monks. Industrious out of desperation, she freezes and cans the last of the produce from the garden, wondering how it is that this task has fallen to her. Their first week here they had spaded up the little plot behind the cabin, working happily, leaning on each other's shoulders to help dig the shovel in, planting their garden together. But by harvest time it's all hers. Now Whitman only comes into the kitchen to get his beer and get in the way, standing for minutes at a time with the refrigerator door open, staring at the shelves. The distraction annoys her. Lydia hasn't canned tomatoes before and needs to concentrate on the instructions written out by Verna.

"It's cold enough, we don't have to refrigerate the state of California," she shouts above the roar of the rain, but feels sorry for him as he silently closes the refrigerator. She tries to be cheerful. "Maybe we ought to bring back the TV next time we go into the city. If Randy would give it back. Think she's hooked on the soaps by now?"

"Probably couldn't get anything up here," he says. He stands at the windows and paces the floor, like David.

"Bedroom," she commands, wishing Whitman would lie down too.

On Monday it's a relief for both of them when school starts again. But the classroom smells depressingly of damp coats and mildew, and after nearly a week off, the kids are disoriented and wild. They don't remember things they learned before. Lydia tries to hold their attention with stories about animal behavior, not because it's part of the curriculum but because it was her subject in graduate school and she's now grasping at straws. She tells them about imprinting in ducks.

"It's something like a blueprint for life," she explains. "This scientist named Konrad Lorenz discovered that right after they hatched the baby birds would imprint on whatever they saw. When he raised them himself, they imprinted on him and followed him around everywhere he went. Other scientists tried it with cats or beach balls or different shapes cut out of plastic and it always worked. And when the baby ducks grew up, they only wanted to mate with those exact things."

The kids are interested. "That's too weird," one of them says, and for once they want to know why.

"Well, I don't know. Nobody completely understands what's going on when this happens, but we understand the purpose of it. The animal's brain is set up so it can receive this special information that will be useful later on. Normally the first thing a baby duck sees would be an adult duck, right? So naturally that would be the type of thing it ought to grow up looking for. Even though it's less extreme, we know this kind of behavior happens in higher animals too." She knows she's losing her audience as she strays from ducks, but feels oddly compelled by the subject matter. "Most animals, when they're confused or under stress, will fall back on more familiar behavior patterns." As she speaks, Lydia has a sudden, potent vision of the entire Father John family, the downtrodden women at their mandala woodstove and the ratty-haired children and the sublime Father John himself. And standing behind him, all the generations of downtrodden women that issued him forth.

A girl in the back speaks up. "How did the scientists get the ducks to, um, go back so they were normal?"

"I'm sorry to say they didn't. It's a lifetime commitment." Lydia really is sorry for the experimental ducks. She has thought of this before.

"So they go around wanting to make it with beach balls all the time?" one boy asks. Several of the boys laugh.

Lydia shrugs. "That's right. All for the good of science."

She wakes up furious, those women and ducks still on her mind. Instead of boiling the water for coffee and oatmeal, she goes to the sink and picks up the handmade soup tureen. "Do you like this bowl?" she asks Whitman, who is standing beside the bed buttoning his shirt.

He looks at her, amazed. They haven't been asking lately for each other's opinions. "I don't know," he says.

"You don't know," she says. "I don't either. I'm ambivalent, that's my whole problem." She holds it in front of her at arm's length, examining it. Then she lifts it to chin level, shuts her eyes, and lets it fall on the stone hearth. The noise is remarkable and seems to bear no relation to the hundreds of pieces of crockery now lying at her feet, cupped like begging palms, their edges as white and porous as bone. Lydia, who has never intentionally broken anything in her life, has the sudden feeling she's found a new career. She goes to the cabinet and finds the matching duck-shaped ladle and flings it overhand against the opposite wall. It doesn't explode as she'd hoped, but cracks like a femur and falls in two pieces. David gets up and stands by the door, looking back over his shoulder, trembling a little. Whitman sits back down on the bed and stares, speechless and bewildered.

"I never applied for this job I'm doing here," she says. "I don't know how I got into it, but I know how to get out." With shaky hands she stacks her papers into neat piles, closes her briefcase, and goes to work.

The walk home from school is not pleasant. The mud sticks to her boots, making her feet heavy and her legs tired. Tonight she'll have a mess to clean up, and she'll have to talk to Whitman. But his silent apathy has infected her and she's begun to suspect that even screaming won't do it. Not talking, and not screaming; what's left but leaving? She can see why people scramble to get self-help books, the same way David falls over his own feet to be obedient. Things are so easy when someone else is in charge.

She decides she's a ripe target for a book called *How to Improvise a Love Affair That's Not Like the Failures You've Already Seen*. That would sell a million, she thinks. Or *How to Live with a Man After He's Stopped Talking.*

David runs down the hill to greet her as she passes the fence separating Verna's farm from theirs. "Come on, David, come on boy," she says, and because of the creek between them David is frantic, running back and forth along the bank. He raises his head suddenly, remembering, and takes off up the hill for the long way around by the orchard road.

Farther up on the opposite bank she can see Whitman's table saw where he set it up above the wrecked bridge. He is salvaging what lumber he can, and cutting up the rest for firewood. At the moment the saw isn't running and Whitman isn't around. Then she sees him, halfway down the bank below the table saw. He is rolled up in such an odd position that she only recognizes him by his shirt. A hot numbness runs through her limbs, like nitrous oxide at the dentist's office, and she climbs and slides down the slick boulders of the creek bed opposite him. She can't get any closer because of the water, still running high after the flood.

"Whitman!" She screams his name and other things, she can't remember what. She can hardly hear her own voice over the roar of the water. When he does look up she sees that he isn't hurt. He says something she can't hear. It takes awhile for Lydia to understand that he's crying. Whitman is not dead, he's crying.

"God, I thought you were dead," she yells, her hand on her chest, still catching her breath.

Whitman says something, gesturing, and looks at her

the way the kids in school do when she calls on them and they don't know the answer. She wants to comfort him, but there is a creek between them.

"Hang on, I'm coming," she says. She begins to climb the bank, but Whitman is still saying something. She can only make out a few words: "Don't leave."

She leans against the mossy face of a boulder, exhausted. "I have to go over there." She screams the words one at a time, punctuating them with exaggerated gestures. "Or you can come here. Or we can stay here and scream till we hyperventilate and fall in the river." She knows he isn't going to get the last part.

"Don't dive into the river," he says, or "I'm not going to throw myself in the river," or something along those lines, spreading his arms in the charade of a swan dive and shaking his head "no." He indicates a horizontal circle: that he will come around to where she is. She should stay there. He seems embarrassed. He points both his hands toward Lydia, and then puts them flat on his chest.

They are using a sign language unknown to humankind, making it up as they go along. She understands that this last gesture is important, and returns it.

David, who had a head start, has already made it to the road. Risking peril without the slightest hesitation, he gallops down the slick creek bank to Lydia. Her mind is completely on Whitman, but she takes a few seconds to stroke David's side and feel the fast heartbeat under his ribs. It's a relief to share the uncomplicated affection that has passed between people and their dogs for thousands of years.

COVERED BRIDGES

Last summer all of our friends were divorcing or having babies, as if these were the only two choices. It's silly, I know, but it started us thinking. From there our thoughts ran along a track that seemed to stop at every depot and have absolutely no final destination.

"Then there's the whole question of how many," said my wife Lena from the bedroom while I was brushing my teeth. "If you have one, you almost have to have another one. People act like you're a criminal if you don't."

The subject had threaded itself completely through our lives, like a snaking green vine through the boughs of a tree. If there was no formal introduction to the subject, if she didn't say "At work today . . ." or "You know, I was thinking . . ." then I knew it was this conversation we were having.

I rinsed my toothbrush and hung it in the brass ring next to Lena's. "Isn't that getting the cart before the donkey?" I asked.

"I suppose."

I came into the bedroom, where she was sitting up in bed with a book. She took off her glasses. Lena is thirty-seven, and an amazing person to see. Every man in love believes his wife is beautiful, I know, but I also know that people look at Lena, and look again. She has long, very straight black hair with one lock of white streaming out like shooting stars above her high forehead. Every member of her mother's family has this forelock, which is controlled by a single dominant gene, but in Lena that gene has found its perfect resting place.

"Whatever else there is to consider," she said, "we both have to agree, before going ahead with it. Either one of us has veto power."

I assumed this meant that she was leaning toward, but that I was probably leaning against, and ought to speak up. Most of the men I knew thought of their children as something their wives had produced, nurtured, and given to the world like tomatoes grown for the market. With Lena it couldn't be this way.

"I don't know what I think," I said. "I guess I've just assumed that if you really wanted children I'd have no right to object."

She looked surprised. "If I wanted to do it solo, what's the point of being married? I could just use a turkey baster." Lena had a friend in St. Louis who had done just that.

"I know," I said. "But it's hard for me to say what I really think."

Lena's eyes are a very serious, oceanic shade of blue. "What do you really think?" she asked me.

"Well. I have to admit the idea overwhelms me. To rock the boat, just when I feel like I've finally gotten my life arranged the right way." I considered this. "From what I can tell, it's not even like rocking the boat. It's like sinking the boat, and swimming for eighteen years."

She started to say something, but didn't.

"But I'm really not sure," I said. "I'll think about it some more."

"Good." She kissed me and turned out the light.

It seemed odd to have this question arise in my life now, when other men my age were beginning to groan about the price of college tuition. I couldn't remember a time in life when I'd ever clearly visualized my own progeny. Lena and I came together relatively late in the scheme of things, without the usual assumptions people have about starting a family and a life. We bought a two-story house in the maple shade of Convocation Street and assembled our collective belongings there, but as for a life, each of us already had one. I am nearly forty, and a professor of botany. Before I met Lena, three years ago, I devoted myself entirely to opening young minds onto the mysteries of xylem and phloem. I teach the other half of the chicken-and-egg story, the miracle of life that starts with pollen and ends with the astonishing, completed fact of a fruit.

Also, I am a great gardener. Some would call it puttering, but I feel that I commune with nature in the tradition of many great thinkers: Thoreau, Whitman, Aristotle. My communion is simply more domestic. I receive inspiration from cauliflowers. I have always had friends among my colleagues, but never a soulmate. Back before Lena, I liked to think of myself as a congenial hermit in blue jeans and Nikes, a latter-day Gregor Mendel among his peas.

Lena is a specialist in toxicology and operates a poison hotline at the county hospital. People from all over the state call her in desperation when their children have consumed baby aspirin or a houseplant or what have you, and she helps them. It might sound morbid, but no one could be more full of the joy of life than Lena, even where her job is concerned. She is magnificent at parties. Her best story is about a Gila monster named Hilda, which served a brief term as the pet of the Norman Clinderback family. Hilda was an illegal gift from an uncle in Tucson, and crossed our nation in a fiberglass container of the type meant for transporting cats. The Gila monster, by all rights a stranger to this part of Indiana, is a highly poisonous lizard, but is thought by most experts to be too lazy to pose a threat to humans. The incident precipitating the call to my wife involved a July 4th picnic in which Hilda was teased beyond endurance with a piece of fried chicken. Hilda had a bite of Norm Junior's thumb instead.

Of course, the story ended happily. Lena wouldn't make light of someone else's grief, having suffered her own. Another thing that runs in her family, besides the white forelock, is a dire allergy to the stings of bees and wasps. In childhood she lost her sister. Suddenly and incomprehensibly this child passed over from life to death before Lena's eyes while they sat in the yard making clover necklaces. Lena could die by the same sword. Theoretically, any outdoor excursion that includes my wife could come to tragedy.

But it was this aspect of her life that led her into the study of toxic reactions, and it was through the poison hotline that we met. I called because I had gotten diatomaceous earth in my eye. I don't know exactly how it happened, whether I rubbed my eye while I was working with it, or if it was carried by a gust of wind—the powder is light. What I remember most clearly is Lena's voice over the phone, concerned and serious, as if there were nothing on earth more important to her than preventing my cornea from being scratched.

If things had gone another way, if I hadn't gathered the courage to call back the next week without the excuse of a poisoning, I might have become one of her stories. Instead, I became her husband. I called and explained to her what I'd been doing with diatomaceous earth, since I thought she might wonder. The name is poetic, but in fact this substance is a lethal insecticide. I was dusting it onto the leaves of my eggplants, which had suffered an attack of flea beetles and looked like they'd been pelleted with buckshot. I'm fond of eggplants, for aesthetic reasons as much as any other. "Really," I said to Lena, my future wife, "could anyone ask for a more beautiful fruit?" Over the phone, her laughter sounded like a warm bath.

Our courtship was very much a vegetable affair. By way of thanks I invited her to see my garden, and to my amazement she accepted. She had never grown vegetables herself, she said, and it impressed her to see familiar foods like cabbages rooted to the earth. I showed her how brussels sprouts grow, attached along the fat main stem like so many suckling pigs. She seemed to need to take in the textures of things, brushing her hands across velvety petals, even rubbing my shirt sleeve absently between her thumb and forefinger as if to divine the essence of a botanist. I promised to cook her an eggplant rollatini by the time of the summer solstice. But before the shortest night of the year I had already lain beside Lena, trembling, and confessed I'd never held anything I so treasured.

Lena says I was the first poison victim ever to call back, except in the case of repeat offenders. And to think I nearly didn't. A person could spend most of a lifetime in retrospective terror, thinking of all the things one nearly didn't do.

Diatomaceous earth, by the way, isn't dirt. It's a remarkable substance made up of the jagged silicon skeletons of thousands of tiny sea creatures. It feels to a human hand like talc, but to insects it's like rolling on broken bottles. It lacerates their skin so the vital juices leak out. This is a fearful way to die, I'm sure, but as I sprinkled the white powder around the leaves on that spring day I wasn't thinking about the insects. I was thinking of eggplants, heavy and purple-black in the midsummer sun. I believe that try as we might to see it differently, life nearly always comes down to choices like this. There is always a price. My elderly neighbor is fond of saying, as he stands at his mailbox riffling through the bright-colored junk mail: "If there's something on this earth that's really for free, I'd pay everything I got to know what it is."

Lena thought that rather than just hypothesizing it might be a good idea for us actually to try out a baby for a weekend. The more I thought about it, the more reasonable it seemed. In fact, I thought maybe it ought to be a requirement. In any event, our friends the MacElroys were happy to oblige us with their daughter Melinda. They offered to drop her off Friday evening, and head post-haste for Chicago.

MacElroy teaches zoology and has an office next to mine. Our college is small; the biology department is comprised solely of the two of us, one ambassador each from the plant and animal kingdoms. MacElroy came here from a state university, and thinks this is extremely amusing. Sometimes in the restroom he will stand at the next urinal and say, "Shall we convene a departmental meeting?"

What is not a joke, to the MacElroys, is that at the age of twenty months Melinda still doesn't walk. At first they were evasive, saying, "She's shy about walking." This soon eroded into outright defensiveness, and from there they went the sad route of trying everything, from specialists in pediatric orthopedics to "Ask Dr. Gott." All the tests that money can buy have been run on Melinda. The doctors all say the same thing: that she is fine, bonewise, and that every child has her own timetable. And still the MacElroys entertain nervous visions of Melinda packing her bags someday and crawling off to college.

Early on Friday afternoon, Lena called me from her office at Poison HQ. "What have you got for the rest of the day?" she asked.

"Office hours," I said.

"What's the chance some student will drop in?"

"There's a chance," I said. I looked around my desk and considered the odds. I have ferns and bromeliads in my office, a quietly carnivorous *Darlingtonia*, a terrarium full of the humid breath of mosses. I spend a good deal of time alone with them. "A meteor could strike the Science Building, too," I said.

"I've traded shifts with Ursula so we can play hooky for the afternoon." Lena sounded breathless. "We might as well enjoy our last hours of freedom, before we take on the awesome responsibilities of a child," she said. Less than ten minutes after hanging up the phone, she was honking the horn outside my office. We set out for the Covered Bridge Festival.

I should explain that this is not a festival in any normal sense, but a weekend during which the residents of southern Indiana drive about celebrating the fact that there are numerous covered bridges in the vicinity. One can enjoy them in any order. My own favorite is the one at Little Patoka, on the Eel River.

"One of the pros," Lena said as she frowned slightly over the steering wheel, "is that our schedules are so flexible. I could always arrange my shift on the poison line around your classes."

"Assuming your staff doesn't all have a crisis at once."

"There will always be Ursula," she said. Ursula was a good friend of Lena's, a widow in her sixties, and the only other member of the poison hotline team who had neither procreated nor cleaved from his or her spouse in the previous year.

"Think of it," she said. "It's perfect. On the days you have evening classes, I could work days. The other days, I could work nights."

"And when would we talk to each other?" I asked.

"On weekends. And whenever you've taken poison."

Little Patoka is about half a mile from the river. We parked in town, where a small fair had been drummed up along the road running out from town toward the bridge. Against the backdrop of harvested fields and roadside tangles of poison ivy and goldenrod, tables were piled high with local produce: handwoven baskets and corn-husk dolls, clear jars of clover honey, giant pyramids of pumpkins. There was an outstanding display of locally grown vegetable oddities. One was labeled "Two-Headed Yolo Wonder Bell Pepper," and really that is very much what it looked like.

As we walked away from town the tables began to keep their distance from one another, and were laden with more unexpected items—the efforts of people who had come from out of town. One young couple, who were selling jewelry, evidently traveled in a VW van to take advantage of occasions like this. They might have been expecting more from the Covered Bridge Festival. They seemed a long way from home, both in terms of geography and era. The woman had pale hair and eyebrows and wore a long skirt and a great deal of dangly jewelry. The man seemed estranged, sitting apart on a folding chair, concentrating on repairing the small silver mechanism of a necklace.

"I'm Earth," the young woman said. "And this is Jacob. We're from Sacramento. This is really lovely country." She seemed hungry to talk.

"It is," Lena agreed.

"We see a lot of country, but what you have here is something special," she told us. "I read auras. People are at peace here." She stopped then, apparently arrested by the sight of my wife's face, and I wondered momentarily about auras. "Your eyes are exactly the color of lapis lazuli," she said. As proof she held up to Lena's temple a smooth, blue oval that matched like a third eye.

I took the necklace when the young woman held it out to me. The stone had a rubbed, comforting feel. I couldn't help thinking that it was shaped very much like a prosthetic eye. For a long time I thought glass eyes were complete and spherical, like real ones, but they are not. I turned it over and read the tag on the back, which was marked with the number 45. This price startled me. There is some persistent part of my soul that expects the products of nature to be free of charge.

"It's beautiful," Lena said, "but we're just out for a stroll today, really." The young man gave us a hostile look from his folding chair.

"We didn't bring our checkbook," I added for emphasis.

"That business about my eyes was just a ruse," Lena told me once we'd gone on our way. "I do feel sorry for the way they must have to live, but you can't buy things on that basis alone. And that hokum about auras! When half the people around here are completely torn up about one thing or another."

"Old Jacob looked like he was ready to hit the high road back to civilization," I said.

"I guess what I resent is the manipulation. You notice she handed the necklace right to you."

If Lena hadn't spoken up I might have bought it, and not because I felt I had to, either. "It was true about your eyes," I said. "At least that much was sincere. The color was an exact match."

"Really," Lena said. "That blue."

We didn't speak for a while. Then I said, "I know 'azul' means blue. The blue . . . what? What's 'lapis'?"

My wife works the *New York Times* crossword puzzle without fail, and knows about the roots of words. She has worlds of knowledge that amaze me. At one time she was torn between a career in poison or something more literary.

"Stone," she said. "It's Latin."

"Of course. Like a lapidary shop."

We walked past an unattended pile of pumpkins. "Lapidary," she said, nodding. "And dilapidated."

"Unstoned?"

She laughed. "I guess it means the stones are falling out. Like an old rock fence." There were fences like that by the legion in southern Indiana. If we wished to do so, we could probably spot half a dozen from where we stood.

"Did you know that Ron Emerson and Gracie are separated?" she asked. She knew Ron from the hospital, and Gracie had worked as a secretary in my department before taking maternity leave.

"That's something new," I said. "A baby *and* a split-up."

"I know. It's almost like divorce is some kind of virus going around, and there's no vaccine you can take. For a while it looked like babies might be the antidote. But I know that isn't true." We were in sight of the covered bridge now, and the long row of trees that marked the course of the Eel River.

"Lots of people are like Ron and Gracie," Lena went on. "If they're in trouble to begin with, then after a baby they don't have a prayer of working things out. There's never time."

I didn't offer an opinion. I was content to walk beside Lena and hold her hand while she thought this through to the end. My own thoughts were completely different. I was thinking that I belonged in this place, among these fields and rivers and covered bridges. I have spent my entire life in small Indiana towns: I grew up in one, was educated in another, and settled at last in a third. My sisters come to visit from far-flung cities where they enjoy extraordinary foods and philharmonic orchestras—Seattle, Atlanta, Cleveland—and they say that, looking back, they can't imagine how they lived with such limited opportunities.

I suppose I accept these limitations without much question. There are always surprises. I was raised in a home of harsh religion and more children than there should have been, and I grew up expecting little in the way of affection, much less Lena. To my mind, a life spent among burgeoning fields is not always, is not *necessarily*, a life of limitation.

"On the other hand," Lena said, "it's scary to think of being old, and having missed the chance. I guess it's reasonable to want to pass yourself on. It's the nearest thing to living forever."

"In a genetic manner of speaking," I said.

"But then, I'm sure my parents thought three kids were enough to guarantee them immortality, and it may not turn out that way."

Lena was her family's only hope of passing on its DNA. There was the sister who had died, and a much younger brother who became sterile in his teens as a complication of mumps. He and his wife recently adopted Korean twins. To the great credit of my in-laws, though, they never put pressure on Lena. They are uncommon people who love their children without possessiveness or a need to interfere. They astonish me continually, and yet Lena doesn't seem to appreciate what she has. She reads the books, like everyone else, on how to overcome the heartbreak of a dysfunctional family, and says things like "Well, you know my Grandfather Butler did drink." I suppose it's like being beautiful; when every other woman on earth is lamenting this or that physical flaw you can't very well admit you don't have any. But it bothers me sometimes that she takes this love for granted. As if everyone in the world had parents who'd call up while you're out for a birthday dinner and sing the Happy Birthday song in three-part harmony, counting the dog, into your answering machine.

My own parents are still living, like Lena's, but they do not communicate. They once communicated over issues surrounding their children, and then they communicated over which channel to watch. Now they have bought a second television set, smaller than the first, and the two stand side by side. My father sits in a chair next to my mother's in the evenings and watches the sports, without sound.

We reached the bridge. Lena dropped my hand and walked ahead of me without speaking. When a bridge reaches this age, it's important to listen to what it has to say to you, as you walk through it. The river below our feet made a wistful, continuous sigh, and our steps were like whispers. The wood of the floorboards was soft with age and had the dusty smell that carries for me all the confused nostalgia of youth, and barns. When we came out the other side, the day seemed brighter. Sunlight picked out the colors of the trees on the opposite bank of the river.

"Look at this," Lena said, "beauty and the beast, all rolled into one." It was a remarkable caterpillar, the size, shape, and color of a bright kosher dill, with blue suction cups for feet and yellow knobs on its back. It was creeping up one of the bridge's structural timbers, and Lena was entranced.

"What's it going to be when it grows up?" she asked. Insects were not my department, but Lena always placed absolute faith in my knowledge of the natural world, and for this reason I read a great deal.

"A cecropia moth," I guessed. "I don't know anything else that would warrant a caterpillar that big."

She looked up. Over our heads were unpainted eaves, sheltered by the tin roof of the bridge, and a full archaeological record of barn-swallow nests. "Do you think it's going up there right now to make its cocoon?"

I assessed the caterpillar's rate of speed. "Maybe by tomorrow afternoon."

She watched it with intense concentration. "I wish I could weave a cocoon around myself and change into something beautiful," she said at last.

I looked at Lena's profile, framed by an auburn halo of honey locust and red oak leaves, and the Eel River running forever away. "In heaven's name," I asked, "what would you change yourself into?"

"Somebody more definite," she said. "The kind of person who's very sure, on the inside, of what she wants to be."

As we walked back toward town her spirits seemed to lift again. A dog ran up to us from nowhere, and Lena spoke to it in such an encouraging tone I was sure it would follow us home. It did follow us, but only until a family with young children crossed our path going out toward the bridge. The dog was fully grown and even showed some gray around its muzzle, but it tripped and panted and seemed to have the intelligence of a puppy.

"Can dogs be retarded?" she asked me, laughing, and then suddenly looked thoughtful. "Could Melinda be, do you think?"

"No, I don't think so. They're just showing natural concern. Everybody is afraid their child will have something wrong with it." MacElroy had told me that before Melinda was born his wife forgot to turn off the electric blanket one night, and spent the next three months worrying about brain damage to the fetus.

"I think I could handle it. Really, I do, don't you?" With the toe of her boot she kicked an apple that lay in the road. It rolled in a wide arc into the weeds. "What we're looking at is the prospect of a new person coming to live with us, right? And, if we were placing an ad for a roommate, we wouldn't say, 'Imperfect or handicapped people will not be considered.' "

"I never thought of it that way," I said.

"What would be hard, though, is that it would take so much more effort than I've ever counted on, over the long term. A lot more than a regular baby. One of us would probably have to give up our career. I suppose me."

"Why you?"

"Is it something you'd be willing to do?"

I thought about this. "Yes," I said. "If we'd decided to commit ourselves to the project, then yes, I would."

Lena looked at me with such surprise I was overwhelmed by the wish that she knew me better. It isn't as though I hold back information. Usually I don't quite know how I feel about things until Lena asks, and often not even then. "It's only logical, isn't it?" I reasoned. "If it comes down to a choice between teaching Bryophyta and Lycophyta or saving the lives of our youth, there's just no contest."

"And you would do that." She put her hand into my hip pocket and leaned on my shoulder as we walked. "No matter what ever happens, I'm so happy you told me that."

The Lapis Lazulis had packed up and moved on by the time we reached their spot, but we resolved anyway to buy something to commemorate the day. We would acquire the two-headed Yolo Wonder at any price, if it was for sale. Lena stopped at each table, weighing in her hands the acorn squash and noble ears of corn, and holding up small maroon apples for me to bite. She was wearing purple, a color that nearly glows when she puts it on. A purple sweater, and a turquoise and lavender scarf. As I looked at her there among the pumpkins I was overcome with color and the intensity of my life. In these moments we are driven to try and hoard happiness by taking photographs, but I know better. The important thing was what the colors stood for, the taste of hard apples and the existence of Lena and the exact quality of the sun on the last warm day in October. A photograph would have flattened the scene into a happy moment, whereas what I felt was gut rapture. The fleeting certainty that I deserved the space I'd been taking up on this earth, and all the air I had breathed.

There are a few things that predictably give me joy. Watching Lena's face while we make love is one. The appearance of the first new, marble-white tomatoes in my garden is another, and the break of comprehension across a student's face when I've planted an understanding that never grew in that mind before. I'm told that seeing one's own child born is an experience beyond description, but knowing these things, I can just begin to imagine.

That evening, little Melinda might have been enlisted in a conspiracy to make us parents. She ate her dinner without complaint, then rubbed her eyes in a dreamy and charming way, and went to bed.

In the morning she awoke transmogrified. She sat in the middle of the living-room floor and displayed her vocabulary in a dizzying, vengeful series of demands. Her dark hair was wild and her temper fierce. Most ferociously of all she demanded Mommy, and over and over again some mysterious item called Belinka. My will was soon crushed like a slave's, but Lena held on bravely. She brought out the whole suitcase of Melinda's animals and toys, which we had been instructed not to do (just bring the things out one by one, her mother had advised, so she won't know this is all there is), and put on a puppet show as earnest as it was extemporaneous. Melinda was a cruel critic. She bit Lena on the hand, and crawled off toward the kitchen.

By noon we were desperate. "Kids are always soothed by the outdoors," Lena said, and I did not dare doubt the source of her knowledge. I packed cheese and fruit and cans of root beer into a picnic basket, and would have thrown in a bottle of Jim Beam if we'd had it, while she called Ursula. "She'll love the idea," Lena assured me. "She's always complaining how she never sees her grandkids." Ursula lived sixteen miles away on a declining apple orchard and cattle farm.

It cost us several damaged fingers to get Melinda into her car seat, but she gratified us by falling instantly to sleep.

"Do you think maybe it's different when they're your own?" Lena whispered as we drove. I did not hazard a guess.

The rural setting did seem to do some good. Melinda

was no longer belligerent, only energetic. We carried her kicking and squirming, and providing commentary on the cats and cow flops, out to what Ursula called the "June orchard." She'd hired a neighbor to keep a picnic spot mowed all summer for the benefit of her grandchildren on the remote chance that they might visit. Ursula led the way in her stout garden shoes, swinging the picnic basket and pointing out blighted trees, their knotted trunks oozing sweet sap and buzzing with insects. Lena was right, she needed company.

We spread the blanket and laid out the food, cracked open soda cans, and bribed Melinda with grapes. Her speed was a problem. Having postponed walking for so long, her crawl was proficient beyond belief.

"Honey, stay in the short grass. There are blackberry briars and stickery things out there," Lena warned. But Melinda continued to streak out for the high brush like a wild thing seeking its origins. Between every two bites of my sandwich I dragged her back by the legs.

"Well, here's to the new generation," Lena said, raising her root beer. She drank a long gulp, throwing her head back. Then she stood up suddenly, gazed at me with a look of intent misery, and spat out something that twitched on the grass. Ursula and I both leaned forward to look. It was a hornet.

We watched, stupefied, as Lena sank to her knees, then sat down, and then lay full length on the ground. The valves of my heart slammed like doors.

Anaphylactic shock is an impossible thing to expect from a human body: a defense mechanism gone terribly wrong. Normally the blood swells around a foreign protein to flush it away, but when that happens in every cell of the body at once it looks from the outside like a horror movie.

I looked around for Melinda. She had reached the edge of the clearing and stopped, looking back at us with fearful expectation. "Get her," I shouted at Ursula, "and get some help, as fast as you can. If you need a car, take ours." I thrust the keys at her. Ursula knew as well as I did the urgency of the situation, but being the one with the most to lose, I suppose I needed to take command. Ursula scooped a hand under each of Melinda's armpits and ran for the house. I knelt beside Lena. Her face and throat were swollen, but she was breathing.

"In my purse," Lena said quietly, and then she said nothing more, and I was afraid she was going to die. That those would be her last words: "In my purse." But then she said, with her eyes still closed, "That purple cloisonné case. Get that."

I did so, having no idea why. I fiddled frantically with the clasp and then nearly dropped it at the sight of what lay inside. There was a cool, hateful-looking needle and a glass bubble of clear liquid.

Lena told me, in a businesslike way except for occasional long pauses, how to attach the bubble to the needle, turn it once, and jab it into her arm. When I couldn't get her sleeve rolled up, she said to shoot through the shirt. My hands were shaking. It was mostly out of an aversion for operations like this that I went into the study of plants, leaving flesh and blood to others.

Almost immediately she started to breathe more deeply. She lay still without opening her eyes, and I would have thought she was sleeping except for the tightness of her grip on my hand.

"Have you always carried that?" I asked.

She nodded.

In three years of intimacy I had never seen these secret instruments. I thought the case contained some feminine thing that wasn't my business. Face powder, maybe, or tampons.

"You could have told me," I said.

"I've lived all my life with this thing," she said, and I

tried to understand this. That some pains are our own. She said, "I didn't want you constantly worrying about it."

I squeezed her hand to bring some strength into mine. I thought of the previous afternoon, of watching her, beautiful and permanent, against the continual loss of the Eel River. The things we will allow ourselves to believe.

In the hospital, Lena's friend Dr. Cavanaugh warned me that although Lena was out of the woods she was even more visibly swollen than when I had seen her last, and would remain so for a while. It takes the body days, he said, to reabsorb the fluids it releases in such haste.

Before I pushed open the door to her room I put in my mind the image of Lena swollen, but still I was startled. She didn't actually look like my wife, but like some moon-faced relative of Lena's.

She smiled, turning the moon to a sun.

"Does that hurt?" I asked, sitting cautiously beside her thigh under the sheet.

"Does what hurt?"

"I don't know, your face. It looks . . . stretched."

"Gee, thanks," she said, laughing. She took my wrist and laid her fingers lightly across my veins. Her hands were still Lena's hands, slender and gracefully curved. In bygone days they would have been the fingers of a movie star, curled around a cigarette.

"Where's Melinda?" she asked suddenly, almost sitting up but restrained by the sheet that was drawn across her chest and tucked into the bed.

"Ursula has her. They're getting along like knaves."

"You know what I think? Immortality is the wrong reason," she said, and suddenly there were two streams of tears on her shiny cheeks. "Having a child wouldn't make you immortal. It would make you twice as mortal. It's just one more life you could possibly lose, besides your own. Two more eyes to be put out, and ten more toes to get caught under the mower."

Lena's Grandfather Butler had lost some toes under a lawn mower once. And, of course, there was her lost sister.

"You're just scared right now. In a few weeks life will seem secure again," I said.

"Maybe it will. But that won't change the fact that it isn't." She looked at me, and I knew she was right, and I knew that for the first time she felt sure she would not bear children. I felt a mixture of relief and confusion. This was the opposite of the reaction I'd expected—I thought brushes with death made people want children desperately. My younger brother and his wife were involved in a near-disaster on a ski lift in northern Wisconsin, and within forty-eight hours they'd conceived their first son.

"You're full of drugs," I said. "Cortisone and Benadryl and who knows what else. And that stuff I shot into your arm."

"Epinephrine," she said. "You did a good job. Did Cavanaugh tell you? That's what saved me." She stroked my hand and turned it over, palm down. The wedding band stood out against the white hospital sheets like an advertisement for jewelry and true love and all that is coveted in the world.

"What I'm saying is," I said, "this isn't the time to be making important decisions. Your head isn't clear. A lot of things have happened."

"Why do people always say that? My head *is* clear. *Because* of what's happened." She laid her head back on the pillow and looked at the ceiling. The white forelock still bloomed above her forehead, but her beauty had gone underground. Dark depressions hung like hammocks under her eyes. I realized that now I had the answer to a ridiculous question that had haunted me for years, concerning whether or not I would still love Lena if she weren't beautiful.

"Just being married, just loving one other person with

all your heart, is risky enough," she said. This I knew. I lay down carefully on the bed, not with her, but beside her, with my head against the white sheet that on some other day might be drawn up to cover a face.

By Sunday evening Lena was discharged on the promise that she would take it easy. She knew about the complex medications she needed to take, there was no problem there. She spent her days explaining antidotes.

Once we'd gotten settled, Ursula brought Melinda over. It was several hours before the MacElroys were due to arrive, but I told Ursula I'd manage, and I did. Melinda's energy seemed spent, and perhaps the slight pall over the house made her feel as though she had done something wrong. She sat by the hearth in the living room driving a Barbie Doll over the bricks in a dump truck. I was reading Darwin. Occasionally I read short passages aloud to Melinda, and she seemed to appreciate this.

"Nature red in tooth and claw," I told her, "is only one way to look at it."

The principal difference between children and adults, I believe, is that children accomplish their greatest feats with little or no fanfare. Melinda looked at me strangely, then stood up and took five careful steps, and then sat down with a bump.

I called out to Lena, "She walked!"

"What?" Lena appeared at the door in her white robe.

"Melinda walked. She took five steps, from there to here."

A doubtful look crossed Lena's face, which was slowly regaining its original shape and becoming easier for me to read. "Are you positive?" she asked.

Melinda looked gravely back and forth between us, apparently fearing she'd made another unknown mistake.

"Oh, honey, we're proud of you," Lena said, crossing

the room to pick her up. Melinda's knees spread automatically to straddle Lena's hip, and as she kissed the top of the baby's head my throat grew tight, seeing how right this looked. Lena was a mother waiting to happen.

Both Lena and Melinda were asleep by the time the MacElroys arrived, which was probably just as well. Melinda might have been expected to give a repeat performance, and Lena's face would have given away the nature of our catastrophic weekend. I didn't tell them the whole story, only that Lena wasn't feeling well. There would be time later to go into it. For now, I didn't want to dampen the thrill of Melinda's having walked. They did not doubt my word for a minute, nor did they seem disappointed that they weren't there to witness it. They were unconditionally elated. So was Melinda. She collapsed groggily into her mother's arms, a warrior weary from battle.

I fell into bed beside Lena with similar relief. Our house was our own again. We were ourselves.

"What I *really* think," Lena said suddenly, long after I'd turned out the light, "is that having children is the most normal thing in the world. But not for us, because we're not in a normal situation. I haven't been facing up to it, but really, I could go at any time, and it wouldn't be fair to saddle you with that kind of responsibility."

"Don't think about what's fair to me," I said. "Think of what you want."

"I am," she said. "This is what I want." She turned over and faced me in the darkness. "You are."

The light from the window behind Lena outlined the curve of her cheek with a silver line, like a new moon. I felt a strangeness in my chest, as though the muscles of my heart had suffered a thousand tiny lacerations and were leaking out pain.

"You're sure?" I asked.

"I'm sure."

I pulled Lena into my arms and held her tightly, thinking of strange things: of diatomaceous earth and insects and the choices we make, and of eggplants, purple and bright in the sun.

QUALITY TIME

Miriam's one and only daughter, Rennie, wants to go to Ice Cream Heaven. This is not some vision of the afterlife but a retail establishment here on earth, right in Barrimore Plaza, where they have to drive past it every day on the way to Rennie's day-care center. In Miriam's opinion, this opportunistic placement is an example of the free-enterprise system at its worst.

"Rennie, honey, we can't today. There just isn't time," Miriam says. She is long past trying to come up with fresh angles on this argument. This is the bland, simple truth, the issue is time, not cavities or nutrition. Rennie doesn't want ice cream. She wants an angel sticker for the Pearly Gates Game, for which one only has to walk through the door, no purchase necessary. When you've collected enough stickers you get a free banana split. Miriam has told Rennie over and over again that she will buy her a banana split, some Saturday when they have time to make an outing of it, but Rennie acts as if this has nothing to do with the matter at hand, as though she has asked for a Cabbage Patch doll and Miriam is offering to buy her shoes.

"I could just run in and run out," Rennie says after a while. "You could wait for me in the car." But she knows she has lost; the proposition is half-hearted.

"We don't even have time for that, Rennie. We're on a schedule today."

Rennie is quiet. The windshield wipers beat a deliberate, ingratiating rhythm, sounding as if they feel put-upon to be doing this job. All of southern California seems dysfunctional in the rain: cars stall, drivers go vaguely brain-dead. Miriam watches Rennie look out at the drab scenery, and wonders if for her sake they ought to live someplace with ordinary seasons—piles of raked leaves in autumn, winters with frozen streams and carrot-nosed snowmen. Someday Rennie will read about those things in books, and think they're exotic.

They pass by a brand-new auto mall, still under construction, though some of the lots are already open and ready to get down to brass tacks with anyone who'll brave all that yellow machinery and mud. The front of the mall sports a long row of tall palm trees, newly transplanted, looking frankly mortified by their surroundings. The trees depress Miriam. They were probably yanked out of some beautiful South Sea island and set down here in front of all these Plymouths and Subarus. Life is full of bum deals.

Miriam can see that Rennie is not pouting, just thoughtful. She is an extremely obliging child, considering that she's just barely five. She understands what it means when Miriam says they are "on a schedule." Today they really don't have two minutes to spare. Their dance card, so to speak, is filled. When people remark to Miriam about how well-organized she is, she laughs and declares that organization is the religion of the single parent.

It sounds like a joke, but it isn't. Miriam is faithful about the business of getting each thing done in its turn, and could no more abandon her orderly plan than a priest could swig down the transubstantiated wine and toss out wafers like Frisbees over the heads of those waiting to be blessed. Miriam's motto is that life is way too complicated to leave to chance.

But in her heart she knows what a thin veil of comfort it is that she's wrapped around herself and her child to cloak them from chaos. It all hangs on the presumption that everything has been accounted for. Most days, Miriam is a believer. The road ahead will present no serious potholes, no detour signs looming sudden and orange in the headlights, no burning barricades thrown together as reminders that the world's anguish doesn't remain mute—like the tree falling in the forest—just because no one is standing around waiting to hear it.

Miriam is preoccupied along this line of thought as she kisses Rennie goodbye and turns the steering wheel, arm over elbow, guiding her middle-aged Chevy out of the TenderCare parking lot and back onto the slick street. Her faith has been shaken by coincidence.

On Saturday, her sister Janice called to ask if she would be the guardian of Janice and Paul's three children, if the two of them should die. "We're redoing the wills," Janice reported cheerfully over the din, while in the background Miriam could hear plainly the words "Give me that Rainbow Brite right now, dumb face."

"Just give it some thought," Janice had said calmly, but Miriam hadn't needed to think. "Will you help out with my memoirs if I'm someday the President?" her sister might as well have asked, or "What are your plans in the event of a nuclear war?" The question seemed to Miriam more mythical than practical. Janice was a careful person, not given to adventure, and in any case tended to stick to those kids like some kind of maternal adhesive. Any act of God that could pick off Janice without taking the lot would be a work of outstanding marksmanship.

Late on Sunday night, while Miriam was hemming a dress of Rennie's that had fallen into favor, she'd had a phone call from her ex-husband Lute. His first cousin and her boyfriend had just been killed on a San Diego freeway by a Purolator van. Over the phone, Lute seemed obsessed with getting the logistics of the accident right, as though the way the cars all obeyed the laws of physics could make this thing reasonable. The car that had the blowout was a Chrysler; the cousin and boyfriend were in her Saab; the van slammed into them from behind. "They never had a chance," Lute said, and the words chilled Miriam. Long after she went to bed she kept hearing him say "never had a chance," and imagining the pair as children. As if even in infancy their lives were already earmarked: these two will perish together in their thirties, in a Saab, wearing evening clothes, on their way to hear a friend play in the symphony orchestra. All that careful mothering and liberal-arts education gone to waste.

Lute's cousin had been a freelance cellist, often going on the road with the likes of Barry Manilow and Tony Bennett and, once, Madonna. It was probably all much tamer than it sounded. Miriam is surprised to find she has opinions about this woman, and a clear memory of her face. She only met her once, at her own wedding, when all of Lute's family had come crowding around like fog. But now this particular cousin has gained special prominence, her vague features crystallized in death, like a face on a postage stamp. Important. Someone you just can't picture doing the humdrum, silly things that life is made of—clipping her toenails or lying on the bed with her boyfriend watching *Dallas*—if you hold it clearly in your mind that she is gone.

Lute is probably crushed; he idolized her. His goal in life is to be his own boss. Freelance husbanding is just one of the things that hasn't worked out for Lute. Freelance fathering he can manage.

Miriam is thinking of Rennie while she waits through a yellow light she normally might have run. Rennie last week insisting on wearing only dresses to nursery school, and her pale, straight hair just so, with a ribbon; they'd seen *Snow*

White. Rennie as a toddler standing in her crib, holding the rails, her mouth open wide with the simplest expectation you could imagine: a cookie, a game, or nothing at all, just that they would both go on being there together. Lute was already out of the picture by that time; he wouldn't have been part of Rennie's hopes. It is only lately, since she's learned to count, that Lute's absence matters to Rennie. On the Disney Channel parents come in even numbers.

The light changes and there is a honking of horns; someone has done something wrong, or too slowly, or in the wrong lane. Miriam missed it altogether, whatever it was. She remembers suddenly a conversation she had with her sister years ago when she was unexpectedly pregnant with Rennie, and Janice was already a wise old mother of two. Miriam was frantic—she'd wanted a baby but didn't feel ready yet. "I haven't really worked out what it is I want to pass on to a child," she'd said to Janice, who laughed. According to Janice, parenting was three percent conscious effort and ninety-seven percent automatic pilot. "It doesn't matter what you think you're going to tell them. What matters is they're right there watching you every minute, while you let the lady with just two items go ahead of you in line, or when you lay on the horn and swear at the guy that cuts you off in traffic. There's no sense kidding yourself, what you see is what you get."

Miriam had argued that people could consciously change themselves if they tried, though in truth she'd been thinking more of Lute than herself. She remembers saying a great many things about choices and value systems and so forth, a lot of first-pregnancy high-mindedness it seems to her now. Now she understands. Parenting is something that happens mostly while you're thinking of something else.

Miriam's job claims her time for very irregular hours at the downtown branch of the public library. She is grateful that the people at Rennie's day care don't seem to have opinions about what kind of mother would work mornings one day, evenings the next. When she was first promoted to this position Miriam had a spate of irrational fears: she imagined Miss Joyce at TenderCare giving her a lecture on homemade soup and the importance of routine in the formative years. But Miss Joyce, it seems, understands modern arrangements. "The important thing is quality time," she said once to Miriam, in a way that suggested bedtime stories read with a yogic purity of concentration, a mind temporarily wiped clean of things like brake shoes and MasterCharge bills.

Miriam does try especially hard to schedule time for the two of them around Rennie's bedtime, but it often seems pointless. Rennie is likely to be absorbed in her own games, organizing animated campaigns on her bed with her stuffed animals, and finally dropping off in the middle of them, limbs askew, as though felled by a sniper.

Today is one of Miriam's afternoon-shift days. After leaving Rennie she has forty minutes in which she must do several errands before going to work. One of them is eat lunch. This is an item Miriam would actually put on a list: water African violets; dry cleaner's; eat lunch. She turns in at the Burger Boy and looks at her watch, surprised to see that she has just enough time to go in and sit down. Sometimes she takes the drive-through option and wolfs down a fish sandwich in the parking lot, taking large bites, rattling the ice in her Coke, unmindful of appearances. It's efficient, although it puts Miriam in mind of eating disorders.

Once she is settled inside with her lunch, her ears stray for company to other tables, picking up scraps of other people's private talk. "More than four hundred years old," she hears, and "It was a little bit tight over the instep," and "They had to call the police to get him out of there." She thinks of her friend Bob, who is a relentless eavesdropper, though because he's a playwright he calls it having an ear for dialogue.

Gradually she realizes that at the table behind her a woman is explaining to her daughter that she and Daddy are getting a divorce. It comes to Miriam like a slow shock, building up in her nerve endings until her skin hurts. This conversation will only happen once in that little girl's life, and I have to overhear it, Miriam is thinking. It has to be *here.* The surroundings seem banal, so cheery and hygienic, so many wiped-clean plastic surfaces. But then Miriam doesn't know what setting would be better. Certainly not some unclean place, and not an expensive restaurant either—that would be worse. To be expecting a treat, only to be socked with this news.

Miriam wants badly to turn around and look at the little girl. In her mind's eye she sees Rennie in her place: small and pale, sunk back into the puffy pink of her goosedown jacket like a loaf of risen dough that's been punched down.

The little girl keeps saying, "Okay," no matter what her mother tells her.

"Daddy will live in an apartment, and you can visit him. There's a swimming pool."

"Okay."

"Everything else will stay the same. We'll still keep Peppy with us. And you'll still go to your same school."

"Okay."

"Daddy does still love you, you know."

"Okay."

Miriam is thinking that ordinarily this word would work; it has finality. When you say it, it closes the subject.

It's already dark by the time Miriam picks up Rennie at TenderCare after work. The headlights blaze accusingly against the glass doors as if it were very late, midnight even. But it's only six-thirty, and Miriam tries to cheer herself by thinking that if this were summer it would still be light. It's a trick of the seasons, not entirely her fault, that Rennie has been abandoned for the daylight hours.

She always feels more surely on course when her daughter comes back to her. Rennie bounces into the car with a sheaf of papers clutched in one fist. The paper they use at TenderCare is fibrous and slightly brown, and seems wholesome to Miriam. Like turbinado sugar, rather than refined.

"Hi, sweetie. I missed you today." Miriam leans over to kiss Rennie and buckle her in before pulling out of the parking lot. All day she has been shaky about driving, and now she dreads the trip home. All that steel and momentum. It doesn't seem possible that soft human flesh could travel through it and come out intact. Throughout the day Miriam's mind has filled spontaneously with images of vulnerable things—baby mice, sunburned eyelids, sea creatures without their shells.

"What did you draw?" she asks Rennie, trying to anchor herself.

"This one is you and me and Lute," Rennie explains. Miriam is frowning into the river of moving headlights, waiting for a break in the traffic, and feels overcome by sadness. There are so many things to pay attention to at once, and all of them so important.

"You and me and Lute," Miriam repeats.

"Uh-huh. And a dog, Pickles, and Leslie Copley and his mom. We're all going out for a walk."

A sports car slows down, letting Miriam into the street. She waves her thanks. "Would you like to go for a walk with Leslie Copley and his mom sometime?"

"No. It's just a picture."

"What would you like for supper?"

"Pot pies!" Rennie shouts. Frozen dinners are her favorite thing. Miriam rather likes them too, although this isn't something she'd admit to many people. Certainly not her mother, for instance, or to Bob, who associates processed foods with intellectual decline. She wonders, though, if her privacy is an illusion. Rennie may well be revealing all the details of their home life to her nursery-school class, opening new chapters daily. What I had for dinner last night. What Mom does when we run out of socks. They probably play games along these lines at TenderCare, with entirely innocent intentions. And others, too, games with a social-worker bent: What things make you happy, or sad? What things make you feel scared?

Miriam smiles. Rennie is fearless. She does not know how it feels to be hurt, physically or otherwise, by someone she loves. The people at TenderCare probably hear a lot worse than pot pies.

"Mom," Rennie asks, "does God put things on the TV?"

"What do you mean?"

Rennie considers. "The cartoons, and the movies and things. Does God put them there?"

"No. People do that. You know how Grandpa takes movies of you with his movie camera, and then we show them on the screen? Well, it's like that. People at the TV station make the programs, and then they send them out onto your TV screen."

"I thought so," Rennie says. "Do you make them sometimes, at the library?"

Miriam hears a siren, but can't tell where it's coming from. "Well, I organize programs for the library, you're right, but not TV programs. Things like storybook programs. You remember, you've come to some of those." Miriam hopes she doesn't sound irritated. She is trying to slow down and move into the right lane, because of the ambulance, but people keep passing her on both sides, paying no attention. It makes Miriam angry. Sure enough, the ambulance is coming their way. It has to jerk to a full stop in the intersection ahead of them because of all the people who refuse to yield to greater urgency.

"Mom, what happens when you die?"

Miriam is startled because she was thinking of Lute's poor cousin. Thinking of the condition of the body, to be exact. But Rennie doesn't even know about this relative, won't hear her sad story for years to come.

"I'm not sure, Rennie. I think maybe what happens is that you think back over your life, about all the nice things you've done and the people who've been your friends, and then you close your eyes and . . . it's quiet." She was going to say, ". . . and go to sleep," but she's read that sleep and death shouldn't be equated, that it can cause children to fear bedtime. "What do you think?"

"I think you put on your nicest dress, and then you get in this glass box and everybody cries and then the prince comes and kisses you. On the lips."

"That's what happened to Snow White, isn't it?"

"Uh-huh. I didn't like when he kissed her on the lips. Why didn't he kiss her on the cheek?"

"Well, grownups kiss on the lips. When they like each other."

"But Snow White wasn't a grownup. She was a little girl."

This is a new one on Miriam. This whole conversation is like a toboggan ride, threatening at every moment to fly out of control in any direction. She's enjoying it, though, and regrets that they will have to stop soon for some errands. They are low on produce, canned goods, aluminum foil, and paper towels, completely out of vacuum-cleaner bags and milk.

"What I think," says Miriam, after giving it some consideration, "is that Snow White was a little girl at first, but then she grew up. Taking care of the seven dwarfs helped her learn responsibility." Responsibility is something she and Rennie have talks about from time to time. She hears another siren, but this one is definitely behind them, probably going to the same scene as the first. She imagines her sister Janice's three children bundling into her life in a whirlwind of wants and possessions. Miriam doesn't even have time for another house plant. But she realizes that having time is somehow beside the point.

"So when the prince kissed her, did she grow up?" Rennie asks.

"No, before that. She was already grown up when the prince came. And they liked each other, and they kissed, and afterward they went out for a date."

"Like you and Mr. Bob?"

"Like Bob and I do sometimes, right. You don't have to call him Mr. Bob, honey. He's your friend, you can call him just Bob, if you want to."

Instead of making the tricky left turn into the shopping center, Miriam's car has gone right, flowing with the tide of traffic. It happened almost before she knew it, but it wasn't an accident. She just isn't ready to get to the grocery store, where this conversation will be lost among the bright distractions of bubble gum and soda. Looping back around the block will give them another four or five minutes. They could sit and talk in the parking lot, out of the traffic, but Miriam is starting to get her driving nerves back. And besides, Rennie would think that peculiar. Her questions would run onto another track.

"And then what happened to the seven dwarfs?" Rennie wants to know.

"I think Snow White still took care of them, until they were all grown up and could do everything by themselves."

"And did the prince help too?"

"I think he did."

"But what if Snow White died. If she stayed dead, I mean, after the prince kissed her."

Miriam now understands that this is the angle on death that has concerned Rennie all along. She is relieved. For Miriam, practical questions are always the more easily answered.

"I'm sure the dwarfs would still be taken care of," she

says. "The point is that Snow White really loved them, so she'd make sure somebody was going to look after them, no matter what, don't you think?"

"Uh-huh. Maybe the prince."

"Maybe." A motorcyclist dodges in front of them, too close, weaving from lane to lane just to get a few yards ahead. At the next red light they will all be stopped together, the fast drivers and the slow, shooting looks at one another as if someone had planned it all this way.

"Rennie, if something happened to me, you'd still have somebody to take care of you. You know that, don't you?"

"Uh-huh. Lute."

"Is that what you'd like? To go and live with Lute?"

"Would I have to?"

"No, you wouldn't have to. You could live with Aunt Janice if you wanted to."

Rennie brightens. "Aunt Janice and Uncle Paul and Michael-and-Donna-and-Perry?" The way she says it makes Miriam think of their Christmas card.

"Right. Is that what you'd want?"

Rennie stares at the windshield wipers. The light through the windshield is spotty, falling with an underwater strangeness on Rennie's serious face. "I'm not sure," she says. "I'll have to think it over."

Miriam feels betrayed. It depresses her that Rennie is even willing to take the question seriously. She wants her to deny the possibility, to give her a tearful hug and say she couldn't live with anyone but Mommy.

"It's not like I'm sending you away, Rennie. I'm not going to die while you're a little girl. We're just talking about what-if. You understand that, right?"

"Right," Rennie says. "It's a game. We play what-if at school." After another minute she says, "I think Aunt Janice."

They are repeating their route now, passing again by the Burger Boy where Miriam had lunch. The tables and chairs inside look neater than it's possible to keep things in real life, and miniature somehow, like doll furniture. It looks bright and safe, not the sort of place that could hold ghosts.

On an impulse Miriam decides to put off the errands until tomorrow. She feels reckless, knowing that tomorrow will already be busy enough without a backlog. But they can easily live another day without vacuum-cleaner bags, and she'll work out something about the milk.

"We could stop here and have a hamburger for dinner," Miriam says. "Or a fish sandwich. And afterward we could stop for a minute at Ice Cream Heaven. Would you like that?"

"No. Pot pies!"

"And no Ice Cream Heaven?"

"I don't need any more angel stickers. Leslie Copley gave me twelve."

"Well, that was nice of him."

"Yep. He hates bananas."

"Okay, we'll go straight home. But do you remember that pot pies take half an hour to cook in the oven? Will you be too hungry to wait, once we get home?"

"No, I'll be able to wait," Rennie says, sounding as if she really will. In the overtones of her voice and the way she pushes her blond hair over her shoulder there is a startling maturity, and Miriam is frozen for a moment with a vision of a much older Rennie. All the different Rennies—the teenager, the adult—are already contained in her hands and her voice, her confidence. From moments like these, parents can find the courage to believe in the resilience of their children's lives. They will barrel forward like engines, armored by their own momentum, more indestructible than love.

"Okay then, pot pies it is," Miriam says. "Okay."

STONE DREAMS

When I was sixteen my mother found birth-control pills in my sock drawer and declared that early promiscuity would ruin me psychologically. She said I'd been turned loose too young in the candy store and would go spoiled, that later in life I'd be unable to hold down a monogamous relationship. She said many things, but that one stayed with me. At the age of thirty-nine I was going on vacation with a man who wasn't my husband. There we sat in his Volvo, bald proof of my psychological ruin, headed north on the interstate along with the crowd of holiday travelers breaking the speed limit slightly.

My lover's name was Peter, which we felt to be ironic because of my husband's great knowledge of rocks. Also, our destination was the Petrified Forest. None of this irony was intended, though. Life always provides me with better jokes than any I could invent.

Peter was an intellectual and custom cabinetmaker with a lean body and appealing hands and a head of hair like some sweet, dark animal doomed for its pelt. The first time I saw him, his muscular abdomen set my fingers to wondering how it would like to have them go rippling across it. He'd shown up at our unfinished house to conceive the cabinetry, and was fully clothed, as you would expect, but I have a sixth sense about pleasing men in ways that aren't my business. I'm rarely wrong. My mother would say I can't help it, that my moral fiber decayed in adolescence like a twelve-year molar.

I settled my neck into the soft leather headrest of my lover's car, letting my hair blow out the window. Peter's Volvo was old but the seats were reupholstered in an unbelievably soft material that he claimed, with a straight face, to be kitten leather. The car had everything except air conditioning, which in his opinion put an artificial distance between the passenger and the passage. Men can say things like that; they don't have to put up with hair whipping in their eyes for hours on end. I was hoping I looked attractively disheveled, and not browbeaten. I'd dressed for this adventure in a black tank top and a pair of jeans whose most striking feature was a zipper that ran all the way from front to back. Technically I suppose you could zip them right in two. I'd bought the outfit at my daughter's insistence on one of our afternoons in the mall.. The real name of this style, she informed me, was "drive-in pants." I had grave reservations. "Nobody but Cher ought to be wearing an outfit like this at my age," I said.

"No, Mom, it's great," she said. "You look sexy."

Julie is thirteen, a dangerous time, I'm told, because soon she'll discover sex, just as surely as she learned ten years ago to pull the protective caps out of the electric sockets and toy with the powers lying hidden in the wall. I look at Julie's long flying hair, her coltish gait, and refuse to believe it. She and I are close. She leaves me notes, sweet things decorated with hearts, in places where I'll discover them as I go through the business of my day: in my change purse or the pocket of her jeans in the clothes hamper. Where would she hide sex? And how could she urge me into vampish clothes, if she truly understood the implications for family disaster? Still, her sock drawer I'd begun to avoid like the plague.

"Julie wants to be a linguist," I told Peter, needing to

alter my train of thought. For two weeks each summer Julie visited my mother in Kentucky, and in the early years would come home with cheerful reports of butter-and-sugar-on-bread for dessert, but more recently she'd brought back a fascination for country speech. "I'd knock you down for that shirt," my daughter will cry, and "Just a minute? I'll just-a-minute you over the head with something!" Last year she filled up a little notebook, studying Mother and her rook-playing cronies like Margaret Mead among the Samoans. I was floored to see my mother, policewoman of my adolescence, reduced to a list of quaint phrases.

"A linguist?" Peter, who was tall, leaned back from the steering wheel as if its only purpose were for resting his hands.

"That's what she says. She just made the announcement, and it's been one big argument between her and Nathan ever since."

"Why is that?" he asked. "Does he want her in the family cornea business?" My husband is an eye surgeon. Rocks and minerals are just a consuming passion.

"Oh no, I don't think there's anything he especially wants her to *be.* He just has to tell her what *not* to be. He says Noam Chomsky is a socialist. And Julie says that's the point, linguistics is a truly egalitarian science." The Upper Sonoran Desert was ripping by us at 3,000 rpm and my right ear was roaring from the wind. I was relieved to see Peter put on his blinker for the scenic route through Sedona. If scenery was an objective, he'd need to slow down. "Did you know phrases like that when you were twelve?" I asked, forgetting she'd turned thirteen.

"Perhaps. But I'm not a fair example." It's true, Peter was probably not a fair example of anything, linguistically speaking. He was born in St. Louis but carried a trace of German accent, having been raised in a part of the city where, he claimed, you'd go for weeks hearing no English other than "Coca-Cola" and "Scram." Julie was fascinated.

Whenever he came over on his visits, feigning interest in the woodwork—hugging us all and exclaiming, "Nathan, Diana! How is that veneer holding up?"—Julie would make him repeat her favorite phrase: "*Varoom nicht?*"

"Well," I said. "I'm scared to death she's going to say something like that to *me* one morning at breakfast. A truly egalitarian science. That's exactly how she is, you know? She'd expect me to carry on a conversation on the same intellectual level as Nathan does."

"But you would agree with her, and that would take the sport out of it. So there's no danger."

"I suppose that's true," I said.

Nathan and Julie and I live in a new house that is too large and dramatic for a family of three. There's lots of plate glass, with views of mountains and canyons if you're feeling naturalistic, or of the twinkling, seemingly distant lights of the city if you're feeling superior. In the living room are expensive copies of pre-Columbian art and genuine fossils—delicate fish that look like etchings—on slabs of pink and beige stone that harmonize with the carpet. I think the drama of the house gets to us, forcing us to rise to occasions we'd all rather just let pass. Nathan and Julie stalk around each other with faces like tragic masks. She's going through a stage in which she claims to hate Nathan. He really was good with her when she was a baby, but now that she's threatening to turn into a woman he seems to feel a great need to boss her around.

I take classes in things that go well with Danish Modern—weaving and natural dyes, for instance, but never macramé—and envision myself writing poetry in some other, probably smaller house. Three days a week I teach steno and typing to junior-high students without an ambitious bone in their bodies.

Now, I have a sister Eva, six years younger, who of all things works as a reporter for Japanese TV. They say she is the Jane Pauley of Japan. She has a Japanese boyfriend and can use chopsticks without giving it a thought, her mind totally on something else. I'm not sure how Eva got from here to there; I was already in Phoenix when she finished high school. We have the same features, everyone sees her picture and thinks it's me in a kimono, and yet Eva has gone so far in her life whereas I have only traveled. I'm the oldest and, according to all the books, should be the achiever, but there you go. I've never quite gotten over my hometown's limited expectations of me—of any girl, really. "Marry a millionaire" was the best they could come up with, "or teach school." I expected to settle for the latter, there seeming to be too much competition for the former.

I went to college on my dead father's Social Security and did try adventurous electives—pre-Columbian history and modern poetry—but I never left home until I married Nathan and moved to Phoenix. Deserts of the world have a high incidence of cornea disease. Mother felt I'd chosen Nathan purposefully as part of an overall scheme centering on her abandonment, but the truth is I met him at a fraternity mixer and couldn't turn him down once we saw how perfectly I fit in with his plans. I would have sex with him now, marry him later, and type his way through med school. After that would come residency, and Julie, and Phoenix. It was as much a surprise to me as to Mother. I could only tell her it was lucky we didn't end up in Saudi Arabia—eye-disease capital of the earth—and then give her Julie for two weeks a year, the way the Aztecs every so often offered up to the grumpy gods a human heart.

Apart from that first decision to submit to the pressures of a high-school linebacker and go to his family's doctor for birth-control pills, I don't believe I'd ever acted in a bold or decisive way. I have wished for a womanly friendship with my mother. I'd like to confess to her my doubts about who's in the driver's seat of my life, but she thinks I am Jezebel. That discovery of hers in my bureau really started us out on the wrong foot.

Technically, Peter has pointed out, I'm not promiscuous. I'm serially monogamous. I hadn't consciously made love with Nathan in over a year, and my earlier affairs took place during similar dry spells. There had been a good number. Nathan didn't know about Peter, but I had a feeling he wasn't altogether in the dark either. We stayed together because he didn't seem to have other plans, and because I couldn't picture myself as being husbandless. There was my daughter to consider, still young, in need of years of shelter.

Peter had two grown sons. People my age, I've found, can turn out to be the parents of children anywhere along the way from cradle to college, but this doesn't necessarily tell you the first thing about them. Peter's wife and boys barely made a dent in him. Now he was interested in Jung and Nietzsche and lived alone in his workshop, a rented studio with sawdust in the kitchen. He ate cold baked potatoes for breakfast. And he did not, by any means, wish to be saved. He wasn't someone I could marry.

But we were in love by modern standards, and had been planning this trip for months—our first opportunity for daytime adventures and whole nights together. It was Memorial Day weekend: Julie was off to Mother's and Nathan to an eye-surgery meeting. Normally I might have gone along, but I'd begged off. There was my weaving class, I pointed out. Our answering machine had beeperless remote so my plan was to check in and answer calls as needed, pretending to be home. It would work as long as there were no catastrophes, no calls in the middle of the night, but then that's only life's ordinary degree of risk.

Really I wasn't worried; I felt free. At that moment Peter and I were driving through the impressively inanimate landscape of Sedona; all that red, and it had nothing to do with blood. "Iron," Nathan would have announced. I could almost picture him in the back seat. "When the seas first learned to breathe oxygen, a carpet of rust was laid down over the face of the earth." I made fun of his way of talking, but in sixteen years I'd picked up his penchant for dramatizing things, and I did it better. Peter loved it. In Peter's presence my stories took on mythic significance. He called them "Diana's legends."

"I think the happiest afternoon of Nathan's and my marriage was last Thanksgiving," I said, reminded by the cliffs. "When I found the petroglyph." Whenever Peter was driving, the burden of conversation fell to me. I settled back, looking out the window. "We'd eaten too much, and drunk too much, and these people I'd invited Nathan couldn't really abide so they'd left already, and Nathan and I went hiking up the arroyo behind the house. We hadn't hiked in years, I don't know what got into us. I think we felt like after all that food we had to do something virtuous."

"After this trip," Peter pointed out, "you will have to hike the Grand Canyon."

"Or the Himalayas," I said. "With ankle weights. But only if Nathan's flirting with a hula girl in Waikiki." His meeting was in Honolulu. If you move in the right circles you'll know that discussing torn retinas within a hundred yards of the pounding surf is not an unusual thing.

"You're laughing," Peter said. "But it might be true. Don't you ever wonder if he's having affairs?"

"Oh, God, if only he were. I really do wish he would."

"Why, because you would feel less guilty?"

I'd thought about this. "No. Because then we'd have to do something, he and I. About us."

The sun was beginning to set on the red rocks of Sedona, firing them to a crimson exactly the color of Peter's Volvo. If this were a family vacation we would stop now and take a picture: with a red scarf draped theatrically around my neck, the crimson cliffs in the background, Nathan and I would pose in a contrived arrangement of passion on the hood of the red car. Julie would snap the shot.

"And you can't do anything about *you* by yourself?"

Peter really didn't know me. Our relationship was not primarily based on conversation. "I am a non-mover," I said. "An immobilized person."

"He does have that effect." Peter had told me he was bored by only about eight things on earth, including Nathan.

"No, I can't blame it all on him. It's me. I was that way before I met Nathan. I cling to steady things, like a barnacle clings to a boulder."

"A barnacle will cling to anything," he said. "Flotsam and jetsam."

"Only if it *thinks* those things are a boulder."

"Nevertheless," Peter said. "That's something you ought to keep in mind." I wondered what he meant by that, until he added, "When you write poems about barnacles."

He knew I didn't write poems about barnacles or anything else. I only read them. I fiddled with the radio. We were gradually losing the public radio station from Phoenix, so that the strains of Schubert's *Trout Quintet* were interspersed with what seemed to be a call-in show about garden difficulties. "You don't believe me, about being a barnacle, but it's true," I said. "When I went to college, which was supposed to make you feel, you know, uplifted, I felt like my loafers were screwed to the floor. The other students would ask these questions that made the professors *pause* and *reflect*, and they'd see symbolism without having it pointed out, but I just couldn't conceive of anything beyond what I saw on the page. I kept thinking there was some explanatory brochure I'd forgotten to pick up during registration. Or maybe it was because they all lived in dorms and I lived at home. Those other girls probably sat around in the halls with their hair in rollers and talked about symbolism."

Peter laughed. "So let's go back to Thanksgiving," he said, in a laid-on-thick accent like Dr. Freud. "The happiest afternoon of your marriage." He knew it was not going to be a happy story.

"Okay, we'd had this huge dinner. We were hiking up the arroyo, and we'd stopped for some reason. Oh, I know, Nathan had these new seventy-five-dollar running shoes and they weren't wearing right. He said if they weren't broken in correctly they would be no better than shoes from K-Mart. Believe it or not, there was something on those shoes you could actually adjust. So I was standing there looking up at the rocks. It's that part where it's narrow, like a little canyon. You know where I mean?"

Peter nodded. He'd spent a good deal of time on the land where our house was built. He said he needed a sense of the topography before he could build cabinets that would complement the home's natural setting. I believe that some of his topographical devotion had to do with our kissing and kneading of each other's thigh muscles between the boulders.

I shifted my hips on the kitten leather. "So there it was, I just saw it," I said, trying to concentrate on the dramatic core of my story. "The petroglyph. It was one of those, I can't think what they're called—the way a child will draw the sun, with the rays sticking out."

"A sunburst."

"A sunburst. But a child hadn't drawn it, it was carved there by the Indians hundreds of years ago as an act of worship, or whatever. The personal statement of an Indian, back when it wasn't vandalism to carve on the rocks in Camelback Park."

Peter said, "In a time when personal statements were more scarce than rocks."

"Yes," I said.

It hadn't been our first, by any means—petroglyphs were an avid hobby of Nathan's, along with rocks in general. Prehistoric rock carvings, he said, were the aesthetic bridge between humans and the earth. But this makes him sound metaphysical, whereas the truth was he *collected* petroglyphs, the way birders will fiercely accumulate a life list. We were lost for seven hours once in Arkansas looking for a state park that was established on the basis of one decorated rock. What we finally found was a boulder pathetically cordoned off like the Plymouth Rock, out of its element, and miserably defaced. The teenagers of Arkansas had immortalized their current passions alongside the holy artwork of the Osage. We'd made out lizards with tails like corkscrews, and something that looked like an umbrella, but the carvings were overwritten like a brutally graded essay test, in Nathan's opinion too damaged even to photograph. He blamed the Park Service, and pouted for days, though it wasn't unexpected. We'd had more than one vacation ruined by this form of vandalism.

But Peter had heard that story. "What was so beautiful about finding that petroglyph," I said, "was that we hadn't even been looking. There it was, perfect, maybe nobody even knew about it, and I could just present it to him like a gift. Peter, you wouldn't have recognized him—you wouldn't believe Nathan could be that joyful. He didn't even run back to get his camera. Because it would always be there, two hundred yards from our living room. For weeks and weeks he made almost this *show* of postponing going back to photograph it. I think it gave him a thrill to be so casual."

"As if he owned it," Peter said.

"Exactly."

Peter was waiting for the rest of the story.

"But then what happened is, he got busy and forgot. He didn't remember until just a couple of weeks ago. They're putting in a new split level up there above the arroyo, and the blasting for the foundations split the face right off the rocks. Nathan had a fit."

"Poor inconsolable Nathan."

"Poor me! You're not going to believe this, now he's accusing me of having carved it there, and pretending to find it that day. He says I go out of my way to ridicule his avocation."

"I'll bet you did," Peter said. "You climbed up there in the dark of night with a cold chisel and carved a petroglyph, to make a mockery of his avocation. That's something you would do."

I laughed. The whole point of these stories, I knew, was to betray Nathan. I never mentioned his kindnesses or his broad intelligence, it was the unreasonable parts of our marriage I needed to pester and pick at like a scab. It wasn't that Peter wanted that, really. He was a generous human being, unusually self-assured, not requiring constant favorable comparisons with the husband the way some men do. After all, I was there in his Volvo instead of in Waikiki. But Peter understood, I think, that in some way these stories kept my head above water. As if I were really that far removed from my life, that much in command.

"That truly is the essence of Nathan," I said. "Everything has to revolve around his pursuit of the perfect petroglyph."

"The rock that will complete his life."

"That's it," I said. "The Rock of Ages, there, from whence they flow."

"From whence what flows?"

"I'm not sure. That's Robert Southey." Sometimes lines of poems I'd read long ago would flutter up from the air and perch in my brain like sparrows. "From whence poetic things flow, I guess, rocky reveries. Chiseled hopes and stone dreams."

"*Obsidian* dreams," said Peter, who had a working knowledge of rocks himself. "Sedimentary obsessions, and obsidian dreams."

Our plan was to go as far as Flagstaff the first day and camp near the Wupatki ruins. We would hike out to Wupatki in the moonlight, and in the shadow of the ancient city carved into the hillside, we would make love. The next day we would continue on to our destination.

I had carried with me from childhood a fascination for the Petrified Forest. I can't imagine how I even knew of its existence, but in sixth grade I wrote a poem about it. It was deemed excellent, and I was required to read it to the entire class. I had in mind that the Petrified Forest was an elaborate affair, comprised of entire, towering trees; I remember a line about "the twisted igneous of their trunks, their glistening granite leaves." (My mother owned a thesaurus.) I believe I even had their firm branches offering shelter to stone deer and little stone squirrels. I'd had such splendid confusions about the geological world back then, before marrying a man who'd minored in igneous and granite.

But Nathan, it turned out, was unconcerned about formerly living things turned to stone. The fossil fish in our living room were my idea of a representation of his interests, not his. In all our years in Arizona he'd steadfastly refused to take me to see the fossil forest. "It's not a forest at all," he explained. "The very name makes it sound like something it isn't. No person alive has ever visited the Petrified Forest and not come away disappointed."

This sort of statement was so typical of Nathan that it didn't dissuade me. I wanted to see it. When it became clear that Peter and I were going to have a clandestine adventure, it seemed fitting that we should go to the stone forest of my dreams. Peter was only too happy to fill the various empty places Nathan left in my life.

But Peter and I, unlike Nathan and me, were a couple without a practical half; vacations do go more smoothly when someone takes an interest in things like museum schedules and motel reservations. It turned out that Peter and I had chosen an utterly moonless night for our moonlight hike, and the drive to Wupatki was hours longer than we thought. We reached Flagstaff after dark and had trouble finding the state park. We ended up in a deserted county fairground. A sign said it was the home of the Rotary Ranglers, and served also, for a few weeks of the year, as a Boy Scout camp.

A man at the entrance waved us in, and we were too tired and lost to resist the motion of his hand.

"It's free, anyway," Peter said.

"It's late," I added. It was, and I was hungry. Peter had brought some corn on the cob to roast slowly in the coals, but I had a feeling we'd be content with cold chicken and one another.

I was right. After we'd picked the wishbone clean and found the paper towels to clean our fingers and chins, Peter pulled me along, kissing my neck, to the edge of the fairground and up through a dry stream bed. We'd climbed thousands of feet in elevation since Phoenix, and it was cold. We walked side by side, or single file where the path was narrow, touching each other's palms in the darkness and sometimes slipping our icy hands inside each other's clothes. They practically made steam against our hot bodies. I don't think we'd ever gotten over those early days in the arroyo; we were turned on by uncomfortable outdoor locales.

The night was black. I'd forgotten that the moon sometimes failed to show up at all. From the dim lighting over the fairground we could make out silhouettes of the boulders along the creek bank, but little else, and I did consider rattlesnakes, but not very much. We rolled ourselves down onto a wide, flat boulder, which I informed him was granite. I'd learned a thing or two in sixteen years of marriage, I said.

"Like what?" asked Peter, who was on the verge of discovering the modern engineering miracle of drive-in pants.

We lay in a small clearing, with tall pines standing around the edge like dignified voyeurs.

I unbuttoned my coat and pulled up Peter's sweater and mine so that our abdomens could commune. He was astonishingly soft to the touch, like kitten leather himself. I always forgot this, in between times, or thought I'd imagined it. He said his mother used to tell him that *Gott im Himmel* meant for Peter to be a girl, but at the last minute realized little Werner needed a baby brother. Little Werner got his brother all right but died young of rheumatic fever, so God's last-minute decision went to waste, except insofar as heterosexual womankind was concerned. Peter was another one turned loose too young in the candy store, I suspect.

Peter's kisses were cold on my skin, and my fingers in his hair tingled as though they'd found a pair of fur-lined mittens. Through several layers of clothes I could feel his muscles. It never failed to arouse me, to think my contours were appreciated by one of the city's most excellent builders of cabinets.

He sat up, stroking my hair and looking at me, forming over me a dark man-shape that blotted out the stars. He ran a finger from my jawbone to my ear and said something in German, "*Geliebte Hafen.*" My body lay flat against the rock and was cold enough to be part of it, like a fossil fish, but at that moment I belonged to the living world nearly more than I could bear.

Peter bent over and picked up something from the ground and polished it on his jeans, then touched it to my lips—something cold and surprisingly smooth. It was a pebble. He put it down the neck of my sweater and I shivered as it slid between my breasts and touched my belly.

"What kind of rock is that?" I asked.

"Melted rock," he said, warming it with his breath and drawing it in a circle around my navel. "Obsidian."

Obsidian is rare, and fairly precious. Technically it is

volcanic glass, cooled suddenly to brilliance when it is pulled from the earth and thrown across miles of sky.

I'd worn my old camping coat, a Navy surplus pea-jacket, and was glad to have it. With our passions spent and our furnaces running low on fuel, I pulled it over us like a blanket. Even through the wool the brass buttons stood out as individual points of cold. We were lying back on the boulder and on Peter's sweater, looking at the stars. It was nothing like Phoenix; the stars here were crowded. It looked like there was a shortage of space up there for all of them.

"Last time I wore this coat I was stargazing with Julie," I said. "We went up Camelback Mountain, I think it might have been New Year's Day. I can't remember where Nathan was."

"I wish I knew the constellations," Peter said. "Not from a need to be scientific, but for the stories. There is so much poetry up there, and history, and to me it's only stars."

"That's almost exactly the same thing I told Julie. I said I hated not being able to teach her the constellations, that they stood for all these ancient myths. But she didn't care, she said she wanted to know about idioms."

"Idioms?" Peter pulled the sweater down, tucking it under our backs. The granite felt cold and grainy, like frozen sand.

"She said they show how the language changes. She wanted to know what funny expressions we used to use when I was a girl in Kentucky. She made it sound like I'd lived in a covered wagon. I told her they didn't seem that funny to us at the time, it was just the way we talked. I couldn't remember any. Just one."

"Which one?"

" 'My stars.' My mother used to say that, 'My stars!' "

"What did she mean?"

"Oh, just surprise. Like, 'My goodness' or 'My word.' I have no idea where it comes from. But I liked it. I used to think Mother really did have some stars of her own tucked away. That a little section up there was fenced off like a garden, and those were my mother's stars."

Peter's lips smiled against my neck.

Eventually the cold was too much for us and we got up. Peter buried the fruits of our labors under a rock. A friend of mine, new to extramarital sex, said she loved how condoms kept everything neatly packaged up, but I didn't. I knew I would wake up in the morning missing the stickiness, proof that someone had needed me in the night.

"Latex isn't biodegradable," I reminded my lover as we zipped and buttoned ourselves for the hike back. I slipped the pebble into my coat pocket, determined to look at this alleged obsidian someday in better light. "I'm sure there's a huge fine for littering a county fairground with prophylactics."

"But, my love," he said, "we use sheep gut. It will have disappeared by morning."

"But the question is, will you?"

This, in its variations, was an old joke.

Back in the tent I couldn't sleep. Like the pea princess I was aware of every stone underneath the air mattress and the down sleeping bag, and I felt myself growing bruised and old while Peter breathed heavily in a distant, happy land. I knew we would never really be together; we needed different things. I loved the time I spent with him, but felt in some other chamber of my heart that it was time wasted. That I ought to be doing something else while there was time.

Sometimes I get this way, letting my mind run in frantic fast-forward like a videotape gone wild. In a year, I say to myself, I will be forty. In a decade, fifty. Peter may be the last man ever attracted to me purely on the basis of sex. I wonder what else there is to me, what will become of me, and of Julie. I can't see staying in my marriage, but neither could I ever be the one to bring it down just to please myself. Nathan would say I was selfish, and he would be right. All I can imagine for certain is Nathan's anger, the roof caving in and plate glass flying as the house implodes on itself the way a light bulb will when the vacuum inside is disrupted.

I woke up in the heat, with morning sun on the tent and Peter tasting my ear. Peter's sexual appetite was surpassed only by his supply of condoms, which seemed to swarm around him in their bright yellow wrappers like a hive of personal bees. Sometimes they surprised me in my purse or the glove box of my car, lying dangerously close to the little folded notes in which my daughter the linguist had declared, "I ♥ MY MOM."

I turned over and ran my tongue along his collarbone. He rolled me onto his chest and bingo, we were connected. Peter's body and mine were like those spacecraft that lock or dock, moving together all of their own accord. I've heard that up there in the absence of air molecules objects develop their own gravity.

Peter turned his face into my hair and whispered, "The Boy Scouts are here."

Mother of God, it was true. I could hear sounds of hatcheting and seventh-grade swearing and, I imagined, of two sticks being rubbed together, all in the near vicinity of our tent. They had arrived early this morning, obviously, or very late last night. The man at the front gate must have thought we were the first wave of Scouts.

Peter began to roll under me like the ocean and I had a good deal of difficulty being quiet. We were lying right out on the same ground where boyhood industry was getting fires built and kindling split; copulating, very likely, in the middle of a merit badge. The only thing between them and our nakedness was a membrane of blue nylon, and it seemed so thin.

Peter's hands held the small of my back like some piece of maple or walnut they understood. "Peter," I pleaded, about to laugh out loud, or cry, "have pity on the children. They're trying to remain clean in thought, word, and deed."

"How do you know?"

I tried to hold my breath. "I'm sure of it. It's one of their laws."

"Girl Scout laws," he said, his fingers sending chills up my spine that threatened to disturb the peace. "I don't think the Boy Scouts have that one."

On the way to the Petrified Forest we had a fight. Peter drove faster and faster as we argued, and my ears were roaring so ferociously that I demanded we roll up the windows and sweat until the argument was over. We were back in the low country, in the heat.

It started when I found a condom in my purse. I wasn't really angry, but we'd talked about this. "I've asked you not to put them in there," I said.

"You put it there. Three weeks ago. Remember, when we met at the bicycle race and walked down to the river?"

Men will make fun of you for lugging around a purse, and then the minute you've set off for somewhere they'll ask if you could just stick in for them this little thing or that.

"Just try to keep them out of my territory, okay?" I asked. "That's all Julie needs, to find her own mother's illicit contraceptives."

I felt the weight of last night's depression moving back into my chest. Also I was getting a headache, an actual migraine—something I'd rarely had since Julie's birth rewrote the recipe of my body chemicals. As a teenager I'd had them like clockwork. First came the aura: an arc of blue lights strung across my field of vision. Slowly it would curve around into circles, so I'd see the world as if through two long glass tunnels in a sparkling ocean. Then the pain would clamp down.

"It wouldn't be the end of the world if Julie found a condom," Peter said. "She would probably think they were for you and Nathan."

"She knows about Nathan." Nathan had had a vasectomy, performed for free by a colleague in exchange for his mother's cataract operation; Nathan felt he'd gotten the short end of the bargain. "She knows way too much," I said. "Sometimes I think she reads my mind."

"What do you mean when you say, 'That's all Julie needs'? You talk as though she's constantly about to step over a cliff."

"I just think there's enough stress in her life right now. For example, she thinks she hates her own father."

"Why do you deny the validity of her feelings? Maybe she really does hate him."

"She can't really hate him. He's her father."

"He is her biological father, which doesn't prove he is good for her. Male guppies eat their children."

"He's cold-blooded, but he's not a guppy."

"Children," said Peter the authority, who hadn't laid eyes on his sons in a month of Sundays, "have excellent instincts about what is good for them."

"Children need their parents."

"Do you think your mother was good for you? You're always saying she robbed you of self-confidence."

"She was all I had. Daddy couldn't do a whole lot for us."

My father was killed in a train derailment when my sister was still too young to know him from any other man without a beard. After that, Mother had a career behind the soda fountain at Woolworth's. On weekdays you could see her there drawing out sodas with no expression on her face, or standing at the juicer making orange juice, stacking up the emptied-out halves like a display of bright beanies, their cheerfulness lost on her. The franchise was owned by a Mr. Fuller, who people said was a philanderer. Mother told us this meant he gave away his savings. His wife threw herself off a bridge and lay at the bottom of the Licking River for nine days before they dragged her out, the reason being that she had tied a whole cement block around her neck with binder's twine and it took her down like an anchor. She was a small, weak woman, and people speculated about how she'd lifted the thing up in the first place. She must have made a great effort. On the day of her funeral, my mother got the job.

She worked there still. I had the crazy idea—I knew I wouldn't do it—of sending Mother a postcard from the Petrified Forest.

Peter was still involved in winning the argument. "But what if you *had* had a choice?" he insisted. "As Julie does."

"What do you mean?"

"What if you'd had two parents, one who was good for you, and one who was not?"

It seemed unfair of him to egg me on like this. He certainly wouldn't be there to offer her fatherhood, if I bailed out of my marriage.

I sighed and rolled down the window. "I don't know what people do when they have choices," I said. "I don't think I've ever had any."

I don't suppose I had honestly expected whole trees, standing upright, but really there was so little to see. A young Navajo woman in a Smokey Bear hat at the park entrance handed us a brochure. "There's a map of the auto route in your brochure," she said. "There are nine stops. Please stay on the trails, and have a great day." She sounded as if she would willingly surrender her job to progress, if a robot could be found.

At each stop we parked the Volvo and hiked the hundred yards or so through the desert to the vista, hoping every time that we were about to see the real petrified forest. Peter tried to make it seem more impressive by reading passages from the brochure about the mineralization process, how actual living tissue had over the millennia turned to stone. But it wasn't trees, just trunks, scattered here and there over the desert. Not even whole trunks, really, just short lengths of log toppled over and broken into parts. "Take Nothing but Pictures, Leave Nothing but Footprints," we were instructed by signs at every turn, but if there had ever been anything to take it must have been carted off long ago. At the later stops, some people weren't even getting out of their cars. A giant mobile home hummed like a vibrator next to us in the Stop Eight parking lot, its windows rolled up to hold in the air conditioning. High up in the passenger seat, a woman in a sun visor sat petting a cocker spaniel, waiting while her husband went out for one more try.

I hated to admit Nathan was right, but they had no business calling this a forest. It reminded me of a Biblical disaster area—a tribe of toppled-over women who'd all looked back and got turned into pillars of salt.

Finally, on our way back, something went right: we found the Wupatki campground. Peter bustled around setting up camp, pleased with himself. He lit the lantern and built a fire and pitched the tent while I slowly wrapped each ear of corn in aluminum foil. He buried them in the coals like little mummies, making a ritual of it, saying that by the time we returned from our hike to Wupatki it would be done to perfection.

The pain in my head was subsiding. I knew when it was gone I'd be left with a migraine aftermath, the sense that my brain had been peeled like a fruit. And there was another sensation too, which might stay with me for days—an animal feeling, a need to hide and rest somewhere, and think.

I wasn't sure I felt like going out to the ruins with Peter. I knew that would be all right with him; the hike was no longer an important point on the agenda. There was still no moon to speak of and we had, after all, already made love under the stars. Peter's interest in Wupatki was at this point more archaeological. He brought my peajacket and draped it around my shoulders, telling me to sit and take it easy. He could be a family sort of man at certain moments. He brought me a tin cup and the bottle of brandy.

I slipped my arms into the coat sleeves and sat on the picnic table with my feet on the bench, and drank brandy in hopes that it would warm my hands. I hadn't thought to bring gloves. It is impossible to foresee, in hundred-degree weather, that you'll ever want gloves. I'd done well to think of bringing along my peajacket.

I had a sudden thought, and reached into my pocket for the pebble, to see if it was obsidian. I held it in the lantern light. It wasn't. It was an ordinary smooth gray pebble with white lines running through it. There was also in my pocket a piece of folded paper. I unfolded the note and read:

MOM, I KNOW YOU LOVE PETER. WHATEVER YOU WANT TO DO ABOUT DAD IS OKAY. JUST YOU AND ME IS OKAY. I ♥ YOU.

Peter was off somewhere outside the circle of light. I could hear him crackling quietly through the woods in search of fallen timber. He returned to camp with an armload of branches and set about breaking them into lengths and stacking them according to thickness.

Eventually he was ready to go. "I think I just need to sit here awhile in the peace and quiet," I told him. "Till my ears stop roaring from the car. You go on without me."

"I will," he said, "but I'll miss you."

He kissed me and left the flashlight, teasing that I'd need

to look out for bears, before he set off like a cheerful German hiker to find the trail head. He promised that even if he made it to Wupatki, he wouldn't stay long.

When he was gone I turned down the lantern until the white flame hissed and died. I sat on the picnic table hugging my knees, out there in the pitch dark with nothing familiar over my head but my mother's garden of stars. The roaring in my ears, I knew, wasn't going to stop. It wasn't from the drive. It was the crashing of the petrified forest. Stone limbs were dropping heavily and straight to the ground; trunks crumbled, and granite leaves splintered like glass. When it was over, there would be only Julie and me left standing in the desert, not looking back.

SURVIVAL ZONES

Millie Ormsby is trying to tell her friends Roberta and Ed the joke she heard from her thirteen-year-old grandson, Clay. The joke is about why the punk rocker crossed the road, but she can't remember the punch line.

"Well, now it's slipped my mind," she says, annoyed. When she deals the cards she loses count and has to start over. "It had something to do with an animal."

"It probably wasn't any count," Ed says. "They all ought to go in the army and get a decent haircut. That would be funny." Ed is in a bad mood because they're playing three-handed hearts instead of Buck Euchre, boys against girls, which is the normal routine on Saturday nights. Tonight Darrell is in bed with the stomach flu. Every so often he lows like a calf from the bedroom and Millie has to go get him some more Seven-Up.

Millie can't stop worrying over the joke, and is going through a list of every animal she can think of. "What animal would you all be, if you could be anything?" she asks. Millie is a reasonable person, but easily sidetracked.

"I'd be one of them dern ear worms eating my corn," Ed says, pulling in another trick of hearts. "They've eat better than us this year."

Ed's wife, Roberta, knows he would like to have said

"damn." "You'll get the last laugh on them," she says. "As soon as we get a good hard freeze."

"Isn't that the truth," Millie says. "You'd just as well be a turkey, long about this time of year, Ed." It's the Saturday before Thanksgiving.

Roberta passes off another heart to Ed. "I'd be a kangaroo," she decides on impulse. "I've always wanted to see that part of the world."

Ed snorts. "You ought to be a cola bear," he says, in a tone that indicates he knows more about it than his wife. "They live in that part of the world."

"Oh, that's what I'd be," cries Millie. "They're real cute. We seen them on TV the other night."

Now that she's mentioned it, Roberta thinks her friend actually looks something like a koala bear. She and Ed saw the same *Wild Kingdom* show at their house. The koala bears sometimes spend their entire lives in a single tree. "No, I'd want to be bigger than that," she says. "A kangaroo could get around. There's one for you, Millie. A kangaroo'd get across the road."

"Why, it was a chicken, of course," Millie says, suddenly stricken with memory. "It was because he had a chicken stapled to his ear." When she sees their empty faces she pinches her right earlobe. "The punk rocker. Right here, you see? Like it was a earring, I guess."

"Ha ha," Ed says. "So funny I forgot to laugh."

Millie is flustered and a little embarrassed. She accidentally lays down the Black Lady when she could have made someone else take it. "Oh, that one was bad. I never would've told it if I'd remembered how it ended up."

Roberta is still thinking about the joke. "But it doesn't say why the *chicken* crossed the road, in the first place."

"Everybody knows that," Ed tells her. It seems that way to Roberta too, but when she really thinks about it she doesn't know the answer. She doubts that Ed does, either.

On the way home in the car she says to Ed, "Listen to us talk," although they aren't talking. "We sound like a bunch of old folks. Talking about what animals we'd be. We don't even understand our own kids' jokes anymore."

Ed has had enough of playing cards with two women and is in no mood to talk about being old. He is five years older than Roberta, crowding fifty, as they say.

Their family has missed out on a generation, it seems to Roberta. Their daughter Roxanne is still in high school, and Millie already has an adolescent grandson. Roberta and Ed waited awhile before having Roxanne, thinking they would have plenty of time for family, but it didn't work out that way. Two years later they'd lost a boy. He was due on George Washington's birthday but came on Thanksgiving instead, the wrong holiday. He was perfectly formed—Roberta had wanted to see him, even though Ed thought she shouldn't—and as she lay in bed bleeding out the rest of what her uterus no longer needed she could only think of that one word: perfect. Inside his chest he had two tiny, perfectly flattened lungs, like butterfly wings—pushed out before he was ready to fly. Roberta was shocked that her body could have let them all down this way. It was like taking a bad fall on level ground: an unexpected thing for a body to do, and not easily forgiven. After that she'd lost heart for the family project. Roxanne, she'd decided, Roxanne who confronted life confidently on solid little legs, would be enough.

Roberta is going through the change of life now. It's a bit early but no special cause for concern, her doctor says. He made light of the whole business, in fact, pointing out that women rarely have children after forty anyway, if they can help it.

Their car passes through town quickly because all four of Elgin's stoplights are set to stay on green after ten o'clock. Ed turns onto Star Route 1, which will take them home to their farm. On a portion of the large piece of land that was once Ed's family's farm they raise livestock and feed corn and have a small apple orchard.

Although the road is just barely blacktopped now, it makes Roberta feel old to remember when it used to be dirt. She and her brother Willis rode their bikes out this way often when they were children, exploring the routes by which they would lead their parents and friends out of Elgin when the Russians dropped the H-bomb. Later they learned that if this were to occur, people would be coming *into* town, not going out. Elgin was in what was called a "survival zone": a band of small communities around Cincinnati to which people from the populated areas would flee for sustenance and shelter.

An H-bomb is what it would take, Roberta thinks. She has lived in Elgin for more than forty years, and during that time no one she knows of has ever moved here from Cincinnati.

When they pass by the drive-in Roberta notices the movie that's playing, something called *Octopussy*. She pays attention because Roxanne has gone to see it with her boyfriend. Roxanne will graduate in the spring ("If I don't flunk math," she tells everyone), and is going with a very polite boy on the football team who is also a senior. Since there wasn't a game tonight, they went to the drive-in and are probably still there. Or they may be home now, necking on the davenport with the lights out and the front curtains open, so they can see the car lights come up the driveway.

Sure enough, when Ed and Roberta pull up she sees the drapes snap together and then glow yellow as the light comes on behind them. She is pretty sure Ed doesn't notice this, nor will he see the flush on Roxanne's face when she greets her parents inside, looking happy.

Danny is just getting ready to leave as they come in. He's a quarterback; Roberta has seen him on the ball field in tight football pants, spinning around with the ball held high over his head, as graceful as one of the male ballet dancers on educational TV. But when he's in their house, in their presence, Danny pulls at himself as if he's suddenly outgrown his clothes. It makes Roberta sad. But he's a Talmadge, she tells herself, and Talmadges are shy. When she was in high school she dated Roland, Danny's father, for a time. It took him six months to get up the nerve to give her a dry, woody-tasting peck on the mouth. Ed Gravier, even though he was a Methodist, was older and had seemed fast by comparison. The same pompadour he wears now had given him a worldly air back then, like James Dean. If James Dean had lived, Roberta supposes this would be his lot now. Slicking his hair into a kindly, old-fashioned style while his teeth go bad and his children ignore his advice.

Roland Talmadge had gone on to marry the most timid girl in Roberta's class. Roberta has secretly joked to Millie that it's a miracle her daughter's beau was ever born. In this respect Danny seems to have made progress beyond his parents' generation.

Roberta turns on the late movie. Roxanne has gone to her room and Ed has turned in for the night, too, but Roberta has been having trouble falling asleep. Ed says she should take a shot of Old Grand-dad, but that only causes her heart to beat fast and make her anxious.

The movie is *The Way We Were.* Roberta saw it at the drive-in years ago. She enjoys the movie more because of this; she's able to fill in the colors, even though they only have black-and-white. She knows, for instance, that Barbra Streisand's fingernails are red. Roberta remembers clearly how she ran them over Robert Redford's back in the bedroom scene, but of course they've cut that part. One minute they're kissing and the next minute they're in the kitchen, with Barbra fixing breakfast. Roberta feels that her own life has been like that, with the exciting parts cut out. She will soon wake up and be old, with no inkling of what she missed.

She would love to go out and see real movies but Ed says no, wait a few years and it will be out on TV. He doesn't seem to miss the colors or the bedroom scenes. They could probably afford a color set now, but Ed claims to be able to see the colors perfectly well in black-and-white. Sometimes to prove it he'll call them out. "That's a green shirt he's wearing," he says. "That girl's hair is red." Sometimes Ed is wrong, though. For years he thought Peter Graves on *Mission Impossible* was blond, until one evening they watched it at Darrell and Millie's and saw that his hair was snow white like an old man's. "Well, that just don't look right," Ed had said. "You've got it adjusted wrong."

She turns off the set and stands at the front window for a long time, looking out. A tall azalea bush stands like a spook by the front door, spreading its dark hands out under the greenish porch light. It was planted by Ed's old mother—Roberta remembers her as old, anyway—when she first moved here from the South. Roberta loves the azalea in the spring when it's covered with white blossoms, but it gives her a good deal of trouble in the winter. She has to remember to cover it before frost comes. This year she has about decided to let it go. She doesn't believe anyone else will ever bother with protecting it, so eventually the azalea will die anyway: either before Roberta or the first winter after. She's running out of energy for unwinnable battles against nature.

She goes into the kitchen and is surprised to find Roxanne sitting at the table in her yellow terry robe. There is a full glass of milk in front of her, untouched, and it reminds Roberta of times in Roxanne's childhood when she would go through stages of refusing to eat or drink certain things she'd always liked, for no good reason. Roberta discovered over the years that it generally meant something was bothering her.

"I thought you were in bed, hon. How was the movie?" Roberta asks.

"Oh, it was dumb. It was one of those James Bonds, where he goes gallavanting all over the world with women dripping off of him. I don't think Danny cared for it either."

Roberta often thinks Roxanne sounds mature for her age, stuffy even, and wonders if she has suffered for having older-than-average parents. She begins to put away the supper dishes that were left in the drainer. "Well, maybe the next one that comes will be something better."

Roxanne gets up to help her mother, drying out the insides of the glasses, which are still fogged. This has always been Roxanne's job because she has such slender hands, "piano hands" people call them, though Roxanne has never learned to play any instrument.

"Mama, Danny and me are talking about getting married."

"Now? Before you even graduate?"

"No, not now. Right after, in June."

"What's your hurry?" Roberta watches her daughter's back as she reaches to put away a glass. She wonders if Roxanne would be able to tell her if she were pregnant.

But that doesn't seem to be it. "He's going away next year, most likely to Indianapolis," Roxanne says, in a tone of voice Roberta can't quite decipher. "They're giving him a football scholarship to IUPUI."

"Well, honey, that's real exciting."

"I know it. But I'm scared to death. What in the world would I do in Indianapolis?"

"You'd do just fine, I imagine. Nothing ever slows you down."

"No I wouldn't, Mama. I'm so stupid. Remember that time you and Daddy took me up to Cincinnati to see the Christmas lights? And I cried? I get all bewildered in a city."

"You weren't but nine, Roxanne. You're a lot different

from what you were then. There's only one person in the world I ever heard say you were stupid, and that's Miss Roxanne."

"But see, Mama, I'd have to *do* something. I couldn't just be Danny's wife. I don't think they're paying him that much."

"Well, you could wait awhile. You could always stay here and work at Hampton's for a year or two, till everything's situated." Hampton Mill, just outside of Elgin, produces men's knitwear; it's the largest employer of women in the Ohio Valley, and virtually the only one in the vicinity of Elgin. Roberta worked there before she married, and off and on for many years after because the income from farming is so unpredictable.

"I thought about Hampton's," Roxanne says. "I know I could stay, but it's scary; he might meet somebody else. Or I might." She looks at her mother, checking to see if she understands. "You know the way things happen."

Roberta is drying a wooden spoon and notices that the bowl of it has begun to go to splinters. "Do you know, I never told you this, but once upon a time I had the chance to marry Danny's daddy. Now, where would we all be if I'd gone and done that?"

"Danny's *daddy?* Roland *Talmadge?*" Roxanne makes a face.

Roberta shakes the spoon at her, laughing. "Just you watch. Give him twenty years and Danny will be just as bald and just as much of an old string bean. If you're married to him all those years, you'll never even notice. And, if you're not, you'll run into him one day and say to yourself, 'Thank goodness I threw that one back in the river!' "

Roxanne looks upset. "That's enough to scare you out of marrying *any*body."

"Honey, what I'm trying to say is, things generally work out for the best, whichever way they go. Don't do something just because you think it's going to be your last chance in the world at being happy. There's lots of chances. You've got time." Roberta believes this is good advice, though when she listens to her own voice it sounds doubtful.

In any case, Roxanne isn't paying much attention. "But that doesn't help me *now*," she wails. "I've still got to decide." She polishes off her glass of milk and wipes off her white mustache with the sleeve of her robe, looking so young it makes Roberta's chest hurt. "Mama, I'm just so petrified about the whole thing."

In the years since her daughter developed a woman's body and a magazine-cover face, Roberta has seen Roxanne become self-assured, coy, serious, and occasionally angry, but never truly afraid, though she frequently claims to be petrified. Roberta suspects that this time it might be genuine.

"What would you do, if it was you?" Roxanne asks her.

Roberta has no idea what she will say. She feels as though a part of her is standing back with crossed arms, listening. "The way I've been feeling lately, I'm inclined to say I'd catch any train headed out of Elgin," she says. "But you know I wouldn't mean it. Look at me, born right down the road, and after all these years of chasing my tail doing nothing, here I still am."

Roxanne's lips are pursed. She is too absorbed in the difficulties of being seventeen to want to hear the confusions of forty-four. Roberta gives her daughter a hug, and feels like crying. By the time they ask you what they ought to do, she thinks, you're too old to know what to tell them.

On Thanksgiving morning Ed and his younger brother, Lonnie, watch football while Lonnie's wife, Aggie, helps in the kitchen. "Glued to the tube," Aggie says, rolling her eyes. "You'd think two grown men could find something constructive to do."

Roberta has no interest in sports either, and never has,

except for the 1972 Olympics, which the women of Elgin watched with unprecedented eagerness. That was the year Hampton Mill got the contract for the Olympic swimwear. It sent chills up their spines to think the swimsuit they were cutting or stitching would soon be on its way to Germany and could end up with Mark Spitz's privates in it. Later on, their husbands shook their heads in amazement when the women could not be pried away from TV sets whenever the Olympics came on. Roberta watched too, as he dived into the water, and she blew her nose when he stood with the ribbons and gold around his neck, dripping and smiling, in trunks made especially for him.

Thinking of this as she scoots the heavy turkey around in the oven, it occurs to Roberta that working at Hampton's wasn't so bad, even though all anybody ever talked about was how soon they could quit. But she remembered exactly the way her arms felt, steady and knowing, on the cutting and pressing machines. She liked the women she worked with, especially Dottie Short, who was the organizer of the Textile Workers at Hampton's and worked the pressers with Roberta. Dottie claimed to know a lot about history and was fond of saying peculiar things. She once told Roberta that the vacuum cleaner was invented to get women out of the factories and back into the home after World War II. Without a lot of new kinds of machines and gadgets, Dottie said, they'd have gotten bored stiff and wanted their old jobs back.

People often said behind Dottie's back that she was a Red, but Roberta saw what she meant about the vacuum cleaners. It was hard to imagine Rosie the Riveter in an apron and hair ribbon, sweeping with a broom, but you could just about picture her behind a big old Hoover.

Roberta's own kitchen has technology enough: the self-cleaning oven, the refrigerator with an ice maker. No dish-washer yet. Only last year did they finally replace the gas stove Ed's mother had cooked on when he was a boy. It was an antique with little enameled feet, and in a way Roberta hated to see it go, but she needed something with even heat and better temperature controls. She has modernized gradually, simply by making it clear to Ed that these are things she needs. She wonders, though, if she is somehow replacing herself. Even a complicated thing like Thanksgiving dinner practically cooks itself. A kangaroo could do my job, Roberta thinks, amused by the picture in her mind.

Aggie is scooping out the insides of a cooked pumpkin for pies while Roberta rolls out dough for the crust.

"I ought to be making apple instead of pumpkin. With all those apples we got this year," Roberta says.

"Thanksgiving with no pumpkin pie? The boys would have a conniption!"

Aggie, who has twin sons, is fond of saying "boys" in an emphatic way that suggests male children are her own special cross to bear. She rarely recalls that Roberta lost a son. Roberta can't blame her, really. Even Ed and Roxanne seem to have forgotten. It's so long in the past, a river that has gone underground, surfacing only rarely, at times when they intend to count their blessings.

"No," Roberta agrees. "You can't always do the practical thing. We'll leave the apples sit for today." They have a whole cellarful—mostly Red Delicious, although there are some very old trees in the orchard that bear a small, nonsalable variety Roberta calls "antique." She's heard old people call them "witch apples." For a long time she's been experimenting with new varieties, planting two new saplings each year. She orders them from a catalogue while the ground is still under snow, and they arrive so certain of spring: little switches of trees wrapped in paper, their buds aching to burst. They are Roberta's project. Ed is the type inclined to say, "Apples is apples."

Lonnie comes into the kitchen to get a couple of Buds from the refrigerator. He complains to Roberta about their

TV. "I can't even tell the players on that little thing. The white uniforms looks just like the yeller ones. You ought to tell Ed to get a new set." Lonnie manages a gas station, but he still talks like a boy who grew up on a farm.

"Tell him yourself," Roberta says. "He won't listen to me. He says he can see the colors just fine."

"Lonnie's just as stubborn," Aggie confides after he leaves the kitchen. "You ought to have seen how we went round and round about getting another car, even after the old one got to where it wouldn't go three blocks without stopping dead in the street."

Lonnie and Aggie are a good deal younger than Roberta and live in town, near Lonnie's station. It sounds peculiar to Roberta to hear distance measured in blocks. She's suddenly much too hot in the kitchen, finding it hard to concentrate on either cooking or conversation. She stands up straight with a hand on her back and feels a great weight moving through her, an enormous lifelessness. She has felt it before, but can't name it. All she can think of is the way she's heard people speak of whole rivers becoming dead, of something destroying all the oxygen.

She can see much of the family land through the kitchen window: a landscape of brown stubble fields, harvested alfalfa hay, fencerows of leafless hickories. She searches among them for some premonition of the killing frost that's predicted. If it comes, it will be the first. It has been an unusually warm fall. The tomato plants in Roberta's kitchen garden are still blooming, with a perky effort that makes her feel depressed. As if they intended to go on producing forever.

"I expect I'd better get out there directly and cover up that azalea by the front door," she says to Aggie. "They're saying frost tonight." Roberta is trying the decision aloud, to see how it sounds, though really she's leaning the other way.

"To everything there is a season." Aggie says this in an offhand way, the way a farm-bred person could never do.

"I've kept that thing alive for twenty-odd years now. It'd be a shame to see it killed by frost; it's real pretty in the spring. But azalea bushes oughtn't to be growing this far north."

"What do you mean, oughtn't to be?" Aggie, who is paring radish rosebuds now for the relish tray, seems indifferent to the azalea.

"Most of the azaleas aren't hardy. All the nursery catalogues say that white one won't survive north of zone seven. Right around the Mason-Dixon, in other words."

"Well, how'd it get up here, walk?" Aggie laughs.

"Didn't I ever tell you? Ed's mother planted it when they first moved up here. She brought it with her from her people's place in Virginia. There were some other things that were here when Ed and I first got the place. Magnolias, I don't even remember what all. That azalea's the only one of them left."

"I didn't know Lonnie and Ed's mother came from Virginia."

"Didn't you? She was a Franklin." Roberta checks the oven again, feeling better. The hot flashes have subsided. "You remember her, don't you? She was a good woman, but Lord help me, she was ornery as a tree stump. She'd come back and haunt me if I let that azalea die."

"I'll have to tell the boys they had a grandma from Virginia," Aggie says. Her twins, Benny and Andrew, are chasing each other around the circle of the kitchen, dining room, and what used to be called the parlor. Benny misjudges the kitchen door and bangs into the door frame, with Andy right behind.

"Come here, Ben, let me see you. Are your teeth all right?" Aggie takes his head between her hands and examines his teeth while Benny squirms. The boys are ten years old, but only during the past year, since Aggie stopped dressing them alike, has Roberta begun to see her nephews as separate people. She was amazed when she realized this. That a mother had the power to make two people one, or vice versa.

"Your Aunt Roberta's house is no place to be running horse races," Aggie says. "You boys go on outside."

"We're not running races, Mom."

"Whatever you're doing, then. Go do it outside."

Ben pushes Andy against the refrigerator on his way out the back door.

"It would be okay with me if they wanted to play inside," Roberta says. "It's too quiet around here now that Roxanne's grown up."

"Count your blessings," Aggie says. "Boys are so rambunctious."

"Whatever you say," Roberta says.

Ed and Roberta's old farmhouse truly is too large. In winter they have to move downstairs into the guest bedroom, next to Roxanne's, so they can heat only a small section of the house and close off the upstairs. There was a time when this inconvenience seemed romantic to Roberta. They were like the lovers in Dr. Zhivago, with snow all around and wolves howling. But over the years it's become just one more way of marking the passing seasons.

Aggie has made a green Jell-O–cottage cheese mold that is shaped like a fish, and moves like one too, flopping on the plate when she turns it out.

"That's real pretty, Aggie. Something different."

"Mama always used to make this for Thanksgiving, but it seems like nobody around here's ever heard of it. Mama just used a plain round mold."

Roberta turns the pumpkin pies deftly, pressing a fork around the edges to pleat the crust. She remembers once watching Roxanne out the kitchen window, when she was four or five, pressing a plastic fork around the rim of a mud pie. Just a few years ago Roxanne would have been snitching fingerfuls of whipped cream from the pies in the refrigerator, and fighting with her Daddy to watch the Macy's parade instead of football. Roberta finally settled that argument with a compromise: they would watch the parade until Roxanne got to see the Bullwinkle balloon, and then could switch over. It was a successful solution because it entertained them both. It was a gamble. Sometimes Bullwinkle's giant antlers were the first thing to come bobbing down the street between the rows of skyscrapers, while other years they saved him until nearly the end.

This year Roxanne is having Thanksgiving dinner at Danny's house, and she and Danny will drop by later. The shape of things to come, Roberta thinks. We're all Graviers here. Roxanne will soon be a Talmadge, or if not, then something else, most likely. Ed's sister is a Richie now, and usually spends the holidays with her husband's people across the river in Kentucky. Families swallowing other families, endlessly, like the Pac Man game Millie and Darrell gave Clay last Christmas. Ed, Lonnie, Roland Talmadge, Danny, one day even Benny and Andrew: they're all like the Pac Man, running around the blocks of Elgin and the county roads, gobbling up little dots of women.

But the women don't disappear, they only rearrange. Roberta doesn't believe she's changed much for being a Gravier. And Roxanne will still be Roxanne, even if she goes to Indianapolis. Maybe she'll go to college one day; she has always been quick to pick things up, doing passably well in school without half trying. Or possibly she'll work in a factory. Indianapolis is probably jam-packed with industry, big plants that make important things, TV sets and cars. Roberta knows for a fact, from reading the package, that Granny Brown frozen mince pies are manufactured in Indianapolis. As she polishes the Gravier china and sets the table, she imagines her pretty daughter in coveralls and a head scarf, like Rosie the Riveter, operating a big machine that turns out Granny Brown pies a hundred at a time.

Soon after they all sit down to dinner the telephone rings. It's Roxanne, explaining that she and Danny are going to be late. "We'll be there in an hour or two," she says. She calls Roberta "Mom," instead of "Mama," which she tends to do if any of her peers are within earshot.

"That's fine. We're just sitting down now," Roberta says. "Where are you?"

"I'm calling from the pay phone at the Tastee-Freez."

"Well, Lord have mercy, didn't they feed you over at Talmadge's?"

"Oh Mom, sure they did, we're just out driving around." She hesitates. "The Tastee-Freez is closed on Thanksgiving. Didn't you know that?"

"Sure, honey, I knew. I was teasing."

"Oh." Roxanne's voice is up in her nose. Roberta can tell she has been crying.

"Are you all right?" she asks.

"Yeah." Roxanne pauses. "I guess so. We're having a fight."

Roberta waits for her to go on.

"I told Danny I might not go to Indianapolis right away, that I might want to stay and work at Hampton's, and he's real mad. He says he won't go without me. I feel awful. It's his one chance to play college ball."

"Well, try not to get too worked up about it. You'll get it straightened out. You've got six months or better to decide."

"No we don't. He's got to let them know pretty soon about the scholarship."

"That's his decision, Roxanne. He's got his to make, and you've got yours."

"Mom, it just isn't that simple." Roxanne is lecturing now. "Everything depends on everything else."

"Well, if it helps any, I imagine he's just as scared as you are."

"I know it." She hesitates again, and Roberta can tell from the change in Roxanne's voice that she's smiling. "He is, and he won't admit it."

"Don't be too long, now," Roberta says. "And be careful. The roads might be freezing up."

"Okay."

Roberta waits for her daughter to hang up, listening to the quiet static that is swimming in the few miles of wire between her house and the Tastee-Freez.

"Mama? I was thinking about what you said."

"About what, hon?"

"When you said you'd been in Elgin all this time chasing your tail. It isn't like you've been doing *nothing*. Maybe it's not like a job that, well, like the jobs people have, you know. But it's something. To me it is."

When Roberta comes back to the table and sits down, the landscape of white linen and silver has been transformed into a war zone. The turkey looks more like a carcass than a bird, and the Jell-O fish is gutted and beheaded like a bluegill ready for the skillet. Already there is gravy on the tablecloth. She helps herself to some cornbread stuffing. The twins are trying to pull the big turkey wishbone, but it's rubbery in their greasy fingers, and won't break. It becomes a contest to see who can jerk it out of the other's hand.

"You boys can be excused now," Aggie says.

Roberta is always amazed that a dinner that took days to prepare can be eaten in minutes. "Come back after while for pumpkin pie," she tells them, before they vanish. "If you've still got room for it."

"They'll have room," Lonnie says. "Them two has hollow legs." He reaches across the table to refill the glasses from the second of two bottles of wine he brought. Ed and Lonnie had a strict Methodist upbringing, but their wives have been an influence. They're more relaxed about things than their parents were. And, although none of the Graviers is accustomed to much drinking, Thanksgiving is clearly a time when excesses are forgiven.

Roberta sips the wine happily. It's too sweet, but she likes the way it warms the inside of her chest as it goes down, and numbs her lips. Her cheeks feel flushed, like Roxanne's after she and Danny have been necking.

Lonnie is telling a complicated story about a man with three dogs named Larry, Curly, and Moe, which he takes to the grocery store with him. Aggie corrects him on factual points several times, but Roberta is uncertain as to whether this is just a joke, or a real story about someone Lonnie and Aggie really know. In the end she decides it must have been real life, because the story just fades out without a punch line.

"I've got one for you, Lonnie," Roberta says. She touches her tongue to her numb lips to make sure they're still in working order. "Why did the punk rocker cross the road?" Lonnie says he doesn't know.

Roberta starts to laugh. "Because he had a chicken stapled to his ear. For an earring, see? And the chicken . . ." she can't stop laughing. "The hen is the only one of the two that knows where she's going."

"I don't get it," Lonnie says, but Aggie is laughing.

"Now I can just see that," Aggie says. "That hen flapping, and the man trying to keep up. 'Come on, boy, time to get across this road!' " She gets the giggles so badly that when she takes a drink of water it goes down the wrong way, and Lonnie has to slap her on the back.

"That's an old one," Ed says. "I've heard that one before."

"Oh, I expect you have," Roberta says. She smiles out over the expanse of gristle and balled-up napkins and the cage of bird bones sitting in the place of honor, a bedraggled centerpiece. It's really more meat than bone; only a few magnificent slabs have been carved from it. Roberta imagines the army of women across the country marching into their kitchens with turkeys like this, preparing to pick the bones clean for sandwiches and soup stocks that will nourish their families halfway to Christmas.

A sunbeam slants through the west window looking weak, as though it has had to pass through a great ordeal to reach this dining room. It's late. Roberta catches Aggie's eye and feels a secret between them that neither could own up to if they were asked. Possibly it's just that. That no one will ask.

"Aggie," she says, "come help me throw a quilt over that azalea bush. There's no point letting it stand out there and die."

ISLANDS ON THE MOON

Annemarie's mother, Magda, is one of a kind. She wears sandals and one-hundred-percent-cotton dresses and walks like she's crossing plowed ground. She makes necklaces from the lacquered vertebrae of non-endangered species. Her hair is wavy and long and threaded with gray. She's forty-four.

Annemarie has always believed that if life had turned out better her mother would have been an artist. As it is, Magda just has to ooze out a little bit of art in everything she does, so that no part of her life is exactly normal. She paints landscapes on her tea kettles, for example, and dates younger men. Annemarie's theory is that everyone has some big thing, the rock in their road, that has kept them from greatness or so they would like to think. Magda had Annemarie when she was sixteen and has been standing on tiptoe ever since to see over or around her difficult daughter to whatever is on the other side. Annemarie just assumed that she was the rock in her mother's road. Until now. Now she has no idea.

On the morning Magda's big news arrived in the mail, Annemarie handed it over to her son Leon without even reading it, thinking it was just one of her standard cards. "Another magic message from Grandma Magda," she'd said, and Leon had rolled his eyes. He's nine years old, but that's only part of it. Annemarie influences him, telling my-most-embarrassing-moment stories about growing up with a mother like Magda, and Leon buys them wholesale, right along with nine-times-nine and the capital of Wyoming.

For example, Magda has always sent out winter solstice cards of her own design, printed on paper she makes by boiling down tree bark and weeds. The neighbors always smell it, and once, when Annemarie was a teenager, they reported Magda as a nuisance.

But it's April now so this isn't a solstice card. It's not homemade, either. It came from one of those stores where you can buy a personalized astrology chart for a baby gift. The paper is yellowed and smells of incense. Leon holds it to his nose, then turns it in his hands, not trying to decipher Magda's slanty handwriting but studying the ink drawing that runs around the border. Leon has curly black hair, like Magda's—and like Annemarie's would be, if she didn't continually crop it and bleach it and wax it into spikes. But Leon doesn't care who he looks like. He's entirely unconscious of himself as he sits there, ears sticking out, heels banging the stool at the kitchen counter. One of Annemarie's cats rubs the length of its spine along his green high-top sneaker.

"It looks like those paper dolls that come out all together, holding hands," he says. "Only they're fattish, like old ladies. Dancing."

"That's about what I'd decided," says Annemarie.

Leon hands the card back and heads for fresh air. The bang of the screen door is the closest she gets these days to a goodbye kiss.

Where, in a world where kids play with Masters of the Universe, has Leon encountered holding-hands paper dolls? This is what disturbs Annemarie. Her son is normal in every obvious way but has a freakish awareness of old-fashioned things. He collects things: old Coke bottles, license-plate slogans, anything. They'll be driving down Broadway and he'll call out "Illinois Land of Lincoln!" And he saves string. Annemarie found it in a ball, rolled into a sweatsock. It's as if some whole piece of Magda has come through to Leon without even touching her.

She reads the card and stares at the design, numb, trying to see what these little fat dancing women have to be happy about. She and her mother haven't spoken for months, although either one can see the other's mobile home when she steps out on the porch to shake the dust mop. Magda says she's willing to wait until Annemarie stops emitting negative energy toward her. In the meantime she sends cards.

Annemarie is suddenly stricken, as she often is, with the feeling she's about to be abandoned. Leon will take Magda's side. He'll think this new project of hers is great, and mine's awful. Magda always wins without looking like she was trying.

Annemarie stands at the kitchen sink staring out the window at her neighbors' porch, which is twined with queen's wreath and dusty honeysuckle, a stalwart oasis in the desert of the trailer court. A plaster Virgin Mary, painted in blue and rose and the type of cheap, shiny gold that chips easily, presides over the barbecue pit, and three lawn chairs with faded webbing are drawn up close around it as if for some secret family ceremony. A wooden sign hanging from the porch awning proclaims that they are "The Navarrete's" over there. Their grandson, who lives with them, made the sign in Boy Scouts. Ten years Annemarie has been trying to get out of this trailer court, and the people next door are so content with themselves they hang out a shingle.

Before she knows it she's crying, wiping her face with the backs of her dishpan hands. This is completely normal. All morning she sat by herself watching nothing in particular on TV, and cried when Luis and Maria got married on *Sesame Street*. It's the hormones. She hasn't told him yet, but she's going to have another child besides Leon. The big news in Magda's card is that she is going to have another child too, besides Annemarie.

When she tries to be reasonable—and she is trying at the moment, sitting in a Denny's with her best friend Kay Kay—Annemarie knows that mid-forties isn't too old to have boyfriends. But Magda doesn't seem mid-forties, she seems like Grandma Moses in moonstone earrings. She's the type who's proud about not having to go to the store for some little thing because she can rummage around in the kitchen drawers until she finds some other thing that will serve just as well. For her fifth birthday Annemarie screamed for a Bubble-Hairdo Barbie just because she knew there wouldn't be one in the kitchen drawer.

Annemarie's side of the story is that she had to fight her way out of a family that smelled like an old folks' home. Her father was devoted and funny, chasing her around the house after dinner in white paper-napkin masks with eye-holes, and he could fix anything on wheels, and then without warning he turned into a wheezing old man with taut-skinned hands rattling a bottle of pills. Then he was dead, leaving behind a medicinal pall that hung over Annemarie and followed her to school. They'd saved up just enough to move to Tucson, for his lungs, and the injustice of it stung her. He'd breathed the scorched desert air for a single autumn, and Annemarie had to go on breathing it one summer after another. In New Hampshire she'd had friends, as many as the trees had leaves, but they couldn't get back there now. Magda was vague and useless, no protection from poverty. Only fathers, it seemed, offered that particular safety. Magda reminded her that the Little Women were poor too, and for all practical purposes fatherless, but Annemarie didn't care. The March girls didn't have to live in a trailer court.

Eventually Magda went on dates. By that time Annemarie was sneaking Marlboros and fixing her hair and hanging around by the phone, and would have given her eye teeth for as many offers—but Magda threw them away. Even back then, she didn't get attached to men. She devoted herself instead to saving every rubber band and piece of string that entered their door. Magda does the things people used to do in other centuries, before it occurred to them to pay someone else to do them. Annemarie's friends think this is wonderful. Magda is so old-fashioned she's come back into style. And she's committed. She intends to leave her life savings, if any, to Save the Planet, and tells Annemarie she should be more concerned about the stewardship of the earth. Kay Kay thinks she ought to be the president. "You want to trade?" she routinely asks. "You want my mother?"

"What's wrong with your mother?" Annemarie wants to know.

"What's wrong with my mother," Kay Kay answers, shaking her head. Everybody thinks they've got a corner on the market, thinks Annemarie.

Kay Kay is five feet two and has green eyes and drives a locomotive for Southern Pacific. She's had the same lover, a rock 'n' roll singer named Connie Skylab, for as long as Annemarie has known her. Kay Kay and Connie take vacations that just amaze Annemarie: they'll go skiing, or hang-gliding, or wind-surfing down in Puerto Peñasco. Annemarie often wishes she could do just one brave thing in her lifetime. Like hang-gliding.

"Okay, here you go," says Kay Kay. "For my birthday my mother sent me one of those fold-up things you carry in your purse for covering up the toilet seat. 'Honey, you're on the go so much,' she says to me. 'And besides there's AIDS to think about now.' The guys at work think I ought to have it bronzed."

"At least she didn't try to *knit* you a toilet-seat cover, like Magda would," says Annemarie. "She bought it at a store, right?"

"Number one," Kay Kay says, "I don't carry a purse when I'm driving a train. And number two, I don't know how to tell Ma this, but the bathrooms in those engines don't even *have* a seat."

Annemarie and Kay Kay are having lunch. Kay Kay spends her whole life in restaurants when she isn't driving a train. She says if you're going to pull down thirty-eight thousand a year, why cook?

"At least you had a normal childhood," Annemarie says, taking a mirror-compact out of her purse, confirming that she looks awful, and snapping it shut. "I was the only teen-ager in America that couldn't use hairspray because it's death to the ozone layer."

"I just don't see what's so terrible about Magda caring what happens to the world," Kay Kay says.

"It's morbid. All those war marches she goes on. How can you think all the time about nuclear winter wiping out life as we know it, and still go on making your car payments?"

Kay Kay smiles.

"She mainly just does it to remind me what a slug I am. I didn't turn out all gung-ho like she wanted me to."

"That's not true," Kay Kay says. "You're very responsible, in your way. I think Magda just wants a safe world for you and Leon. My mother couldn't care less if the world went to hell in a handbasket, as long as her nail color was coordinated with her lipstick."

Annemarie can never make people see. She cradles her chin mournfully in her palms. Annemarie has surprisingly fair skin for a black-haired person, which she is in principle. That particular complexion, from Magda's side of the family, has dropped unaltered through the generations like a rock. They are fine-boned, too, with graceful necks and fingers that curve outward slightly at the tips. Annemarie has wished for awful things in her lifetime, even stubby fingers, something to set her apart.

"I got my first period," she tells Kay Kay, unable to drop the subject, "at this *die-in* she organized against the Vietnam War. I had horrible cramps and nobody paid any attention; they all thought I was just dying-in."

"And you're never going to forgive her," Kay Kay says. "You ought to have a T-shirt made up: 'I hate my mother because I got my first period at a die-in.' "

Annemarie attends to her salad, which she has no intention of eating. Two tables away, a woman in a western shirt and heavy turquoise jewelry is watching Annemarie in a maternal way over her husband's shoulder. "She just has to one-up me," says Annemarie. "Her due date is a month before mine."

"I can see where you'd be upset," Kay Kay says, "but she didn't know. You didn't even tell me till a month ago. It's not like she grabbed some guy off the street and said, 'Quick, knock me up so I can steal my daughter's thunder.' "

Annemarie doesn't like to think about Magda having sex with some guy off the street. "She should have an abortion," she says. "Childbirth is unsafe at her age."

"Your mother can't part with the rubber band off the Sunday paper."

This is true. Annemarie picks off the alfalfa sprouts, which she didn't ask for in the first place. Magda used to make her wheat-germ sandwiches, knowing full well she despised sprouts and anything else that was recently a seed. Annemarie is crying now and there's no disguising it. She was still a kid when she had Leon, but this baby she'd intended to do on her own. With a man maybe, but not with her mother prancing around on center stage.

"Lots of women have babies in their forties," Kay Kay says. "Look at Goldie Hawn."

"Goldie Hawn isn't my mother. *And* she's married."

"Is the father that guy I met? Bartholomew?"

"The father is not in the picture. That's a quote. You

know Magda and men; she's not going to let the grass grow under *her* bed."

Kay Kay is looking down at her plate, using her knife and fork in a serious way that shows all the tendons in her hands. Kay Kay generally argues with Annemarie only if she's putting herself down. When she starts in on Magda, Kay Kay mostly just listens.

"Ever since Daddy died she's never looked back," Annemarie says, blinking. Her contact lenses are foundering, like skaters on a flooded rink.

"And you think she ought to look back?"

"I don't know. Yeah." She dabs at her eyes, trying not to look at the woman with the turquoise bracelets. "It bothers me. Bartholomew's in love with her. Another guy wants to marry her. All these guys are telling her how beautiful she is. And look at me, it seems like every year I'm crying over another boyfriend gone west, not even counting Leon's dad." She takes a bite of lettuce and chews on empty calories. "I'm still driving the Pontiac I bought ten years ago, but I've gone through six boyfriends and a husband. Twice. I was married to Buddy twice."

"Well, look at it this way, at least you've got a good car," says Kay Kay.

"Now that this kid's on the way he's talking about going for marriage number three. Him and Leon are in cahoots, I think."

"You and Buddy again?"

"Buddy's settled down a lot," Annemarie insists. "I think I could get him to stay home more this time." Buddy wears braids like his idol, Willie Nelson, and drives a car with flames painted on the hood. When Annemarie says he has settled down, she means that whereas he used to try to avoid work in his father's lawnmower repair shop, now he owns it.

"Maybe it would be good for Leon. A boy needs his dad."

"Oh, Leon's a rock, like me," says Annemarie. "It comes from growing up alone. When I try to do any little thing for Leon he acts like I'm the creature from the swamp. I know he'd rather live with Buddy. He'll be out the door for good one of these days."

"Well, you never know, it might work out with you and Buddy," Kay Kay says brightly. "Maybe third time's a charm."

"Oh, sure. Seems like guys want to roll through my life like the drive-in window. Probably me and Buddy'll end up going for divorce number three." She pulls a paper napkin out of the holder and openly blows her nose.

"Why don't you take the afternoon off?" Kay Kay suggests. "Go home and take a nap. I'll call your boss for you, and tell him you've got afternoon sickness or something."

Annemarie visibly shrugs off Kay Kay's concern. "Oh, I couldn't, he'd kill me. I'd better get on back." Annemarie is assistant manager of a discount delivery service called "Yesterday!" and really holds the place together, though she denies it.

"Well, don't get down in the dumps," says Kay Kay gently. "You've just got the baby blues."

"If it's not one kind of blues it's another. I can't help it. Just the sound of the word 'divorced' makes me feel like I'm dragging around a suitcase of dirty handkerchiefs."

Kay Kay nods.

"The thing that gets me about Magda is, man or no man, it's all the same to her," Annemarie explains, feeling the bitterness of this truth between her teeth like a sour apple. "When it comes to men, she doesn't even carry any luggage."

The woman in the turquoise bracelets stops watching

Annemarie and gets up to go to the restroom. The husband, whose back is turned, waits for the bill.

The telephone wakes Annemarie. It's not late, only a little past seven, the sun is still up, and she's confused. She must have fallen asleep without meaning to. She is cut through with terror while she struggles to place where Leon is and remember whether he's been fed. Since his birth, falling asleep in the daytime has served up to Annemarie this momentary shock of guilt.

When she hears the voice on the phone and understands who it is, she stares at the receiver, thinking somehow that it's not her phone. She hasn't heard her mother's voice for such a long time.

"All I'm asking is for you to go with me to the clinic," Magda is saying. "You don't have to look at the needle. You don't have to hold my hand." She waits, but Annemarie is speechless. "You don't even have to talk to me. Just peck on the receiver: once if you'll go, twice if you won't." Magda is trying to sound light-hearted, but Annemarie realizes with a strange satisfaction that she must be very afraid. She's going to have amniocentesis.

"Are you all right?" Magda asks. "You sound woozy."

"Why wouldn't I be all right," Annemarie snaps. She runs a hand through her hair, which is spiked with perspiration, and regains herself. "Why on earth are you even having it done, the amniowhatsis, if you think it's going to be so awful?"

"My doctor won't be my doctor anymore unless I have it. It's kind of a requirement for women my age."

A yellow tabby cat walks over Annemarie's leg and jumps off the bed. Annemarie is constantly taking in strays, joking to Kay Kay that if Leon leaves her at least she won't be alone, she'll have the cats. She has eleven or twelve at the moment.

"Well, it's probably for the best," Annemarie tells Magda, in the brisk voice she uses to let Magda know she is a citizen of the world, unlike some people. "It will ease your mind, anyway, to know the baby's okay."

"Oh, I'm not going to look at the results," Magda explains. "I told Dr. Lavinna I'd have it, and have the results sent over to his office, but I don't want to know. That was our compromise."

"Why don't you want to know the results?" asks Annemarie. "You could even know if it was a boy or a girl. You could pick out a name."

"As if it's such hard work to pick out an extra name," says Magda, "that I should go have needles poked into me to save myself the trouble?"

"I just don't see why you wouldn't want to know."

"People spend their whole lives with labels stuck on them, Annemarie. I just think it would be nice for this one to have nine months of being a plain human being."

"Mother knows best," sighs Annemarie, and she has the feeling she's always had, that she's sinking in a bog of mud. "You two should just talk," Kay Kay sometimes insists, and Annemarie can't get across that it's like quicksand. It's like reasoning with the sand trap at a golf course. There is no beginning and no end to the conversation she needs to have with Magda, and she'd rather just steer clear.

The following day, after work, Kay Kay comes over to help Annemarie get her evaporative cooler going for the summer. It's up on the roof of her mobile home. They have to climb up there with the vacuum cleaner and a long extension cord and clean out a winter's worth of dust and twigs and wayward insect parts. Then they will paint the bottom of the tank with tar, and install new pads, and check the water lines. Afterward, Kay Kay has promised she'll take Annemarie to the Dairy Queen for a milkshake. Kay Kay is looking after her friend in a carefully offhand way that Annemarie hasn't quite noticed.

It actually hasn't dawned on Annemarie that she's halfway through a pregnancy. She just doesn't think about what's going on in there, other than having some vague awareness that someone has moved in and is rearranging the furniture of her body. She's been thinking mostly about what pants she can still fit into. It was this way the first time, too. At six months she marched with Buddy down the aisle in an empire gown and seed-pearl tiara and no one suspected a thing, including, in her heart-of-hearts, Annemarie. Seven weeks later Leon sprang out of her body with his mouth open, already yelling, and neither one of them has ever quite gotten over the shock.

It's not that she doesn't want this baby, she tells Kay Kay; she didn't at first, but now she's decided. Leon has reached the age where he dodges her kisses like wild pitches over home plate, and she could use someone around to cuddle. "But there are so many things I have to get done, before I can have it," she says.

"Like what kind of things?" Kay Kay has a bandana tied around her head and is slapping the tar around energetically. She's used to dirty work. She says after you've driven a few hundred miles with your head out the window of a locomotive you don't just take a washcloth to your face, you have to wash your *teeth*.

"Oh, I don't know." Annemarie sits back on her heels. The metal roof is too hot to touch, but the view from up there is interesting, almost like it's not where she lives. The mobile homes are arranged like shoeboxes along the main drive, with cars and motorbikes parked beside them, just so many toys in a sandbox. The shadows of things trail away everywhere in the same direction like long oil leaks across the gravel. The trailer court is called "Island Breezes," and like the names of most trailer courts, it's a joke. No swaying palm trees. In fact, there's no official vegetation at all except for cactus plants in straight, symmetrical rows along the drive, like some bizarre desert organized by a child.

"Well, deciding what to do about Buddy, for instance," Annemarie says at last, after Kay Kay has clearly forgotten the question. "I need to figure that out first. And also what I'd do with a baby while I'm at work. I couldn't leave it with Magda, they'd all be down at the Air Force Base getting arrested to stop the cruise missiles."

Kay Kay doesn't say anything. She wraps the tarred, spiky paintbrush in a plastic bag and begins to pry last year's cooler pads out of the frames. Annemarie is being an absent-minded helper, staring into space, sometimes handing Kay Kay a screwdriver when she's asked for the pliers.

With a horrible screeching of claws on metal, one of Annemarie's cats, Lone Ranger, has managed to get himself up to the roof in pursuit of a lizard. He's surprised to see the women up there; he freezes and then slinks away along the gutter. Lone Ranger is a problem cat. Annemarie buys him special food, anything to entice him, but he won't come inside and be pampered. He cowers and shrinks from love like a blast from the hose.

"How long you think you'll take off work?" Kay Kay asks.

"Take off?"

"When the baby comes."

"Oh, I don't know," Annemarie says, uneasily. She could endanger her job there if she doesn't give them some kind of advance notice. She's well aware, even when Kay Kay refrains from pointing it out, that she's responsible in a hit-or-miss way. Once, toward the end of their first marriage, Buddy totaled his car and she paid to have it repaired so he wouldn't leave her. The next weekend he drove to Reno with a woman who sold newspapers from a traffic island.

Annemarie begins to unwrap the new cooler pads, which look like huge, flat sponges and smell like fresh sawdust. According to the label they're made of aspen, which Annemarie thought was a place where you go skiing and try to get a glimpse of Jack Nicholson. "You'd think they could make these things out of plastic," she says. "They'd last longer, and it wouldn't smell like a damn camping trip every time you turn on your cooler."

"They have to absorb water, though," explains Kay Kay. "That's the whole point. When the fan blows through the wet pads it cools down the air."

Annemarie is in the mood where she can't get particularly interested in the way things work. She holds two of the pads against herself like a hula skirt. "I could see these as a costume, couldn't you? For Connie?"

"That's an idea," Kay Kay says, examining them thoughtfully. "Connie's allergic to grasses, but not wood fibers."

Annemarie's bones ache to be known and loved this well. What she wouldn't give for someone to stand on a roof, halfway across the city, and say to some other person, "Annemarie's allergic to grasses, but not wood fibers."

"I'll mention it," Kay Kay says. "The band might go for it." Connie Skylab and the Falling Debris are into outlandish looks. Connie performs one number, "My Mother's Teeth," dressed in a black plastic garbage bag and a necklace of sheep's molars. A line Annemarie remembers is: "My mother's teeth grow in my head, I'll eat my children's dreams when she is dead."

Connie's mother is, in actual fact, dead. But neither she nor Kay Kay plans to produce any children. Annemarie thinks maybe that's how they can be so happy and bold. Their relationship is a sleek little boat of their own construction, untethered in either direction by the knotted ropes of motherhood, free to sail the open seas. Some people can manage it. Annemarie once met a happily married couple who made jewelry and traveled the nation in a dented microbus, selling their wares on street corners. They had no permanent address whatsoever, no traditions, no family. They told Annemarie they never celebrated holidays.

And then on the other hand there are the Navarretes next door with their little nest of lawn chairs. They're happy too. Annemarie feels permanently disqualified from either camp, the old-fashioned family or the new. It's as if she somehow got left behind, missed every boat across the river, and now must watch happiness being acted out on the beach of a distant shore.

Two days later, on Saturday, Annemarie pulls on sweat pants and a T-shirt, starts up her Pontiac—scattering cats in every direction—and drives a hundred feet to pick up Magda and take her to the clinic. There just wasn't any reasonable way out.

The sun is reflected so brightly off the road it's like driving on a mirage. The ground is as barren as some planet where it rains once per century. It has been an unusually dry spring, though it doesn't much matter here in Island Breezes, where the lawns are made of gravel. Some people, deeply missing the Midwest, have spray-painted their gravel green.

Magda's yard is naturally the exception. It's planted with many things, including clumps of aloe vera, which she claims heals burns, and most recently, a little hand-painted sign with a blue dove that explains to all and sundry passers-by that you can't hug your kids with nuclear arms. When Annemarie drives up, Magda's standing out on the wooden steps in one of her loose India-print cotton dresses, and looks cool. Annemarie is envious. Magda's ordinary wardrobe will carry her right through the ninth month.

Magda's hair brushes her shoulders like a lace curtain as she gets into the car, and she seems flushed and excited, though perhaps it's nerves. She fishes around in her enormous woven bag and pulls out a bottle of green shampoo.

"I thought you might like to try this. It has an extract of nettles. I know to you that probably sounds awful, but it's really good; it can repair damaged hair shafts."

Annemarie beeps impatiently at some kids playing kickball in the drive near the front entrance. "Magda, can we please not start right in *immediately* on my hair? Can we at least say, 'How do you do' and 'Fine thank you' before we start in on my hair?"

"Sorry."

"Believe it or not, I actually *want* my hair to look like something dead beside the road. It's the style now."

Magda looks around behind the seat for the seat belt and buckles it up. She refrains from saying anything about Annemarie's seat belt. They literally don't speak again until they get where they're going.

At the clinic they find themselves listening to a lecture on AIDS prevention. Apparently it's a mandatory part of the services here. Before Magda's amniocentesis they need to sit with the other patients and learn about nonoxynol-number-9 spermicide and the proper application of a condom.

"You want to leave a little room at the end, like this," says the nurse, who's wearing jeans and red sneakers. She rolls the condom carefully onto a plastic banana. All the other people in the room look fourteen, and there are some giggles. Their mothers probably go around saying that they and their daughters are "close," and have no idea they're here today getting birth control and what not.

Finally Magda gets to see the doctor, but it's a more complicated procedure than Annemarie expected: first they have to take a sonogram, to make sure that when they stick in the needle they won't poke the baby.

"Even if that did happen," the doctor explains, "the fetus will usually just move out of the way." Annemarie is floored to imagine a five-month-old fetus fending for itself. She tries to think of what's inside her as being an actual baby, or a baby-to-be, but can't. She hasn't even felt it move yet.

The doctor rubs Magda's belly with Vaseline and then places against it something that looks like a Ping-Pong paddle wired for sound. She frowns at the TV screen, concentrating, and then points. "Look, there, you can see the head."

Magda and Annemarie watch a black-and-white screen where meaningless shadows move around each other like iridescent ink blots. Suddenly they can make out one main shadow, fish-shaped with a big head, like Casper the Friendly Ghost.

"The bladder's full," the doctor says. "See that little clear spot? That's a good sign, it means the kidneys are working. Oops, there it went."

"There what went?" asks Magda.

"The bladder. It voided." She looks closely at the screen, smiling. "You know, I can't promise you but I think what you've got here . . ."

"Don't tell me," Magda says. "If you're going to tell me if it's a boy or a girl, I don't want to know."

"I do," says Annemarie. "Tell me."

"Is that okay with you?" the doctor asks Magda, and Magda shrugs. "Close your eyes, then," she tells Magda. She holds up two glass tubes with rubber stoppers, one pink and the other blue-green. She nods at the pink one.

Annemarie smiles. "Okay, all clear," she tells Magda. "My lips are sealed."

"That's the face, right there," the doctor says, pointing out the eyes. "It has one fist in its mouth; that's very common at this stage. Can you see it?"

They can see it. The other fist, the left one, is raised up alongside its huge head like the Black Panther salute. Magda is transfixed. Annemarie can see the flickering light of the screen reflected in her eyes, and she understands for the first time that what they are looking at here is not a plan or a plot, it has nothing to do with herself. It's Magda's future.

Afterward they have to go straight to the park to pick up Leon from softball practice. It's hot, and Annemarie drives distractedly, worrying about Leon because they're late. She talked him into joining the league in the first place; he'd just as soon stay home and collect baseball cards. But now she worries that he'll get hit with a ball, or kidnapped by some pervert that hangs around in the park waiting for the one little boy whose mother's late. She hits the brakes at a crosswalk to let three women pass safely through the traffic, walking with their thin brown arms so close together they could be holding hands. They're apparently three generations of a family: the grandmother is draped elaborately in a sari, the mother is in pink slacks, and the daughter wears a bleached denim miniskirt. But from the back they could be triplets. Three long braids, woven as thin and tight as ropes, bounce placidly against their backs as they walk away from the stopped cars.

"Was it as bad as you thought it would be?" Annemarie asks Magda. It's awkward to be speaking after all this time, so suddenly, and really for no good reason.

"It was worse."

"I liked the sonogram," Annemarie says. "I liked seeing it, didn't you?"

"Yes, but not the other part. I hate doctors and needles and that whole thing. Doctors treat women like a disease in progress."

That's Magda, Annemarie thinks. You never know what's going to come out of her mouth next. Annemarie thinks the doctor was just about as nice as possible. But in fairness to Magda, the needle was unbelievably long. It made her skin draw up into goose pimples just to watch. Magda seems worn out from the experience.

Annemarie rolls down the window to signal a left turn at the intersection. Her blinkers don't work, but at least the air conditioning still does. In the summer when her mobile home heats up like a toaster oven, the car is Annemarie's refuge. Sometimes she'll drive across town on invented, insignificant errands, singing along with Annie Lennox on the radio and living for the moment in a small, safe, perfectly cooled place.

"I'd have this baby at home if I could," says Magda.

"Why can't you?"

"Too old," she says, complacently. "I talked to the midwife program but they risked me out."

The sun seems horribly bright. Annemarie thinks she's read something about pregnancy making your eyes sensitive to light. "Was it an awful shock, when you found out?" she asks Magda.

"About the midwives?"

"No. About the pregnancy."

Magda looks at her as if she's dropped from another planet.

"What's the matter?" asks Annemarie.

"I've been trying my whole life to have more babies. You knew that, that I'd been trying."

"No, I didn't. Just lately?"

"No, Annemarie, not just lately, forever. The whole time with your father we kept trying, but the drugs he took for the cancer knocked out his sperms. The doctor told us they were still alive, but were too confused to make a baby."

Annemarie tries not to smile. "Too confused?"

"That's what he said."

"And you've kept on ever since then?" she asks.

"I kept hoping, but I'd about given up. I feel like this baby is a gift."

Annemarie thinks of one of the customers at Yesterday! who sent relatives a Christmas fruitcake that somehow got lost; it arrived two and a half years later on the twelfth of

July. Magda's baby is like the fruitcake, she thinks, and she shakes her head and laughs.

"What's so funny?"

"Nothing. I just can't believe you wanted a bunch of kids. You never said so. I thought even having just me got in your way."

"Got in my way?"

"Well, yeah. Because you were so young. I thought that's why you weren't mad when Buddy and I had to get married, because you'd done the same thing. I always figured my middle name ought to have been Whoops."

Magda looks strangely at Annemarie again. "I had to douche with vinegar to get pregnant with you," she says.

They've reached the park, and Leon is waiting with his bat slung over his shoulder like a dangerous character. "The other kids' moms already came ten hours ago," he says when he gets into the car. He doesn't seem at all surprised to see Magda and Annemarie in the same vehicle.

"We got held up," Annemarie says. "Sorry, Leon."

Leon stares out the window for a good while. "Leon's a stupid name," he says, eventually. This is a complaint of his these days.

"There have been a lot of important Leons in history," Annemarie says.

"Like who?"

She considers this. "Leon Russell," she says. "He's a rock and roll singer."

"Leon Trotsky," says Magda.

Annemarie has heard all about Leon Trotsky in her time, and Rosa Luxemburg, and Mother Jones.

"Trotsky was an important socialist who disagreed with Stalin's methodology," Magda explains. "Stalin was the kingpin at the time, so Trotsky had to run for his life to Mexico."

"This all happened decades ago, I might add," Annemarie says, glancing at Leon in the rear-view mirror.

"He was killed by his trusted secretary," Magda continues. "With an axe in the head."

"Magda, please. You think he'll like his name better if he knows many famous Leons have been axed?"

"I'm telling him my girlhood memories. I'm trying to be a good grandmother."

"Your girlhood memories? What, were you there?"

"Of course not, it happened in Mexico, before I was born. But it affected me. I read about it when I was a teenager, and I cried. My father said, 'Oh, I remember seeing that headline in the paper and thinking, What, Trotsky's dead? *Hal* Trotsky, first baseman for the Cleveland Indians?' "

"Live Free or Die, New Hampshire!" shouts Leon at an approaching car.

Magda says, "Annemarie's father came from New Hampshire."

Annemarie runs a stop sign.

It isn't clear to her what's happened. There is a crunch of metal and glass, and some white thing plowing like a torpedo into the left side of the Pontiac, and they spin around, seeing the same view pass by again and again. Then Annemarie is lying across Magda with her mouth open and her head out the window on the passenger's side. Magda's arms are tight around her chest. The window has vanished, and there is a feeling like sand trickling through Annemarie's hair. After a minute she realizes that a sound is coming out of her mouth. It's a scream. She closes her mouth and it stops.

With some effort she unbuckles Magda's seat belt and pulls the door handle and they more or less tumble out together onto the ground. It strikes Annemarie, for no good reason, that Magda isn't a very big person. She's Annemarie's own size, if not smaller. The sun is unbelievably bright. There's no other traffic. A woman gets out of the white car with the New Hampshire plates, brushing her beige skirt in a businesslike way and straightening her hair. Oddly, she has on stockings but no shoes. She looks at the front end of her car, which resembles a metal cauliflower, and then at the two women hugging each other on the ground.

"There was a stop sign," she says. Her voice is clear as a song in the strange silence. A series of rapid clicks emanates from the underside of one of the cars, then stops.

"I guess I missed it," Annemarie says.

"Are you okay?" the woman asks. She looks hard at Annemarie's face. Annemarie puts her hand on her head, and it feels wet.

"I'm fine," she and Magda say at the same time.

"You're bleeding," the woman says to Annemarie. She looks down at herself, and then carefully unbuttons her white blouse and holds it out to Annemarie. "You'd better let me tie this around your head," she says. "Then I'll go call the police."

"All right," says Annemarie. She pries apart Magda's fingers, which seem to be stuck, and they pull each other up. The woman pulls the blouse across Annemarie's bleeding forehead and knots the silk sleeves tightly at the nape of her neck. She does this while standing behind Annemarie in her stocking feet and brassière, with Magda looking on, and somehow it has the feeling of some ordinary female ritual.

"Oh, God," says Annemarie. She looks at the Pontiac and sits back down on the ground. The back doors of the car are standing wide open, and Leon is gone. "My son," she says. The child inside her flips and arches its spine in a graceful, hungry movement, like a dolphin leaping for a fish held out by its tail.

"Is that him?" the woman asks, pointing to the far side of the intersection. Leon is there, sitting cross-legged on a mound of dirt. On one side of him there is a jagged pile of broken cement. On the other side is a stack of concrete pipes. Leon looks at his mother and grandmother, and laughs.

Annemarie can't stop sobbing in the back of the ambulance. She knows that what she's feeling would sound foolish put into words: that there's no point in living once you understand that at any moment you could die.

She and Magda are strapped elaborately onto boards, so they can't turn their heads even to look at each other. Magda says over and over again, "Leon's okay. You're okay. We're all okay." Out the window Annemarie can only see things that are high up: telephone wires, clouds, an airplane full of people who have no idea how near they could be to death. Daily there are reports of mid-air collisions barely averted. When the ambulance turns a corner she can see the permanent landmark of the Catalina Mountains standing over the city. In a saddle between two dark peaks a storm cloud spreads out like a fan, and Annemarie sees how easily it could grow into something else, tragically roiling up into itself, veined with blinding light: a mushroom cloud.

"Magda," she says, "me too. I'm having a baby too."

At the hospital Magda repeats to everyone, like a broken record, that she and her daughter are both pregnant. She's terrified they'll be given some tranquilizer that will mutate the fetuses. Whenever the nurses approach, she confuses them by talking about Thalidomide babies. "Annemarie is allergic to penicillin," she warns the doctor when they're separated. It's true, Annemarie is, and she always forgets to mark it on her forms.

It turns out that she needs no penicillin, just stitches in her scalp. Magda has cuts and serious contusions from where her knees hit the dash. Leon has nothing. Not a bruise.

During the lecture the doctor gives them about seat belts, which Annemarie will remember for the rest of her life, he explains that in an average accident the human body becomes as heavy as a piano dropping from a ten-story building. She has bruises on her rib cage from where Magda held on to her, and the doctor can't understand how she kept Annemarie from going out the window. He looks at the two of them, pregnant and dazed, and tells them many times over that they are two very lucky ladies. "Sometimes the strength of motherhood is greater than natural laws," he declares.

The only telephone number Annemarie can think to give them is the crew dispatcher for Southern Pacific, which is basically Kay Kay's home number. Luckily she's just brought in the Amtrak and is next door to the depot, at Wendy's, when the call comes. She gets there in minutes, still dressed in her work boots and blackened jeans, with a green bandana around her neck.

"They didn't want me to come in here," Kay Kay tells Annemarie in the recovery room. "They said I was too dirty. Can you imagine?"

Annemarie tries to laugh, but tears run from her eyes instead, and she squeezes Kay Kay's hand. She still can't think of anything that seems important enough to say. She feels as if life has just been handed to her in a heavy and formal way, like a microphone on a stage, and the audience is waiting to see what great thing she intends do with it.

But Kay Kay is her everyday self. "Don't worry about Leon, he's got it all worked out, he's staying with me," she tells Annemarie, not looking at her stitches. "He's going to teach me how to hit a softball."

"He doesn't want to go to Buddy's?" Annemarie asks.

"He didn't say he did."

"Isn't he scared to death?" Annemarie feels so weak and confused she doesn't believe she'll ever stand up again.

Kay Kay smiles. "Leon's a rock," she says, and Annemarie thinks of the pile of dirt he landed on. She believes now that she can remember the sound of him hitting it.

Annemarie and Magda have to stay overnight for observation. They end up in maternity, with their beds pushed close together so they won't disturb the other woman in the room. She's just given birth to twins and is watching *Falcon Crest*.

"I just keep seeing him there on that pile of dirt," whispers Annemarie. "And I think, he could have been dead. There was just that one little safe place for him to land. Why did he land there? And then I think, *we* could have been dead, and he'd be alone. He'd be an orphan. Like that poor little girl that survived that plane wreck."

"That poor kid," Magda agrees. "People are just burying her with teddy bears. How could you live with a thing like that?" Magda seems a little dazed too. They each accepted a pill to calm them down, once the doctor came and personally guaranteed Magda it wouldn't cause fetal deformity.

"I think that woman's blouse was silk. Can you believe it?" Annemarie asks.

"She was kind," says Magda.

"I wonder what became of it? I suppose it's ruined."

"Probably," Magda says. She keeps looking over at Annemarie and smiling. "When are you due?" she asks.

"October twelfth," says Annemarie. "After you."

"Leon came early, remember. And I went way late with you, three weeks I think. Yours could come first."

"Did you know Buddy wants us to get married again?" Annemarie asks after a while. "Leon thinks it's a great idea."

"What do you think? That's the question."

"That's the question," Annemarie agrees.

A nurse comes to take their blood pressures. "How are the mamas tonight?" she asks. Annemarie thinks about how nurses wear that same calm face stewardesses have, never letting on like you're sitting on thirty thousand feet of thin air. Her head has begun to ache in no uncertain terms, and she thinks of poor old Leon Trotsky, axed in the head.

"I dread to think of what my hair's going to look like when these bandages come off. Did they have to shave a lot?"

"Not too much," the nurse says, concentrating on the blood-pressure dial.

"Well, it's just as well my hair was a wreck to begin with."

The nurse smiles and rips off the Velcro cuff, and then turns her back on Annemarie, attending to Magda. Another nurse rolls in their dinners and sets up their tray tables. Magda props herself up halfway, grimacing a little, and the nurse helps settle her with pillows under her back. She pokes a straw into a carton of milk, but Annemarie doesn't even take the plastic wrap off her tray.

"Ugh," she complains, once the nurses have padded away on their white soles. "This reminds me of the stuff you used to bring me when I was sick."

"Milk toast," says Magda.

"That's right. Toast soaked in milk. Who could dream up such a disgusting thing?"

"I like it," says Magda. "When I'm sick, it's the only thing I can stand. Seems like it always goes down nice."

"It went down nice with Blackie," Annemarie says. "Did you know he's the one that always ate it? I told you a million times I hated milk toast."

"I never knew what you expected from me, Annemarie. I never could be the mother you wanted."

Annemarie turns up one corner of the cellophane and pleats it with her fingers. "I guess I didn't expect anything, and you kept giving it to me anyway. When I was a teenager you were always making me drink barley fiber so I wouldn't have colon cancer when I was fifty. All I wanted was Cokes and Twinkies like the other kids."

"I know that," Magda says. "Don't you think I know

that? You didn't want anything. A Barbie doll, and new clothes, but nothing in the way of mothering. Reading to you or anything like that. I could march around freeing South Africa or saving Glen Canyon but I couldn't do one thing for my own child."

They are both quiet for a minute. On TV, a woman in an airport knits a longer and longer sweater, apparently unable to stop, while her plane is delayed again and again.

"I knew you didn't want to be taken care of, honey," Magda says. "But I guess I just couldn't accept it."

Annemarie turns her head to the side, ponderously, as if it has become an enormous egg. She'd forgotten and now remembers how pain seems to increase the size of things. "You know what's crazy?" she asks. "Now I want to be taken care of and nobody will. Men, I mean."

"They would if you'd let them. You act like you don't deserve any better."

"That's not true." Annemarie is surprised and a little resentful at Magda's analysis.

"It *is* true. You'll take a silk blouse from a complete stranger, but not the least little thing from anybody that loves you. Not even a bottle of shampoo. If it comes from somebody that cares about you, you act like it's not worth having."

"Well, you're a good one to talk."

"What do you mean?" Magda pushes the tray table back and turns toward her daughter, carefully, resting her chin on her hand.

"What I mean is you beat men off with a stick. Bartholomew thinks you're Miss America and you don't want him around you. You don't even miss Daddy."

Magda stares at Annemarie. "You don't know the first thing about it. Where were you when he was dying? Outside playing hopscotch."

That is true. That's exactly where Annemarie was.

"Do you remember that upholstered armchair we had,

Annemarie, with the grandfather clocks on it? He sat in that chair, morning till night, with his lungs filling up. Worrying about us. He'd say, 'You won't forget to lock the doors, will you? Let's write a little note and tape it there by the door.' And I'd do it. And then he'd say, 'You know that the brakes on the car have to be checked every so often. They loosen up. And the oil will need to be changed in February.' He sat there looking out the front window and every hour he'd think of another thing, till his face turned gray with the pain, knowing he'd never think of it all."

Annemarie can picture them there in the trailer: two people facing a blank, bright window, waiting for the change that would permanently disconnect them.

Magda looks away from Annemarie. "What hurt him wasn't dying. It was not being able to follow you and me through life looking after us. How could I ever give anybody that kind of grief again?"

The woman who just had the twins has turned off her program, and Annemarie realizes their voices have gradually risen. She demands in a whisper, "I didn't know it was like that for you when he died. How could I not ever have known that, that it wrecked your life too?"

Magda looks across Annemarie, out the window, and Annemarie tries to follow her line of vision. There is a parking lot outside, and nothing else to see. A sparse forest of metal poles. The unlit streetlamps stare down at the pavement like blind eyes.

"I don't know," Magda says. "Seems like that's just how it is with you and me. We're like islands on the moon."

"There's no water on the moon," says Annemarie.

"That's what I mean. A person could walk from one to the other if they just decided to do it."

It's dark. Annemarie is staring out the window when the lights in the parking lot come on all together with a soft blink. From her bed she can only see the tops of the cars glowing quietly in the pink light like some strange crop of luminous mushrooms. Enough time passes, she thinks, and it's tomorrow. Buddy or no Buddy, this baby is going to come. For the first time she lets herself imagine holding a newborn against her stomach, its helplessness and rage pulling on her heart like the greatest tragedy there ever was.

There won't be just one baby, either, but two: her own, and her mother's second daughter. Two more kids with dark, curly hair. Annemarie can see them kneeling in the gravel, their heads identically bent forward on pale, slender necks, driving trucks over the moonlike surface of Island Breezes. Getting trikes for their birthdays, skinning their knees, starting school. Once in a while going down with Magda to the Air Force Base, most likely, to fend off nuclear war.

Magda is still lying on her side, facing Annemarie, but she has drawn the covers up and her eyes are closed. The top of the sheet is bunched into her two hands like a bride's bouquet. The belly underneath pokes forward, begging as the unborn do for attention, some reassurance from the outside world, the flat of a palm. Because she can't help it, Annemarie reaches across and lays a hand on her little sister.

BEREAVED APARTMENTS

That woman in the gable-ended house is not all there.

In the beginning there is nothing else for Sulie to think. Her other neighbor, Estelle Berry, who spends a good part of each day picking yellow leaves off her jasmine bushes and looking down the street, comes over and says like it's Sulie's fault, "If you ask me it makes the place look slummish. She's started setting them out on her porch under a door stop, to flap in the breeze."

"Well, Mrs. Berry, it's just notes," says Sulie. "Maybe it's notes to the milkman."

"Lord in heaven, child, you haven't lived here long enough to know. It's not to the milkman, it's to *Him.*"

For a dollar Sulie has changed a light bulb for the woman in the gable-ended house, whose name is Nola Rainey, and for free she has knocked down two paper-wasp nests from behind the ivy with a mop handle. In the eyes of the rest of the neighborhood, that is enough. Sulie is on Nola Rainey's side. But Sulie doesn't know the woman all that well, and when Estelle says *Him,* Sulie thinks she means Nola is leaving notes to God.

So it's a surprise when, on another day, Estelle knocks on Sulie's door and sticks one of the notes straight into her hand. "This blew over on my jasmines. I won't tolerate litter on my shrubs," says Estelle. Her square-hipped figure in beige stretch pants marches away. Sulie reads:

I KNOW WHAT YOU ARE DOING. YOU WILL BE SORRY BY AND BY. EVEN IF THE POLICE DON'T CARE WHAT HAPPENS TO A WIDOW WOMAN. YOU THINK YOU ARE SMART GETTING AWAY WITH PRACTICALLY MURDER SCOT FREE AND YOU THINK I'M BLIND, WELL I'M NOT.

YOURS TRULY,
NOLA RAINEY (MRS. WM.)

Sulie, who doesn't have what she would call friends here yet, decides to show the note to Gilbert McClure. She'll keep an eye out and be on the porch when he comes home from work. Gilbert McClure is the man she shares a house with, in a manner of speaking. It's divided, the way a house can be split down the middle when a landlord sees how he could get twice the rent for the same piece of pie, and makes it a duplex. *There's doors that go right through between my bedroom and his living room, but they're nailed shut and painted over*, she writes Aunt Reima. *Mr. McClure's side must have got the real kitchen because mine's a closet with a hot plate. But it went vice versa on the bathrooms.* And Aunt Reima writes back that yes she's heard those called "love's losts" or some people say "bereaved apartments," because, she supposes, each one is missing something it once had.

Gilbert stands at his window, shaded by Nola's grove of date palms and old cedars, and mixes a gin and tonic. *That woman must be sitting on ten thousand, easy, in antiques.* He's seen plenty of things go in, and nothing come out. This girl who's moved in, Suzie or Sukie, has been over there. Inside. But there's no point in asking; would the child know a Dunand end table if it stood up and talked? She comes from West Virginia. *If people are going to live in these beautiful old houses—going to own them—they could trouble themselves to do it right.* Every house in his line of vision was built before 1940, but decked out in postwar picket fences and venetian blinds, like a gorgeous woman going to dinner in a fireman's jacket. God knows what modern junk they've got inside; that's their problem. And then there is Sukie, who doesn't put up venetian blinds but India-print bedspreads; apparently the sixties have just arrived in West Virginia. *Treasures in Nola's parlor, he's willing to bet.* He stirs his drink with a pencil-thin silver rod, knobbed on the end like a pistol: Prohibition era. The invisible layers of liquid in his glass mix and briefly lose their clarity. Really all he wants is a good look.

If your neighbor is actually insane, I think you have a right to know. Sulie will ask Nola point-blank, she decides. They're standing in Nola's living room. Nola seems small among her overstuffed chairs, but she holds herself straight and her white hair is done up in a whorl at the back that stays put. She wears a navy-blue suit with brass buttons and wide shoulders, very clean, under a clean apron. She's been dusting. What she says, when Sulie asks about the notes, is: "He's broken into my house over two hundred times."

Sulie's arms tingle on the insides. "Who has?"

The feather duster twitches in Nola's hand like a living thing. "Some man," she says. "Or boy. I haven't seen him."

Sulie looks at the windows with their rusted-out locks, hidden from the street by heavy foliage, and sees that this would be a snap if someone were of a mind. Sulie knows something of breaking and entering. "Have you called the police?"

"On more than a dozen occasions," Nola declares proudly. "They have no interest in the elderly."

Sulie says okay she'll have a cup of tea, when Nola offers it, although it's a warm day. The dark kitchen is filled with heavy things, left from a time when a woman needed muscles for cooking. Or needed a cook. Nola turns on the fire and it licks the brass kettle. She has to hold the heavy canister on its side and knock her palm against its bottom to free the last black leaves into the tea strainer. *It must be hard for her to get to the grocery. I could offer to shop for her, for five bucks or something.* Sulie realizes it isn't the money; she's drawn to Nola for other reasons.

They drink warm, weak tea and then Sulie checks the phone, which Nola says has stopped working. It's just come unplugged. Sulie tries to picture in her mind's eye, picture him coming through the window, the person who would break into an old woman's house more than two hundred times.

"You're so able," Nola says. "When I was a girl we never suspected there was any need to know how to fix things." She laughs at herself, waves a hand in front of her face. "And you can drive a truck. I never learned to drive. My husband said I might slaughter someone's livestock for them. This was a long way from town once, this was Senator Pie Allen's ranch."

Sulie smiles. "It's just a pickup. It's not hard to drive. I haul around my stuff in it. I do odd jobs, clean gutters, that kind of thing." She doesn't say what she used to do.

"Oh, I can't imagine. Do you climb up on the ladders? It must be invigorating."

"Well, I guess so." Sulie could leave, but Nola seems unwilling to part company. They return to the kitchen to look at Nola's toaster, which she claims has come unfrazzled near the plug. She says *he* has been meddling with it. But she doesn't go to the toaster, she walks straight to the tea canister, opens it, and cries, "Lord help me, he's stolen all my tea!"

"Sulie, you have to bear in mind that Nola has been in that house for half a century," Gilbert explains. "We've all been wondering which of the two would fall apart first."

"It seems like everybody's mad at her for letting the house run down. Everything on this street's got to be new-looking and just-so. I bet if you painted your gutters some color other than brown or off-white they'd come lynch you."

"Just-so-ugly," he says. "But new-looking, yes."

They're on the porch drinking sherry, compliments of Gilbert, who seems in a friendly mood. Sulie sets her glass on the low wall that divides the porch into halves. "Well, what else can Nola do but let it run down?" she persists. "She says she's got a son someplace but it looks to me like she's on her own."

"She could pay somebody to paint her gutters," Gilbert points out.

"I kind of hinted I'd do it for a good price. I don't think she's got much." Sulie stretches her bare legs, crossing her ankles on the porch railing. Stretching is a habit she's had since living in a place where there wasn't room. Since Women's Correctional. She frees her mass of hair from a rubber band and shakes it off her shoulders, knowing he notices things like that. She wonders if he's ever lived with a woman without the doors nailed shut.

"So tell me the truth, what magic words did you use to get through the front door?" Gilbert asks. "She's never let anybody inside before. Not for years." His back is turned to the gable-ended house and he also, carefully, looks away from Sulie.

"I didn't say hardly anything. She was standing up on a stack of boxes commencing to break her neck so I said I'd change the porch light for her. And one thing led to another, I guess. She's got more ladders over in that garage than you can shake a stick at, but not one of them you'd trust your mother on."

"Is the inside as bad as the outside?"

"Her house? Oh, Lord, on the inside it's decayed. The plumbing, the light switches, all the kinds of little things that go, you know, in a old place. The sash cords on the windows are rotted out. She raises up a window and ten minutes later, bang, back down it comes."

Gilbert touches his mustache lightly, like a pet. "So she thinks this mysterious guy is closing the windows after she's opened them. And tampering with her light switches."

"Uh huh. And stealing things, whatever's run out. Stealing her *toilet paper*. And her tea."

Gilbert looks down the street and laughs to himself.

"But really she's real respectable other than that. I mean, okay, it seems cuckoo leaving those notes on her porch, but how would you feel if your house was running down? Living in this neighborhood where everybody holds it against you?"

"Well, Sulie, I understand the dilemma. Believe me. But I don't think I'd invent a thief to blame my troubles on. I don't think I'd go quite that far off the deep end."

"It's not really off the deep end," Sulie says, looking at her feet. "It could happen. There's thieves in the world."

I can't help the way I was raised. Aunt Reima would take me in a shoe store and try a good new pair on me and leave the old ones sitting on the shelf. Just walk out. I'd keep on thinking of my dirty curled-up shoes back there amongst all the nice ones. Think about somebody finding them.

In front of the bathroom mirror, Sulie is desperate, trying on all her clothes. Everything has specks of paint on it and Gilbert has invited her to dinner. *These are upstanding people here and I have a chance to be who I want because nobody knows what I am. Nobody in Tucson but the parole board.* Seems like he likes her, why would he talk to her otherwise? She doesn't think he's all that old. At first she thought he was, with the mustache, but now she thinks it's like in the black-and-white movies where the men look around fifty but really they're not. And real handsome. *Aunt Reima's idea of dining out was the Mack's Steak House kids-eat-free night. Sulie honey, you go over to the buffet table and pile up your plate. Then hang back behind some family until the daddy pays at the register, and then we'll sit over here at a back booth and we'll feast.* Well, maybe Gilbert and I have got potential, she thinks, who knows? Life's an adventure. Starting clean. She brushes her hair, by turns attacking it and then stroking it with remorse. *Hey, Miss America. They made such a big deal of her hair, and it was envy; you can't get a permanent wave in prison.* Of course they are worlds apart. Gilbert has a regular job he goes to, and nice things. He seems reserved, though, whereas she's outgoing. Well, opposites attract. Between the two of them together maybe they'd make a decent whole person. Sulie laughs. *Like our apartments.*

She is standing in his door, and beautiful. Her hair flowing over her shoulders is a cloud of natural waves—a Botticelli angel—and she has on a pink short-sleeved sweater he likes very much: 1950 or possibly older, angora, with a floral design in seed pearls. Yes, all right, he can go through with this.

"Grand Hotel," he says. His arm pulls the air in front of her through the door, pulls her in with it. "I'm at your service. You'll just have to forgive the fact that there's no dining room."

She is so precious. "I think I got the dining room," she says, looking sideways. "Only I sleep in it."

I stole this sweater. She'd forgotten until his eyes came to rest on it. Now she avoids looking at him. *From a store ten blocks from here called Hearts & Flowers; the price tag said $59 but it was wrong I felt to charge that much for something that had already been owned. Zipped my jacket over it and walked out, thinking how Aunt Reima says: Nine-tenths of successful stealing is believing you're entitled to what you've took. Even now sometimes it's hard to see it any other way.*

Gilbert's living room is all antiques. A light orange rug on the floor, a polished wood coffee table, a curved white sofa shaped like a snail. Gilbert watches her look at it all and seems pleased, walking around laying his hand on things, saying, "This is just a copy." A copy of what? she wonders. The tiles around the fireplace are rounded, old-fashioned-looking, orange like the rug. The exact same tiles as her bathroom, but of course, it used to be all one. His walls in here are painted dark purple, like an eggplant. Sulie supposes that purple walls are usual in better homes. It's hard to believe this is the other half of her own house. That she lives here too.

"*À l'escargot,*" he says, evidently meaning the sofa.

"It's nice. It looks brand new."

"Art Deco, genuine. But it's watermarked." He shows her where. "It sat in my ex-wife's store for eighteen months. If it were perfect it would be worth a few grand, but it's not, so it ends up here. I'm her charity case."

"You used to be married?"

"For about ten minutes." He laughs, waving his hand in front of his face as if he's clearing away smoke.

She stares at the watermarks on the sofa. "If you keep that against the wall, nobody's going to know."

"But it's not perfect." He looks straight at her eyes and

Sulie is startled by what she sees, and he says again, "Nothing you see here is perfect."

He sits down as though he's giving up a fight. He looks like an antique himself. Not old, there are no wrinkles around his eyes; he might be thirty-five, forty, not more. But he looks miserable and handsome in an old-fashioned way, leaning back on the sofa looking up at her. He seems left behind by life.

"So your ex is in the antique business," she says, uncomfortably. "And how about yourself?"

"I *know* the antique business," he says. "Better than she does. But I'm not *in* it. Officially I'm now a bookkeeper at a discount carpet warehouse."

"Oh. Well, that's important. I'm sure they need their money counted up."

He laughs, springs to his feet, and brings out plates and cloth napkins, serving dinner on the polished coffee table. It's Chinese order-out, chicken in an orange sauce that matches the carpet. Even so, she sees him watching her fork each time she lifts it. He seems a little nervous about the red wine. Well, it's true it would stain. They're sitting on opposite ends of the white *l'escargot*.

He raises his glass carefully. "Here's to neighbors."

"Mud in your eye," she says, smiling down at the goblet in her hand. The glass is delicate and old-looking.

"You know," he says, "you have wonderful hair."

"I don't bother it, it don't bother me," she says.

"I'm serious." He squints at her. "I can see you in silk."

"Oh, Lord," she says, laughing, "I'd spill something on it."

They look away from each other and she wonders why she is there. "Could I ask you a question?" she says when it's been too long. "Not to be nosy. But why do you live here? You seem like somebody that could live in a whole house if you wanted to."

"This is a 1929 Meredeth bungalow with a Deco fireplace."

"Oh," she says. She'd driven uptown and down in her second-hand pickup, scouting out FOR RENT signs in yards. Looking for something respectable and nothing like what she left behind.

"Do you know how hard it is to find a nice old house in this cowboy boom-town state? One that hasn't been completely gutted?"

"I guess there's not too many," she says. He could move back East, she thinks, they have plenty of old antique stuff back there, but there is his ex-wife, she remembers—there are all the things you can't know about somebody. The things he can't know about her.

"I'd move and take that fireplace out of here with me if I could," he says, glancing at her. "Just take it. The landlord doesn't know what he's got." The color in Sulie's face deepens.

"Well, it's lucky you got this side, with the real living room," she says. "I don't think there's much of anything special on my side. You could come see it, if you wanted to."

"I'd like that very much," he says politely, and she's embarrassed to think of Gilbert seeing her things. She eats dinner off a cable spool.

"What you could do someday," she says, "is buy this house from the landlord. You could open it back up and make it one house like it's supposed to be." Gilbert just laughs at that.

"Well, anyway you've got a lot of nice things," she says. "It all goes together in here like a magazine house."

"I expect you've seen better over at Nola's," Gilbert says, looking at her oddly.

She considers. "Well, over there it's different. It's an old-lady house. Kind of knickyknacky. It's amazing how people collect so much stuff over the years."

"Stuff stays around," he says, twisting the stem of his antique glass in his fingers. "People don't."

It's quiet again. His ex, Sulie supposes he means. Suddenly he lifts the glass from her hand. The wine is gone, and his head is in her lap. He says, "If you could picture me in another time, when would it be?"

"In a movie, definitely. An old one."

He looks up at her. From this angle, with his Adam's apple exposed, he looks young. "How old?"

"I don't know," she says, afraid of guessing wrong. "One with Greta Garbo."

He smiles and closes his eyes. "Bull's eye. I was born fifty years too late."

"I was born four weeks late," she says, relaxing too, sensing that whatever she says now he'll find charming. "Aunt Reima says Mama was about ready to start jumping off tables."

He gave her a paperweight, the Golden Gate Bridge in blown glass, worth about sixteen dollars, and she thinks it's the Hope diamond. *Trinkets for the Indians,* says an ugly voice behind his ear and he knows there is that, he's charming her to get into Nola's house, but he likes her, too. In the evenings they sit on the porch drinking gin.

On Saturday she knocks on his screen door and walks in with a loaf of banana bread, fresh-baked. Her nonchalant generosity takes him by surprise. Possibly it isn't nonchalant; maybe she's trying as hard as he is. She needs to please everybody, the gossip next door—Estelle—and of course Nola. Sulie looks mid-twenties and has been around men, almost certainly, but she seems impossibly young. As if, like Sleeping Beauty, she's missed out on several years of her life.

"I had to share this, it would have gone stale," she says, and he brings out plates, and tries not to track the course of every crumb she sheds across his rug. In this living room she is modern and incongruous in jeans and bare feet, long legs swinging over the side of his Deco gondola chair. She does the most surprising things for a living—yard work, cleaning, she'll even paint a house. Her resourcefulness makes him feel old. But there is something else about her, some kindred thing, an under-handedness he hasn't named yet.

"How's your friend," he asks. "Nola."

"Oh, Lord, it's a war zone. She's turning the house upside down, and's got me to helping her do it. She says she has to find all her precious things and get them up to the attic."

"The attic?" His eyes wander out the window toward the ivy-covered gable.

"She's got about twenty locks on the door and says HE can't get in there because he hasn't learned how to pick the locks."

Gilbert smiles.

"I know it's crazy. But I still feel like I ought to help her. She's a nice lady, really. Have you noticed how she dresses up? She has the nicest clothes."

"I've noticed," he says. *That pink sweater is what it was. Sulie couldn't afford that vintage sweater. Bless her little West Virginia heart, she's a thief.*

Sulie's eyes are wide. "Listen, Gilbert, could you help me do one thing? I know you think her house is creepy and you'd have to go inside, but I promise it'll just take fifteen minutes."

She's standing on a brocade ottoman when they come in, drawing back a curtain, and she turns, steps down, extends her hand. A dark green suit, padded shoulders, her white hair in a neat chignon; not what he expected. A woman keeping her wits about her in a crisis—Lauren

Bacall in *Key Largo*. Sulie was right, it's a war zone. Or a zone of terrified anticipation, like a news clip of Galveston before a hurricane. The shelves are empty of anything a person might treasure; presumably that's all packed away in the cardboard boxes stacked against the walls. Just a few lamps and chairs left behind, hodgepodge. He does recognize some value in the furniture—it's worn, not the feast he was hoping to let his eyes graze on, but pieces originally of good quality. Things that sigh of old wealth. Worth the trip, anyway. He's had his look.

But they have to sit through chitchat and lemonade, which Nola brings out in a Depression Glass pitcher and glasses. Could be worth some money if there are more glasses packed away. Not in mint condition, though. In mid-sentence Nola stops and reaches out to pick at a chip in the pitcher's rim.

"Now look what he's done to that. I could just cry; this was Mama's."

"You can hardly notice it," Sulie says.

"I can't tell you what my life has been like since he started this." Nola's voice rises to a prayerful monotone. "Not a day goes by without him getting in and monkeying with something."

Gilbert drains his unchipped glass and notes the purple glaze on the bottom. Authentic, and valuable. If he held it up to the light he could know its exact worth.

"It would be another story if he just wanted money. But he's after my precious things." Nola leans forward and pecks on the pitcher with a fingernail. "Oh, there's nothing he wouldn't do. He's *demented*."

Sulie says gently, "I promised Gilbert this wouldn't take long," and Nola's face changes, she squares her padded shoulders. They follow her into the hallway and bend their knees to lift the box that was too heavy for Sulie alone: leather-bound books. Sulie above and Gilbert below make their way up the narrow stairs like an uncoordinated animal. His heart is pumping hard. Nola stands at the top, small and white-haired, prodding keys into locks. Sulie didn't exaggerate; there are more than twenty locks lining the edge of the door from bottom to top.

"He hasn't found a way in here yet," she says, "but he will, he can pick any lock. He'll have his holiday in here." She gives the door a hard tug and it shivers open. Gilbert feels a rush of blood through his knees. It is a wonderland.

If he expected bats in Nola's belfry, what he sees there are rare birds: peacocks, sleek raptors, black satin cormorants. In the furniture alone he recognizes five decades of perfection, and only a small part of it is visible. Cabriole legs turn out like demure ankles under dust skirts; glimpses of ivory-inlaid dresser tops gleam under pyramids of japanned boxes; and Gilbert's heart is struck with the deepest envy he's ever known.

"I told you she'd brought all the good stuff up here," Sulie says, watching his face. Nola has gone downstairs for more small boxes, and Gilbert is walking around touching things in a way that makes Sulie nervous. But she's pleased, too; she wanted him to see. *I've never had a friend like her. She's dignified, more so than somebody like Estelle that just wants to check people's stuff for brand names behind their backs.* Sulie remembers Estelle Berry's mouth pronouncing the word "slummish," her square hips moving away across the lawn toward her jasmine bushes. But Nola has nice things, she and Gilbert know that, even if the outside has gone downhill. *I know what it's like when people look down their nose because you don't have nice things.*

Gilbert lifts a dust cover slowly, the way he might lift a woman's dress. Sulie shivers.

"There's clothes, too. Come look." She pulls him by the hand through the narrow avenues between furniture. The racks of dresses march backward through time like a museum display.

"She let me try on her wedding dress. It's here, I'll show you. You won't believe what color it is: black. Black velvet, and you know it fit me like a glove? Can you believe she was tall as me at one time in her life?"

Gilbert, stopped dead, is staring at a hat. Sulie's seen it before, it's just a cream-colored ordinary man's felt hat with a dark purple band. Nola keeps it on a hat block by the north window.

"Gilbert," Sulie says.

Nola is behind her. She walks to Gilbert and takes the hat in both hands, and they both look like they're in love with the thing. But Nola's eyes go to a spot under the brim, where the face would be. "My husband wore this on our wedding day."

"I bet he looked real good," Sulie says.

"He never would wear it again after that, though. He said it was too dapper for a working man."

"You were married in 1925." Gilbert doesn't ask, he informs them. Sulie stares. Like a subdued child, Nola hands him the hat and Gilbert turns it over, looks inside, and gives a little nod, as if he's found something he knew would be there. He says, "Vallon and Argod, World Exposition." He touches his mustache and settles the hat on his head and it is, really, perfect.

"Did you ever think of selling this, Nola? I know where you could get a hundred dollars for it." His neck twitches slightly. *Fifteen hundred, without even trying.*

Nola, possessed of herself again, takes the hat back and replaces it on the block. She brushes at imaginary dust on its brim, gently, the way she might have preened a lover's combed head. She turns to face him and says, as if she needs to say it, "I wouldn't part with this."

Sulie calls through the screen door, "Gilbert, we need your advice." She's startled him; she sees him jump before he raises his eyebrows and gets up to let her in. He gives her a kiss on the cheek, not seeming to mind her dirty coveralls.

"The problem is, she's worried about the veneer drying out on some of her tables and things. It's real hot up there with no ventilation, and she says if you move something from cool to hot and dry it will ruin. Unless you treat it some way."

"She's right, it will crack all to pieces." He's smiling.

"Well." Sulie stands looking at him. "Can't we help? I know she's never going to use it again, but it'll kill her to see it go to wreck and ruin. I went around back just now to empty my trash and she was standing out there holding a dead poinsettia and a teapot. Crying. She said couldn't I ask you what to do. If she ought to use linseed on it or something."

Sulie can't read Gilbert's face. *A dead plant in one hand and the teapot in the other, and she said, You have to understand, dear, that's all I have; my husband is gone. She looked over here and said, Could you ask the advice of your young man? And I felt so strange, she must think we live together. I said it just looks like that from the outside. Our apartments are completely shut off.*

"Sure," Gilbert says, "there's something you can do, but not necessarily linseed. It depends on the thickness of the veneer, for one thing." He pauses. "I'd have to see it."

They knock on Nola's door and she takes them upstairs, holding her huge key ring in front of her like Diogenes with his lantern searching for an honest man. *She must spend her whole life locking and unlocking things.* When she opens the attic door they're blasted with heat; it's like checking the oven.

"The first thing we have to do is get some cross-ventilation, so we can breathe," Gilbert says. He walks across and throws open the north window. "Now we'll open this one," he says, dragging open a sash on the south side facing the street. "Now let's have a look."

His mouth turns down, like a doctor's, as he listens to Nola and examines a coffee table with a leafy pattern inlaid in light and dark woods. Sulie is touched by his concern. He knows everything in the world about antiques. She jots down notes for Nola on an envelope.

Before they leave the attic Gilbert closes and locks the front window, brushing at the papery shells of dead flies on the sill. As Sulie and Nola start down the stairs Sulie sees, out of the corner of her eye, an amazing thing. Gilbert goes to the north window, but before he closes it he picks up the hat, holds it between his fingertips out the window, and lets it drop. She can only presume it lands two stories below, on the privet hedge behind Nola's garage.

Who would I report it to, if I did? Would I have to go to the police as a witness? An accomplice? Me on parole, casting the first stone. Sulie knocks on his door that evening, knocks and waits, but there's no answer. Then she hears them talking over the fence, out back by the garbage cans. She lingers by the bushes near the water meter. Only because she knows it's there Sulie can see it behind them, in the shrubby dimness behind Nola's house, nested like a white bird down in the privet hedge.

"One of my Fiesta Ware plates, broken right in two," Nola says, rapping her knuckle on the garbage-can lid on her side of the fence.

Gilbert is tall and handsome like a man in a movie. His hand rests on the fence. *He gave me the Golden Gate Bridge.* The paperweight sits under the lamp beside her bed, a globe of light. She can feel the kindness of his hands on her skin as they curled together on the rug. His hands under the soft sweater.

"He knows what's good, I'll give him that much," Nola says. "He goes right for the things I love the most."

"It's like you said," Gilbert tells her. "He knows how to get at you. He's demented."

It's exactly what Nola wants to hear. She leans across the fence toward him with tears in her eyes. Her thin hand reaches out and clasps his wrist.

Well I didn't aim to get caught, I always knew I didn't want to end up in here, but it's hard to see who I'm hurting when I do it. The rehab therapist just nodded, trying not to let anything show on her face, and then another woman in the group dragged on her cigarette and flicked pale straight hair out of her eyes and said Honey I can see who I'm hurting, I just don't give a shit.

Sulie has been hired to paint a house on the north side of town, in a younger neighborhood than this one, with fewer old trees. To paint a house sky blue. She's loading pans and rollers into her truck, ready to leave for work, when her shoulder is touched from behind. It's Nola, dressed in a green silk blouse, a ragged half slip, and spectator shoes. Her hair straggling down her back is surprisingly long. "Now it's happened," she says.

"What's happened?"

"He's found his way into the attic."

Sulie feels her neck go red. "How do you know?"

"Do you remember my husband's fedora, from our wedding day? It's gone. It would have been more like him to ruin it some way, but he took it."

A cluster of sparrows chatters up in one of Nola's date palms, fussing over the ripe dates.

"I'm sorry, Nola. I've got to go to work right now. When I come back this afternoon I'll help you look for it."

Nola ignores her. "He reads my mind," she says. "That hat had been on my mind. Whatever I'm thinking about, he gets to meddling with. I'm afraid to leave my house now. I'm afraid even to turn my back."

Sulie drives twice around the block, parks, and goes back into her house. She can't climb ladders today. She sits on her bed with her arms crossed over her stomach and listens to her young man moving around on the other side of the wall.

He keeps it in the lacquered armoire next to the fireplace. During the day he locks the cabinet and carries the key in his pocket, turning it in his fingertips until the brass shines like an icon. At night he wears it, moving quietly between the bedroom and living-room mirrors. Or he opens the cabinet door and just stares, letting the rest of the room go into soft focus. He has never doubted the rightfulness of this; it's his. He needs it. It is such a completely perfect thing it improves the room. Everything else is perfect by association.

Sulie was gone so must hear secondhand from Estelle about the two police cars and the ambulance. Evidently Nola called the emergency number complaining of a fluttering in her chest and they came in to find her lying in bed, weeping, in a fur hat. She's in the hospital now.

"They said she's got a son," explains Estelle. "Up there someplace, it was either Idaho or Iowa, one. Divorced. They called him and said he's flying right down."

Sulie's stomach hurts. "What's going to happen to her?"

"Well, I told the police they ought to explain to the son about the condition, you know, of the house, and they said he seemed real understanding. I'm sure he had no idea. As soon as she leaves the hospital, if and when, he'll put her in a home. It's the best thing. I guess he'll clean out the house and maybe they'll spruce it up and sell it."

Estelle and Sulie stare at the house. Around the gable windows, where sparrows are nesting, ivy branches wave like arms under the birds' slight weight. To Sulie the house looks completely different without Nola in it.

The two front windows are shuttered from the inside with plywood, making the house seem blind. Sulie leaves early for her housepainting and comes home late, but still she has to come home. On a Saturday afternoon she sees him coming back from the bus stop. The person coming down the sidewalk toward her, wearing the fedora, is Gilbert. He stops in front of Nola's blinded house, clicks his heels together, and lightly touches the brim, smiling, holding her eye. Sulie looks away.

The very night after he'd done it, he talked to her all sweet and innocent. I waited by the water meter because I saw them talking across the fence. Nola with tears in her eyes, reaching over, her hand making a circle around his wrist like a bracelet of bones.

She will go inside now and put what she needs in boxes. There are places for rent on the north side. The pink beaded sweater she'll leave on the bathroom tile, folded, weighted down by the glass paperweight. She'll think about it there, left behind for someone to find. Her own things she'll take. By the end of the month there will be nothing she cares about in either half of that house.

EXTINCTIONS

It may already be too late for the pandas, the man on TV says. When Westerners first discovered them they were so fascinated they just couldn't kill enough; now there are only a few pandas left, and the best efforts of science can't seem to bring them back. Paired up in zoos, they turn their backs on one another and refuse to participate in family life. It's as if the whole species is suffering from a terrible sadness—as though they'd looked around at what had happened and just given up. Grace doesn't blame them. She sits rigidly in bed next to her husband, arms folded tightly over her chest. The program shows an old film clip of men emerging in high leather boots from the bamboo forest, holding up panda skins stretched on wooden frames. The image gives her chills, it is so full of evil. It's like seeing a child's toy flayed.

"They shouldn't tell people it's already too late," Randall says. "If people think that, they won't care anymore."

"But it's the truth," says Grace. "That's how things are with the ocean and the ozone and everything. Once they get around to looking, they find out that things are already way more messed up than anybody thought."

"That's not true. There's somebody someplace that knows when things start to get poisoned, but they try to keep it a secret. They know people would get mad. It's never too late to get mad," he persists, looking at Grace, needing for her to agree that there is hope. There has always been this difference between them, a deep gulf she can't swim.

"I wish Jacob could see this," she says. The boys are in bed. Endangered species are Jacob's hobby—his room swims with posters of every possible kind of whale. When Grace stands in the middle of them, picking up socks in a great fishbowl, she can fathom the depth of the ocean's despair. Jacob knows all the numbers: how many tigers are left, how many mountain gorillas.

"This is the last thing in the world Jacob needs to watch," Randall says. He thinks Jacob carries it too far.

Grace wants the program to stop, but feels it would be wrong to turn it off. It would be turning away from truth. A Chinese woman scientist measures bamboo shoots on a tiny plot of ground. It takes acres of bamboo to keep a panda alive, she explains, and most of it has been cut down to make way for rice paddies. Over Grace's head, rain strikes the roof like bullets and makes her tired. Tomorrow she and the boys have to drive a hundred miles to have dinner and go to church with her relatives. It's Easter weekend, only once a year, she shouldn't resent it. Randall thinks Grace is afraid of her family, which of course is a mistaken opinion, but she does dread the trip. A storm has settled over all of central Kentucky and she knows the drive will be hard.

Every so often, the scientist says, all the bamboo in a whole mountain range will die back to the roots and there is massive starvation. In the old days the pandas could go somewhere else, but now there is no place for them to go. A film clip shows emaciated panda bodies like sad beanbag chairs littering the forest floor. Grace presses her knees together and holds her elbows to resist the urge to get up, again, and see if the boys are still breathing. Ten years ago, when they were babies, she argued with Randall that crib death was real, that something really could happen. Now she knows it isn't rational to need to see, half a dozen times every night, the slight movement of their chests under the covers. Randall calls her a worrier. Now, with so much on TV about addiction, he's decided that's her problem—he has said he thinks Grace is addicted to sadness.

The early weather report said the storm was expected to continue through the weekend. There isn't much rain right now, though, only a fine mist that occasionally freezes on the windshield. The road could be slick, but it's impossible to know that until you try to stop. Red taillights waver and leap in the dimness ahead of her like sparks escaped from a fireplace.

"What did you bring for church?" she asks the boys. Randall says they're old enough to do things for themselves—to pack their own clothes, for example. She does try.

"Our good shirts and jeans," Matt says. She smiles at the tops of their two brush-cut heads in the mirror. "Good shirts" means bright colors—turquoise, fuschia. Matt has a pair of green sneakers with red tongues. She imagines her two sons flowering on the church pew among all the brown-suited farm boys like butterfly weeds in a bean patch. Her grandmother would die if they skipped church, but she would do worse than die if she saw that. They'll have to borrow jackets from Rita's kids.

The boys are good on trips—they can both read in the car without getting sick. Jacob has a new National Geographic book on the condors. Matthew, who's a year younger, is making an elaborate crayon drawing of a brontosaurus, which now the scientists are calling something different, Grace forgets what. Matt knows all the names. His infatuation is not whales but dinosaurs—species that are already gone. It strikes her that by the time her sons are grown there will be little difference. Their own children will view whales as kinds of dinosaurs—mythical beasts—not something real, to mourn. They will never believe those huge, fishlike creatures moved through the seas in modern times, while people were driving around in Hondas and drawing money from bank machines.

They arrive late. Rita, Grace's cousin, has been keeping dinner warm in the oven for two hours. Grace hadn't even worried about the time; she'd forgotten the country habit of eating the main meal in the middle of the day. She hurries the boys to the table while the men bring extra chairs from the kitchen. Grace sees how much she's forgotten—these meals of baked ham with pineapple and marshmallows, and slices of Wonder bread passed around on a plate. Her grandmother Naomi accuses Grace of putting on airs since she moved away from Clement, but Grace has never tried to put the past behind her. Large parts of her childhood just seem to erase themselves quietly while she's not looking. Naomi and Rita will mention important family illnesses, even vacations they took, and to Grace it's as though some child she's never met did all those things.

After Naomi says the blessing, the silence dissolves into a din. The table is crammed with people: Naomi, Rita and her huge husband, Donnie, their three children, and Grace's unmarried cousin Clarence, who's tall and thin, all elbows. Rita and Clarence spent their teenage years as Grace's older brother and sister, more or less, because their father—her Uncle Vale—lost his hands in a hay baler and their mother got to drinking whiskey. It's hard to imagine how they spent those years under one small roof. After concentrating on the long, quiet drive, Grace feels overwhelmed by the sudden commotion and plates of food to be passed. The boys seem right at home, though, talking with Donnie and Donnie, Jr., about the Kentucky versus Louisville basketball game. At the same time, Rita is talking about how easily you could have a moment of carelessness you'd regret your whole life. On *Donahue* she'd seen a woman who allowed her toddler to fall in the washer and drown. "She turns her back one second for the fabric softener, and there he goes in with the sheets," she says.

"No more static cling!" cries Donnie, Jr., who is old enough now to work at a gas station.

"Boo Boo Hardrick blowed his finger off with a M-80," says Rita's daughter Caren. "He pulled off the bandage at playtime and made me look." The way Rita's children talk shocks Grace. Maybe she has put herself above her family, as Naomi says.

"Caren, now hush, if you can't talk about something nice," Rita says. "Is that Michael Hardrick, or Bruce?"

"The big one. Bruce."

"Was it blown clean off, honey?"

"He said clean down to the bone."

Grace notices that Rita's hair is darker than last year. She's started covering the gray. She and her brother look more alike as they get older—as angular as scarecrows. Grace's husband Randall is tall and thin too, but in a nicer way. He has long, slender hands and feet that she finds beautiful.

"I can't believe how grown-up the kids are," she tells Rita. "Donnie Junior working. Our babies aren't babies anymore."

"They get growed up behind your back when you don't come home but ever seven or eight years," says Naomi.

"Grandma, that isn't so, they come ever year," cries Rita. Grace guesses from the way they all shout that Naomi has grown more hard of hearing.

"What's Randall up to?" Donnie asks. Donnie, who seldom talks, has a voice that booms down in his throat like a bass drum. You could just talk with Donnie on the phone and know he was big.

"Same as always," Grace says. "Welding the front of a

car to the back of a car, about a hundred times a day." Randall works at the automotive plant in Louisville. He likes his job. "He wanted to come," Grace lies, "but he couldn't get off."

"Anymore that's about all anybody around here is doing too," says Clarence. "Working over to that Toyota plant the Japs put up down at Campbell. Don't seem like nobody can get a whole living out of farming anymore."

"It's the truth," Rita says. "All the men have to go someplace else to work. There's nobody left in Clement now, of a daytime, but women and children. Somebody could just march in here and take the place I guess."

"Going up to First Methodist with me tomorrow?" asks Naomi suddenly.

Rita leans toward her and shouts, "I told you, Grandma. Me and Grace want to try out Woods Baptist!" This is the first Grace has heard of it.

"Now, who's the pastor there?" the old woman demands without looking up from her plate.

"She knows very well," Rita tells Grace. "She's dying to go see for herself, only she's too proud." She shouts, "You know very well, Grandma. It's the Beltrain boy."

"Oh, yes," Naomi says, reaching for a slice of bread.

"You remember Nestor Beltrain, Grace. He lived next door to us for a while there. Next to your-all's house on Polk Street."

Grace can tell from the way the men are smiling at their plates that there's a joke hanging over the table, but she can't remember the Beltrain boy. If his getting the pastor's job was any big thing, Rita would have told her about it. Rita writes Grace regular letters in her curly cursive hand—the news and calamities of Clement all rendered benign by her fat *o*'s and *c*'s. She keeps in closer touch now with Grace's mother and father—who live in a trailer court in Tucson, Arizona—than Grace does herself. Sometimes Rita lords that over her, too, but Grace tries to be understanding. It would be hard to grow up in somebody else's house without a mother of your own.

They're all looking at Grace. There is some secret here. "Well, I can't place him," she says. "I'm sorry."

"You couldn't have forgot Nestor," says Rita. "Nobody could forget Nestor. His daddy was Colonel Beltrain, remember, that was on the school board and had his own parking place down at the courthouse? Nestor had asthma or something. He was a little skinny old boy with ears that stuck out of his head like tree funguses. The teachers used to grab them like handles. He was so bad."

The men are practically laughing out loud. "You men hush up," Rita says. "It isn't that funny."

Clarence says, "You ought to remember him, Gracie. He liked to have hung you."

Rita interrupts him. "David, stop making such a big show out of it and chew what's in your mouth," she says, and Grace is uncertain of what Clarence has just said.

"I can't stand this stuff," says David, Rita's youngest. "It's stringy and's got too much salt."

"Well, it's Kentucky-cured ham, honey, that's just how it tastes. You liked it fine last year."

"I remember the name," Grace says. "Nestor Beltrain. But I can't picture him. Clarence, what did you say he did?"

Rita gives Clarence an odd, warning look, but he answers anyway. "I said he liked to have hung you from a tree."

Grace's hand rests on her throat. She looks at Jacob and Matt, who seem intent on their food. "What do you mean, hung me?"

"From that old mulberry tree out there," he says, pointing toward the window as if it were still there. But this is a different house.

"I do remember the tree," Grace says.

"You was just little," Clarence says. "He stood you up

on a chair and put a rope around your neck and said to jump any time you was ready."

"You talking about that time he tried to string her up from the tree?" asks Naomi. "You two wasn't living here yet, I'm the one seen it. Grace, your mother and me was setting in the kitchen doing up a mess of break beans and she looked out the window and all the sudden commenced to whooping and hollering." Naomi pauses for breath. "She grabbed up one of her new Revere Ware pots and throwed it at him, right out the back door. I never heard the like of language come out of her mouth."

Apparently this is the story Rita wanted to put a stop to, but now she laughs. "She must have scared him good. I don't think he ever did come back in your-all's yard."

"Law, he used to come over pestering you a awful lot, Grace, and trying to get you to look at dirty magazines under the lilac bushes," says Naomi. "Your mother would get mad, but not like that time."

"Well, he did so come back, Rita," says Clarence. "Me and you and him used to . . ."

"Clarence, I think you'd just better shut up and clean your plate," Rita says.

"Used to what?" Grace asks. She does know that Rita and Clarence were often put in charge of her for whole afternoons, when her mother had to take in ironing. Sometimes Grace thinks Rita hasn't quite given up the job of being boss.

"You wasn't but about three or four," says Naomi. "When he tried to string you up. I don't expect you'd remember it."

Grace doesn't, but she thinks she should. Or that it should have been talked about before now.

"Them magazines don't hurt nobody, Rita, so you can just get down off your high horse," says Clarence.

Grace wishes she knew what they were talking about. She has a sudden, narrow recollection of something else:

the smell of poultry feed. A cardboard box of ducklings in the corner of her classroom. Finding them dead. Nestor was not in her grade, he was older, but he had come into the room somehow and painted the ducklings with thick poster paints. They were dead by morning, their gaudy feathers sticking out like dry quills and their mouths gaping.

She says, "I remember who you mean. His daddy was the Scout leader."

"Boot-camp leader was what he was," says Donnie, helping himself to more ham. "We all quit the Scouts. Nestor was the only one put up with all that nonsense." He takes a bite, and then says, "I guess he didn't have much choice about it. Colonel'd roust him out of bed and make him take a cold shower and go out barefooted in the snow."

"I think some of that was hearsay," Rita says, "the bare feet in the snow. But he drove him hard, that's for sure. We seen it, didn't we, Clarence? Lord, they'd be out there on the sidewalk in their overcoats at the crack of dawn, doing jumping jacks and running around the block. We'd sit over by the front window pretending like we were looking for our galoshes or something so we could watch them out there, before school."

"Hut-*two*, hut-*two*," barks Clarence in a forced imitation of the Colonel, and he and Rita laugh.

Rita smooths her hair back from her forehead with her palm. "It was before this jogging craze hit; we'd never seen such a thing. They'd run around the block eight or nine times and we'd hear Nestor wheezing out there, he'd be breathing so hard. About to drop over dead it sounded like. And old Colonel right behind him, cracking the whip."

Clarence screws up his face and imitates the Colonel again: "You-*will*-keep-up-with-me-or-you-*will*-die-trying!"

Grace remembers a warm kitchen, cocoa and buttered toast, and looking through the house to the fogged front window. Seeing through to the lean gray shapes of them out on the sidewalk. There were things that weren't told.

Her mother stood near the window with crossed arms and a mouth pinched down at the corners by pity or anger. Mrs. Beltrain had a bone disease, people said, that was why her skin looked bruised, and why she was always laid up in one or another combination of plaster casts. "Just like that," they would say, applying a gentle pressure to your forearm. "No more than that, and hers would have snapped like a straw." For weeks at a time she wouldn't appear outside the house.

The younger children are whining. "Mom, can we have turkey next year?" David wants to know. "I hate ham."

"I do too," agrees Caren. "It takes too long to chew."

"Turkey is for Thanksgiving," Rita says. "For Easter we have ham. If you don't like it, move to another house. Go live with your cousins."

Grace feels uneasy. "Matt, Rita told me Donnie Junior has a computer game about dinosaurs. Why don't you all go take a look at it?" The children look happy to leave the table.

"Now the Colonel," says Naomi. "There was a man made out of something."

"The Colonel passed on, you knew about that, Grace. I wrote you about that. They said he cut up his whole steak one night and then put down his knife and died. Seemed like Mrs. Beltrain got a new lease on life; she put the house up for sale and moved to one of those army retirement homes, I forget where."

"It cut Nestor loose from his tether, though," says Clarence. "He went and joined a commune."

"Clarence, I swear," Rita says. "It wasn't a commune, it was that monk place down in Georgia. He was there, oh, I don't know, the longest time, and then next thing we heard he'd finished up at a Baptist seminary and they'd hired him up here at Woods Baptist."

"I don't think they took a good look at him first," Clarence says. "He's got a beard, and speaks in tongues."

"It's true," Rita says. "I think people are going up there for reasons other than to serve Our Lord. It's a show, I'll tell you. He talks Hebrew or something. I went the other Sunday with Sue Carey and we couldn't believe our ears. There's hardly nobody left of the congregation but the old folks, poor things. They just keep on turning up their hearing aids thinking they'll understand him. I swear I think he's still got a mean streak."

The table grows very quiet. From the other room Grace hears the children's voices, quiet with concentration, and the steady beep of the video game. She has the odd sensation of watching this scene—her own family around the dinner table—from a great distance, like one of those people who've watched their own bodies on the operating table before coming back from death.

"The trouble with the boy," says Naomi, "is that he got corrupted blood. They didn't boil it."

"I can't imagine what you mean," Rita shouts at Naomi in an encouraging way.

"When he was just born. His mother liked to of died in labor and the boy was born anemiated. They had to give him blood, in the hospital. And you know very well where they get that blood from." She looks around at her subdued grown grandchildren. "Criminals, that's where. They sell their blood on the streets in Lexington and Louisville when they're on the down and out. They think they're getting away with something, but the people here know about this."

There is a long pause. "What did you mean about boiling it?" Rita asks.

"Boil it," says Naomi. "That's what they do, to get the criminal element out of it. But they got busy that day, and they forgot."

In her dream, Grace sees the elderly people of Clement sitting patiently on folding chairs under the mulberry tree.

He ties nooses around their necks, one at a time, and explains in careful, smiling Hebrew that they're about to be murdered.

She sits up with the memory clear in her head, more real than this strange bed in Rita's guest room. She must have been very young, too little to understand even the basics of gravity. He told her it would be fun. When she jumped off the chair, he said, she would swing to and fro in the breeze. She stood for a while anticipating that pleasure, staring up into the wide mulberry canopy that shaded their yard and the Beltrains' next door, watching while a breeze moved against the leaves. She can feel the knot against her jaw and his eyes on her, alive and quiet, as she prepares to end her life. The memory comes down on her like an ice storm, stiffening her to the center with cold rage. If her mother hadn't looked out the window, Grace thinks. Or if she hadn't survived whatever it was that came later, when Rita and Clarence were in charge. She would have spent these decades as a photograph, smiling its dead child's smile on her parent's mantelpiece, or just put away in a box somewhere. Even tragedies get forgotten. Grace puts her hands on the wall and finds her way to the room where the boys are sleeping.

From the doorway, in the dim light, she can make out which sleeping bags on the floor hold Matthew and Jacob. Matt's has dinosaurs and Jacob's has airplanes. They couldn't find one with endangered species. For a while you saw pictures of whales and wolves and bald eagles everywhere you looked, even bumper stickers about the baby seals, but then endangered species went out of style. Randall is right, somebody knows when things start to get poisoned. What he says might be true. That you should get mad. She stands still with her eyes on the heavy printed fabric until she finds the slow rhythm of their breathing. Her hands are trembling. She's never even known to count, like sheep or blessings, the days of her life that almost didn't happen.

In the morning Rita talks loudly while she and Naomi work around each other in the kitchen. "It turns out it was cancer," she says, breaking eggs into the skillet. "A cancer of the right ovary as big as a mushmelon. Sue said they just sewed her back up and told her to go on back home and get right with God. That poor woman. After all she's been through with Standford."

"What about Standford?" Naomi asks. "Besides just the drinking, I know about that."

"Well, you know about the other too. Him and that lady basketball coach from Campbell. She's not one-half his age if she's a day."

Grace is sitting at the kitchen table with her third or fourth cup of coffee. The easiest thing, she thinks, is if this rage she feels could just be drowned, like an orphaned cat.

"Grace honey, if you don't stop drinking coffee you're going to have to pee before your old buddy Nestor gets through the invocation," Rita says. "He does it in Latin or something, don't say I didn't warn you. Are the kids up? I swear they'd sleep right through church if we let them. Now why is that? Remember when they were babies? They wouldn't sleep late on a weekend if you paid them a hundred dollars."

"You better go roust them out," says Naomi. "Sunday school starts at nine."

"The boys and I aren't going," Grace says without looking up. She can feel the change in the air of the kitchen.

"Not going to church on Easter Sunday?" Naomi asks.

"I better go listen to the early weather and see if this storm's breaking up. I want to know what I'm in for as long as we're driving back this morning." Rita is still staring at her, but Naomi has had the good manners to turn back around and tend to her sausages. Grace gets up, runs scalding water in her coffee cup, and plunks it down hard in the rack. Memories have been coming to her all morning—Nestor's and Clarence's magazines, for one thing. The ugliness that every one of them knew about. She knows there will be more to remember. She could forgive the act, she thinks, but not the attitude. Because an attitude doesn't ask and it doesn't end.

"The boys didn't bring the right clothes for church," she tells Rita and Naomi as she walks out of the room.

The TV weatherman is jokey and annoying, not taking seriously the fact that bad weather can affect people's lives. He tucks his thumbs in the armpits of his tight gray suit and flaps his elbows, saying, "It's a nice day for ducks out there."

But as they turn out onto the interstate she can see for herself that the sky is lighter far to the west, toward Louisville, on the other side of the low thunderheads. Randall would just now be getting the Sunday paper, walking out barefoot on the sidewalk, on dry ground. She braces herself for the road and drives for the light.

JUMP-UP DAY

Jericha believed herself already an orphan—her mother was in the ground by the time she could walk on it—so the loss of her father when it came was not an exceptional thing. This was the nuns' theory, anyway, used to explain her indifference to their sympathy. Also, they reasoned, the father was not actually dead but only gone home to convalesce in England, where the hospitals were superior. (They called it "the mainland," though surely aware that England, too, is an island.) The good doctor had come here in the first place across two seas, Atlantic and Caribbean, to coax the disease out of the reluctant St. Lucians, and for his trouble he fell down trembling with it himself. In the opinion of informed observers, it was the cruel irony of God's will.

Bilharzia is a disease carried by snails. He could not have made this more clear, even going so far as to draw diagrams of the life cycle of the schistosome—an endless circle leading from water to human liver and back again—in an effort to impress upon his young daughter the importance of avoiding the seductive rivers full of cool, frog-naked children and women slapping their slick laundry on the rocks. It was dangerous even to walk without shoes in the back garden where invisible infections were drawn up like cricket songs along the wet grass. But secretly Jericha dug her toes into the cool dirt like earthworms going home, and lay in the vines at the water's edge watching little fish and the birds that hunted them, and it wasn't she but her God-fearing and educated father who had to be bundled up in blankets and flown back to London, leaving Jericha, with nominal instructions, in the care of the Sisters of St. Anthony.

The convent was a centuries-old thing eaten with vines, not right in the town of Soufrière but near enough so that Jericha did not care for the way it smelled. Frankly, she held her nose and said it stank like the henhouse when a mongoose has spoiled the eggs. Sister Armande, who considered this difficult child her special duty, took her into town and marched with her up the slope of the volcano itself in an effort to convince her that it wasn't St. Anthony's or even Soufrière but something deep inside the earth and enormously important that was the source of the odor. Sister Armande put her heart into the trip, drawing out of her black sleeve the twelve cents apiece for entry to the sulfur baths built by Louis XVI for his army. The woman and child stood by the crusted pots of rock, not holding hands but clutching their paper tickets and watching the black water boil up, and Jericha could not see how Louis XVI's men could have thought it a privilege to bathe at all, much less in water that smelled like rotten eggs.

Sister Armande and her sisters of the veil were from France and Ireland but a long time in St. Lucia, accustomed to uplifting the supremely unfortunate. But even the most generous or near-sighted souls in the convent could not fail to notice it: Jericha was trouble. She threw screeching fits when forced into proper clothes, and by virtue of superior stamina spent most of her life running where she pleased in a pair of ragged trousers snatched from the sisters' remnants-and-pieces bin. Her hair presented itself as a defiant, white-blond haystack, until the inventive Sister Josepha tamed it into eight tight braids that had to be renewed only once a week, an honor for which the sisters drew straws. The other orphans called her Anansi the Spider and Jericha did not care. She seemed as greedy for insults as a beggar for bread.

She wanted only one thing, a bicycle. She had been unimpressed by the sulfurous volcano, but the city of Soufrière itself, just a short way from the convent, seemed to promise her something. And, since she asked for little and seemed to need so much, the nuns were persuaded. With a prayer that puberty, when it came, would domesticate her, they looked heavenward and gave her the bicycle, leaving her at first stunned, then grimly preoccupied, as if she'd had it all her life and it required a great deal of attention. While the other orphans in the convent school wrestled with English lessons, the sisters overlooked Jericha's absences. The English language was not what Jericha lacked, and nothing short of lock and key, anyway, could have improved her attendance.

So nearly every afternoon she was left free to pedal the steep brick streets of town. There were shantytowns, and there were villas nested in scarlet clouds of bougainvillaea. At any time, without expecting it, she might round a bend and come onto the view of a pair of pointed mountains, the Pitons, plunging straight down like suicides into the aquamarine bay. And when this happened Jericha stood on the low wall meant to prevent children from falling to their deaths, and she spread her arms and let herself fill with the belief that she could fly.

Jericha was no more aware of loneliness than of her bizarre appearance. She didn't remember having been other than solitary: a peculiarly but unquestionably privileged child, without peers. During the seven years she lived with her father in Vieux Fort she knew only Mr. Ledmond, her British tutor; Sebastian, the gardener who raised spotted rabbits (and whom her father called an insufferably superstitious black); and a handful of children half Jericha's age who swam like sea birds and ran along high tree branches without fear. She coexisted with these remarkable children in a companionship of mutual scorn. Having spent her life as a foreigner, she knew how to behave.

But in Soufrière there were more varieties of people than had existed in Vieux Fort. There were the brightly-dressed foreign women, who moved through town with half-closed eyes and purses hung over their arms like bracelets, buying baskets woven with shells, or egrets carved from goats' horns. White women, whose assured, honey-lazy voices revealed a kinship with the white mistresses of the hilltop villas, who snapped their fingers at servants and held ice in their mouths and watched their children on wide green lawns like cricket fields.

About the dead one who was her mother, Jericha knew nothing; she saw so many kinds of women. These rich ones and their opposites, the lean-armed brown women who loaded boats in the harbor, their hips swinging in wide arcs as the bananas piled high on their heads moved in a perfect straight line up the gangplank toward the ship's dark, refrigerated hold.

Jericha lay hidden in croton and poinsettia hedges, absorbing the colors of linen dresses and January flowers, the nervous parrots in cages, the broad stripes of sunset like paint across the harbor. It was too late, long after the Epiphany mass, when she picked up her bicycle from the hedge and pumped her way home to the convent on Jump-up Day.

She had forgotten the holiday and would have to pay a price for missing the high mass, for even Jericha had to bend to the limited expectations of God, but she wasn't thinking of this until she heard the steel drum and saw the little band of dancers in the road. Their legs and arms were wrapped in tight bands of pink and green paper, and whirling in the center was the Jump-up, painted entirely white, his feet, body, hair, eyelids all cracked and seamed with the thickness of whitewash. His dance was a throbbing of the body, down on the ground and then up, again and again. He contorted his face impressively with cries that made no sound, and he spun from one foot to the other, and the long white strips of cloth tied at his knees and elbows flew in circles like propellers of a frenetic airplane.

The other dancers chanted in patois: *Ka-li-e, ka-quitte, nous ka quitte jusqu'a jour ouvert.* The little band had come by the same road from Soufrière to the ancient stone gate of St. Anthony's, to perform for the nuns and children and a goat or two who watched from within the compound. Jericha watched from a distance. She had seen the Jump-up on nearly every Epiphany holiday, but never at this time of evening, and never was it anything more than steel-drum music and black men dressed up for children and a few of their parents' coins. In this light it seemed something else.

Then it was over. The children applauded with dirt-colored hands and the drummer hammered a livelier song for moving on. The dancers' bare feet rang on the iron bars of the grate, set into the road over a pit, that prevented goats from escaping through the convent gate.

They moved up the road toward her, and Jericha felt an urgent wish to hide. But the Jump-up had already seen her, and behind the dramatic distortion of his face there was something more genuine: he recognized her.

The white face with painted turtle eyelids moved forward and back in the darkness, and the breathy voice touched her skin: "The doctor's child. From Vieux Fort." Jericha filled with the water weight that came to her sometimes in dreams.

"I have a need for you," the Jump-up said. "I'll come, you be here." He spun in the air so close that the white rags touched her face.

She pedaled fast down the road, her skin burning where the cloth had touched it. The bicycle wheels rang trrrat!

over the livestock grate and she was inside the compound, alone in the shadowed outskirts of the yard. Her chest curled over from the pounding against the inside, and she waited for it to stop. She pelted a stone at a jet-black billy named Maximilian grazing under the mango. The pebble shot for the eye but missed, deflected off a horn that gleamed in the shadow. The goat bleated.

"The sisters are going to cook you, Max. We'll have you in a stew," she said. "You're the next one."

In her dreams the Jump-up did come back, always appearing in the sky and commanding her to take hold of the white-feathered streamers that trailed from his wings. They flew across the bay toward the Pitons and whatever lay beyond them, toward a feeling of home. So high over the harbor that there were no people below, no dark women loading boats, only columns of ants filing into the split skins of mangos that floated at the shoreline. Not people but ants, a thing you could step on and smash.

"Not here," the Jump-up said, as their shadows moved over the water and fell on the tin-roofed town, and when they dipped close to the bougainvillaea hilltops and women with ice in their mouths he said again, "Not here," and even when the jungle darkness had swallowed their shadows, he said it. "Not here, somewhere else. Somewhere up ahead."

And then too much time passed by and her fear hardened into a rock in the back of her mind, a certainty, that the Jump-up would break his promise and not return.

But he did. It was nine weeks to the day. Jericha was going home from Soufrière again, late again, standing up on the pedals to try to cover the five miles before it went dark. A rising moon hung over the mountains, higher already than the sun settling down like a roosting red hen onto the sea. She sang, to help herself push the pedals.

Anansi he is a spider,
Anansi he is a man,
Anansi he . . .

She saw the thing stretched full length across the road, slithering and poisonous, with the cross on its head that every child in the southern islands has been taught to recognize: *fer-de-lance*. The snake that just bites once. Her breath cut at her throat and passed down to her legs, and she pulled hard to stop. When the front wheel touched it, the snake collapsed into shadow on the dust.

Planted on the root of the shadow at the edge of the road was a staff, and a man holding it. In the near darkness his face was silver-black and Jericha saw now the two faces at once, white-painted and black. The Jump-up was the same man she had seen once in Vieux Fort, and his name was Benedict Jett. The gardener Sebastian had stood with a rabbit's nape in each hand and pointed out this one standing up straight behind the frangipani, looking at them. Sebastian had called him the Obeah Man.

"Boy or girl? What are you?"

Jericha looked at the bicycle's shadow across her foot. The Obeah Man was speaking to her now, not just looking. "Boy," she said.

"Boy. Ha! What are you called?"

"Jeri."

"Jeri. From now on, from this minute, I want you to study what I say. We have a job to do."

She watched the ground near the bottom of the Obeah Man's staff. The staff was made from knotted black wood, glossy, stripped of its bark.

"What sort of job?" she asked.

"I'm not saying that right now. I'll say that when the time comes. Do you know why I'm coming to you?"

"No."

"Do you know what obeah is?"

"No."

The Obeah Man turned away, speaking in the direction of the trees. "This is what people call working science. You understand?"

She nodded. She did not understand.

"When they are sick, or the business is going bad. Or if a man wants some woman to look at him." He laughed deeply, a laugh full of breath. "They come to me."

Jericha's hands were wet on the rubber handles of her bicycle. "I'm not sick," she said.

The Obeah Man faced her, and looked at her carefully.

"I need to get back," she said. "The sisters will send after me if it gets dark."

"Ha. It will get dark, you don't have to be guessing about that." He smiled, a little more like a man now than a spook. "I am going your same way, and past it," he said. "We can walk along."

They walked along. Jericha held the handlebars and watched for snakes.

"Your father was the white doctor in Vieux Fort," he said quietly. "I made no truck with him, but he was humbugging me. Telling the people not to trust in my medicine. He said, Black man's foolishness. Did he tell you that?"

"No."

"All right, what I'm saying is true. He went to the doctor's shop in Vieux Fort where I say to people go and get their powders, and he told the shop not to sell my powders anymore. He said he could make the law to stop them. He wants the people to use his medicine and no other kind."

Jericha thought for the first time in many months of her father, a spectacled man with clean hands.

"He was a doctor," she said.

"Listen to me. Some people think a white doctor can make you well every time, but he can't. Like praying to God—sometime He will, sometime He won't. If you are smart, you have a powder to back you up."

"Is that why he got sick? My father?"

"He was making cross tracks with me, I said. Saying he was a bigger man than I. You think I am a fool?"

"No."

"And did he get sick?"

"Yes."

"All right."

They walked some more. Suddenly he said, "You are a good strong child. This is the job we have to do. Do you know the thing they call a jumby?"

Jericha shrugged her shoulders.

"Boy, girl! Don't truck with me. If you know a thing, say it."

"I don't know what it is."

"A jumby is a jump-up. Somebody called up from the dead. You call her up to do a job, and then you put her down again. But sometimes she is humbugging you and she won't go down again. You understand?"

"Yes."

A thick darkness was growing up in the treetops. Jericha could see birds moving restlessly, without noise, among the branches over their heads. She knew that snakes could also be in trees.

The man said, "Are you afraid?"

"Of course I'm not."

"Then I want you to come on Sunday to Laborie. You know Laborie? Down this road, after the sisters', first is Choiseul, then Laborie, then Vieux Fort. You know the way?" He asked it kindly, and ordinarily, like an invitation to tea. As a friend would ask, she imagined, though she had not had one.

"I know the way," Jericha said. In truth, she had never explored the road past Choiseul. On her bicycle she always went the other way, toward Soufrière.

"Study this," the Obeah Man said. "On Sunday, go to Laborie. You can find me on the main road in town, the next past Cato's store, where they sell rum. It's near the church. Ask for Benedict."

"I'll have to go to mass first. The sisters will know if I don't."

"All right, that's good. You go to mass first. Take this and wear it inside your shirt." He held out a small bag tied with string. Jericha stopped pushing her bicycle and took the bag carefully in her palms.

"Should I wear it every day, or just to mass?"

"Every day; don't lose it. And to the mass also. And another thing. Do you know *l'eau bénite?*"

"Holy water? Of course."

"Take that water and put it on your head like so. Then come down to Laborie. Don't forget what I'm telling you." He raised his staff over his head so its shadow no longer touched the road. Jericha waited to see if the Obeah Man would fly away.

"Go now. Go!" he cried, and Jericha stumbled onto her bike and fled away through the shadows.

By Friday she could not believe the Obeah Man or a place called Laborie existed. But the pouch filled with sweet-smelling, crumbled leaves was real, and to be safe she wore it around her neck day and night. She was tormented with colored dreams she could not remember. On Saturday, as a test, she asked Sister Armande if she would someday take her to Laborie.

"What would a little girl want in Laborie? It's only a little town." Sister Armande had finished with Jericha's hair and was tending her "God's small extravagances," her orchids. Ragged boys brought them down from the forest for ten cents apiece, and she grew them on planks wired to the veranda posts.

"Is it far? Laborie?"

"Not at all." Sister Armande's hands moved quickly among the leaves. "It's just past Choiseul."

Jericha made up her mind to go. Before mass ended Sunday noon she anointed herself with holy water, genuflected in a hurry, and tore through the yard to her bicycle. Only Maximilian saw her go.

The road rose steeply against the shoulder of the Gros Piton, shortening her breath, then led down into Choiseul. She loudly rang her bicycle bell and shouted at some children and brown goats to get out of the road. They let goats run wild here, her father said one time. They eat boiled leaves while a good meal stands by the back door eating the curtains.

Just beyond the town, broad, banana-planted valleys opened on both sides of the road. It was Sunday, but still there were men and women standing ankle-deep in the ditches between the banana rows, working for someone, hacking with their machetes. Beyond them the ocean glittered, dotted with boats. Sooner than she expected, she was in Laborie.

She easily found the church, the only building of any importance, and a store that said "CATO. SPIRITS" in front on a painted board. Next door, a woman in a tight, straight dress was hanging out laundry.

"I'm looking for Benedict," Jericha said.

The woman waved toward the side street, and took a clothespin out of her mouth. "He's not too good to lie in another man's shade. You'll find him over that way."

She walked her bicycle up an alley that smelled of salt fish, and found Benedict sitting against a wall in the shade of the breadfruit across the way. He wore a weathered hat and was smoking a pipe made of carved white bone, or plastic.

"Hullo," Jericha said. She did not believe now that there was magic in this ordinary man.

Benedict spoke suddenly. "Why did you come here?"

"You told me to."

"Have you been putting it about to people, that you were coming here to see me?"

She shook her head quickly.

"Where is your guardian?"

Jericha hesitated. She felt for the pouch inside her blouse and held it up, her eyebrows questioning.

"Good. You studied what I told you. Come and sit down here. We have plenty of time." He motioned toward the ground beside him where the dirt was worn as smooth as pavement. Jericha sat down and leaned back against the wall, in exactly the same fashion as the Obeah Man.

For a long time they said nothing. While Benedict looked inside his pipe, Jericha studied the leafy hands and large dimpled fruits of the breadfruit tree. Small, glossy blackbirds hung upside-down on some of the fruits, pecking holes through the green skin and pulling out white strings of flesh.

"Are we going to do the thing you said?"

"What thing is that, child?" Benedict looked at her with a slanted eye.

"Kill that thing. The jumby."

Benedict looked up the alley. "You can't kill a thing that's dead."

"Then what?"

"You'll see that in time. It takes time to know a thing well, Jericha."

She glanced quickly away, startled by the sound of her name. This man knew things. They watched a breeze sift through the breadfruit, from bottom to top, scattering the birds.

"I drove your father away," he said. "Do you know about this?"

"He got schistosomiasis."

Benedict looked at her sharply. "What is that?"

"Don't you know?" she asked in a scornful voice she knew. "You get it from some sort of tiny things in the water.

The poor people get it. Sometimes they get it bad the way my father did, but most times it just makes them lazy."

"Whooo," Benedict said. "Who told you this, lazy and poor? That is the *fwedi*. You know who gets sick with this? The man that works hardest and gets a day's pay for standing all the time with his feet wet. Go up on the banana plantation, you'll find plenty *fwedi*. Never did I see so much of this sickness before white man's bananas came to call."

"Did you ever have it?"

"Me? I protect myself."

"And my father?"

"All right. Did he protect himself?"

"He took some kind of medicine."

"Did he have a guardian?"

"No."

"So. He was a fool."

Jericha looked at the Obeah Man's black fingernails.

"I won't tell you a lie," he said suddenly. "The jumby worked on him. I called her up for this. Now she won't go down again."

"How do you know?"

"I know." He fingered the thick pouch that hung on a steel watch chain around his neck. The inside of his arm was erupted with constellations of purple sores. Jericha said nothing.

After a while the Obeah Man pointed down the alley, at the sea. "You smell that? Rain."

Jericha sniffed the air and shook her head.

"Close your eyes."

She squeezed her eyelids shut. Salt and beach mud filled her nostrils. "I can smell it!" She opened her eyes, startled.

The Obeah Man rubbed her shoulder and laughed. "You keep your nose to the sea, child, you'll never get wet." Then his eyes changed and he asked, "Do you know maweepoui root?"

"No."

"You drink it. It takes care of you, if she comes." He extracted from his pocket a bottle of brownish liquid, stoppered with rolled leaves wrapped in string. "Don't lose it, and don't forget. You drink a little every day."

"Does it taste bad?" Jericha had some experience with medicine.

The Obeah Man pointed his finger. "This is death and life, not candy. You don't know what can happen. Now go. Do what the sisters say, but keep your guardians close to you. Come back here Sunday. Just like before, do everything the same."

It was dark before she reached the convent. The stars shone in patches between the clouds rolling up from the ocean. On the deserted banana plantation the long drainage ditches, channels of infected water, shone like an army of luminous snakes marching toward the sea.

She returned three times to Laborie before the job was done. The sisters knew nothing of it, since by good fortune it was Lent and they were preoccupied with penitence. As Easter approached there was also talk of the pageant and feast, in which Maximilian would play a large role.

Loolai Thérèse, a tiny brown girl with a deformed foot, was moribund at the prospect. She couldn't bring herself to confess her anguish to the sisters, but told Jericha many times over.

"They want to eat him," she said one afternoon in the garden. Jericha sat above her on the lowest branch of the mango, to which the goat was tethered.

"I know."

"Maxi-mi." She stroked his nose. Her eyes were as brown and wet as animal eyes. "Don't you feel sorry for him?" she asked, looking up into the branches.

"No." Jericha attempted to drop a ripe mango on the goat's hindquarters. "He's just an old black billy."

"But he'll die. If the sisters kept him he could make milk."

"Only a girl goat makes milk," Jericha informed her. "I'm quite sure of it."

Loolai Thérèse thought about this. "Well, he could be put to some use," she said finally, "besides eating. He could pull a cart."

"That's stupid. That's how you think. In England people eat goats and whatever else they want, whenever they feel like it." She aimed another mango and let it fall.

The final trip to Laborie was on Good Friday. Following instructions, she went straight from the evening service. It was not an actual mass, she'd learned from Sister Armande, since Jesus was in Limbo until the resurrection on Sunday and therefore could not be called upon. But Benedict said it would serve.

Benedict was waiting where he told her, in a truck, a sawed-off thing, just a cab with wheels behind it and no truckbed. But it functioned. They drove on a mud road into the jungle, passing through dark thickets of greenheart and calabash. Small eyes shone from the branches.

While he drove, Benedict leaned forward and pulled another container from his pocket, a tin flask, and unscrewed the cap with his hand on the steering wheel. It smelled like Sister Mary Matthew's cherry brandy. He drank, and then offered the flask to Jericha. The liquid was fiery and tore at her lungs, but she tipped the metal bottle and drank it again.

"Will that protect me too?" She felt dizzy.

He laughed. "The sisters don't give you that, uh?"

She took deep breaths. "No."

He laid the flask down on the seat. There was a good-sized basket there too, riding on the seat between them. It was covered with a cloth and smelled, Jericha thought, like church.

Benedict turned on the headlamps of the truck and darkness drew in around them, covering all but the two mud tracks ahead.

"How did you make her jump up?" she asked. Over the weeks, Benedict had grown more talkative about the jumby.

"This is the easiest thing, to make her come up. She was a troubled soul. She wanted to do harm to a white man."

"Why?"

"She was used by a white soldier boy down at Vieux Fort. He used her and went his way, and she was left with it. She tried to get rid of the baby with St. John's bush. Do you know this bush?"

"No."

"You boil the leaves and the water turns to blood, and then you drink it. But she waited too long. She bled, bled, until she died. So she's troubled, not peaceful dead."

"Do you think she wants to hurt me too?"

"Do you have your guardian? Did you drink the maw-eepoui, like I told you?"

"Yes."

The floor of the truck was pocked with rust and holes, and Jericha could see the dark road beneath her feet as they passed over it. "That kind of medicine is bad, if it made the lady bleed so much and killed her," she said.

"She waited too long, I told you. And it wasn't obeah that killed her. It was the soldier boy. Don't you know that?"

Jericha shook her head. "That medicine is bad."

"I want you to study something." The Obeah Man looked at her. "Nothing is all good or all bad. Maybe the sisters tell you that, and the doctor, but it isn't so."

They stopped. Ahead of them a small clearing was lit by the headlamps. When he turned them off, the distant trees jumped close and crowded around the truck like beggars.

"I want to go back now, please."

The Obeah Man offered her the flask again, but she shook her head. He put his hand on her many-braided head. "Listen, don't fear. She doesn't want to hurt you. We worked on the doctor, but then we felt sorry for what we did to him."

She looked at the dark holes in the floor.

"She is sorry, don't you see this?"

Jericha saw that he wanted very much for her to believe it, and say he was right. She knew that was the most important thing. He kept looking at her, the same eyes that spied through the frangipani that day a long time ago while she stood in the garden with Sebastian. She said nothing.

"She won't be harming us," he said. "Because you are the doctor's child. A good child with no people to look after you."

She felt the Obeah Man's hand on her shoulder. She felt the skin, the fingers, the blood beating inside.

"Do you understand?"

"Not really."

The Obeah Man carried the basket across the small clearing and Jericha followed, the mud sucking at her shoes. The sky was a moonless black. The forest closed over them again, and then drew back, and they were in another open place. She could barely see him bending down to set the basket on the ground. They squatted on their heels, side by side.

"Can you see a tree? This is the silk-cotton tree."

Jericha stared at the dark shape in the center of the open place. Gradually it became a tree. Under it was a large round shape, a woman. Jericha held her breath.

"Is that the jumby?"

The shape moved, laughed, got up. Benedict laughed too, a little. "That's Maman," he said.

"Yours?" Jericha was amazed that a grown man could have a mother.

The woman pressed her nose against Benedict's cheek, then came and squatted down with her face very near. Jericha could see the print of her dress, ships and flags. "Look at this girl, she is good!" the woman cried. The voice was warm, like arms around her, and the laugh too. She spoke in patois to Benedict and took some things from the basket, a roll and some salt fish.

"This tree is where you have to put her down," she said to Jericha. "A jumby can rest well here." Then she set down a little stool she carried with her, and sat and ate the roll. She watched everything they did, but didn't speak anymore.

"Did anybody ever tell you about this tree?" Benedict asked.

Jericha shook her head.

"The most powerful tree," he said. "That's all. Every part is poisonous. You see the snake in the branches? That is Gro Maman. She lives there, in the branch."

"Is it poisonous too?"

"Gro Maman isn't a snake. She's like a man, but stronger. She watches you all the time."

"Like Jesus?"

"Yes. Like Jesus."

He lifted an incense burner out of the basket. He lit the charcoal, blew on it until it glowed orange, then poured the incense over it. Jericha watched; she had longed to do these things altar boys did, but couldn't, of course. The scent stung pleasantly in her nose.

"Follow," the Obeah Man said. He swung the incense in a circle around himself and Jericha, then slowly circled the tree, singing in patois.

"Hoc es corpus meum," Jericha sang very quietly, and "Anansi he is a spider." She felt dizzy and wished for a small

sip again of cherry brandy. She stepped into the holes in the mud left by the Obeah Man's footsteps.

The tree grew more distinct as they walked: its white trunk was dotted with black, waxy thorns that shone like tiny animal horns. At its base, the trunk flared out in flattened, triangular wings like the sails of ships.

They stopped. "Walk toward the tree," the Obeah Man commanded. "Stop when I tell you."

Jericha took one step, then another. Then another.

"Stop!"

She didn't move.

"Stay there. Don't touch any part of the tree. This is a powerful tree."

The Obeah Man sang again, and Jericha understood some of the words. *Ou save ça ou pede:* You have lost something. Now you will find it at last. She sang quietly, *Dona nobis pacem.*

Light came into the clearing: stars, she thought at first, or silvery pieces of falling cloud, but the light was falling down from the tree into a white carpet that floated just above the ground. It moved like water, slowly. She felt it roll over her feet.

"Something is falling on me," she said, standing unsteadily.

"Silk cotton," he told her. "It fell already a long time ago, don't worry. You're just seeing it now."

"It touched my feet," she cried out. "You said it was poison." The air filled with sounds and slithering shadows that drooped from the branches over her head.

"It won't hurt you. Ask for the favor of Gro Maman. Ask her to forgive us," the Obeah Man said.

Ants swarmed up out of the ground and covered her shoes and white legs. Jericha choked on childish sounds in her throat, and slapped at the ants stinging her legs. When she touched them they turned to handfuls of black mud. It was only mud.

"I don't care." She sobbed the words angrily, bent over, rubbing the mud in circles on her legs. "The jumby, or you—I don't care what you did to my father." She rubbed the mud into her knees and then into her arms and the tears on her face, pressing it into a warm mud skin.

"Shh." The Obeah Man was beside her.

"I don't care what you did," she said quietly, not wanting to be crying. "The one I miss is my mother."

"Take this," he said, and formed Jericha's hands into a cradle around something smooth and cold. "It's a hen's egg. Her Good Friday egg. Take it to Gro Maman."

The hand on her shoulder moved her toward the tree, gently, and then let her go. With mud in her mouth she looked up into the branches to find her shape, her eyes. She stooped at the base of the tree among its white, thorned wings and laid the egg in a nest of roots. The silk cotton under her feet was a cloud. There were mountains and harbors, women down there loading boats, women and not ants. There were worlds under her feet, and over her head too—when they flew over the Pitons she had forgotten to look up. There is always something over your head and you're never on top or on the bottom either, you're in the center.

On the seat of the truck she sat between Benedict and his *maman*, holding her sharp knees to her chest and crying without tears. She leaned on the bouncing softness of a shoulder, and then there was a soft arm around her, and then a lap. The incense burner in the basket at their feet made quiet metal sounds.

She awakened when she was lifted out of the truck and carried, along with her bicycle, through the stone gate into the garden.

On Easter Sunday Jericha rose before dawn. She stole from her bed through the corridors, her bare feet noiseless on the cool stone, and out into the garden. She untied the rope around Maximilian's neck and chased him from the compound, hitting lightly at the animal's hind legs with a piece of long grass. At the convent gate the goat hesitated only for a second, almost not at all, before it ran sure-footed over the iron grate into the jungle.

ROSE-JOHNNY

Rose-Johnny wore a man's haircut and terrified little children, although I will never believe that was her intention. For her own part she inspired in us only curiosity. It was our mothers who took this fascination and wrung it, through daily admonitions, into the most irresistible kind of horror. She was like the old wells, covered with ancient rotting boards and overgrown with weeds, that waited behind the barns to swallow us down: our mothers warned us time and again not to go near them, and still were certain that we did.

My own mother was not one of those who had a great deal to say about her, but Walnut Knobs was a small enough town so that a person did not need to be told things directly. When I had my first good look at her, at close range, I was ten years old. I fully understood the importance of the encounter.

What mattered to me at the time, though, was that it was something my sister had not done before me. She was five years older, and as a consequence there was hardly an achievement in my life, nor even an article of clothing, that had not first been Mary Etta's. But, because of the circumstances of my meeting Rose-Johnny, I couldn't tell a living soul about it, and so for nearly a year I carried the secret torment of a great power that can't be used. My agitation was not relieved but made worse when I told the story to myself, over and over again.

She was not, as we always heard, half man and half woman, something akin to the pagan creatures whose naked torsos are inserted in various shocking ways into parts of animal bodies. In fact, I was astonished by her ordinariness. It is true that she wore Red Wing boots like my father. And also there was something not quite womanly in her face, but maybe any woman's face would look the same with that haircut. Her hair was coal black, cut flat across the top of her round head, so that when she looked down I could see a faint pale spot right on top where the scalp almost surfaced.

But the rest of her looked exactly like anybody's mother in a big flowered dress without a waistline and with two faded spots in front, where her bosom rubbed over the counter when she reached across to make change or wipe away the dust.

People say there is a reason for every important thing that happens. I was sent to the feed store, where I spoke to Rose-Johnny and passed a quarter from my hand into hers, because it was haying time. And because I was small for my age. I was not too small to help with tobacco setting in the spring, in fact I was better at it than Mary Etta, who complained about the stains on her hands, but I was not yet big enough to throw a bale of hay onto the flatbed. It was the time of year when Daddy complained about not having boys. Mama said that at least he oughtn't to bother going into town for the chicken mash that day because Georgeann could do it on her way home from school.

Mama told me to ask Aunt Minnie to please ma'am give me a ride home. "Ask her nice to stop off at Lester Wall's store so you can run in with this quarter and get five pound of laying mash."

I put the quarter in my pocket, keeping my eye out to make certain Mary Etta understood what I had been asked to do. Mary Etta had once told me that I was no better than the bugs that suck on potato vines, and that the family was going to starve to death because of my laziness. It was one of the summer days when we were on our knees in the garden picking off bugs and dropping them into cans of coal oil. She couldn't go into town with Aunt Minnie to look at dress patterns until we finished with the potato bugs. What she said, exactly, was that if I couldn't work any harder than that, then she might just as well throw *me* into a can of coal oil. Later she told me she hadn't meant it, but I intended to remember it nonetheless.

Aunt Minnie taught the first grade and had a 1951 Dodge. That is how she referred to her car whenever she spoke of it. It was the newest automobile belonging to anyone related to us, although some of the Wilcox cousins had once come down to visit from Knoxville in a Ford they were said to have bought the same year it was made. But I saw that car and did not find it nearly as impressive as Aunt Minnie's, which was white and immense and shone like glass. She paid a boy to polish it every other Saturday.

On the day she took me to Wall's, she waited in the car while I went inside with my fist tight around the quarter. I had never been in the store before, and although I had passed by it many times and knew what could be bought there, I had never imagined what a wonderful combination of warm, sweet smells of mash and animals and seed corn it would contain. The dust lay white and thin on everything like a bridal veil. Rose-Johnny was in the back with a water can, leaning over into one of the chick tubs. The steel rang with the sound of confined baby birds, and a light bulb shining up from inside the tub made her face glow white. Mr. Wall, Rose-Johnny's Pa, was in the front of the store talking to two men about a horse. He didn't notice me as I crept up to the counter. It was Rose-Johnny who came forward to the cash register.

"And what for you, missy?"

She is exactly like anybody's mama, was all I could think, and I wanted to reach and touch her flowered dress. The two men were looking at me.

"My mama needs five pound of laying mash and here's a quarter for it." I clicked the coin quickly onto the counter.

"Yes, ma'am." She smiled at me, but her boots made heavy, tired sounds on the floor. She made her way slowly, like a duck in water, over to the row of wooden bins that stood against the wall. She scooped the mash into a paper bag and weighed it, then shoved the scoop back into the bin. A little cloud of dust rose out of the mash up into the window. I watched her from the counter.

"Don't your mama know she's wasting good money on chicken mash? Any fool chicken will eat corn." I jumped when the man spoke. It was one of the two, and they were standing so close behind me I would have had to look right straight up to see their faces. Mr. Wall was gone.

"No sir, they need mash," I said to the man's boots.

"What's that?" It was the taller man doing the talking.

"They need mash," I said louder. "To lay good sturdy eggs for selling. A little mash mixed in with the corn. Mama says it's got oster shells in it."

"Is that a fact," he said. "Did you hear that, Rose-Johnny?" he called out. "This child says you put oster shells in that mash. Is that right?"

When Rose-Johnny came back to the cash register she was moon-eyed. She made quick motions with her hands and pushed the bag at me as if she didn't know how to talk.

"Do you catch them osters yourself, Rose-Johnny? Up at Jackson Crick?" The man was laughing. The other man was quiet.

Rose-Johnny looked all around and up at the ceiling.

She scratched at her short hair, fast and hard, like a dog with ticks.

When the two men were gone I stood on my toes and leaned over the counter as far as I could. "Do you catch the osters yourself?"

She hooked her eyes right into mine, the way the bit goes into the mule's mouth and fits just so, one way and no other. Her eyes were the palest blue of any I had ever seen. Then she threw back her head and laughed so hard I could see the wide, flat bottoms of her back teeth, and I wasn't afraid of her.

When I left the store, the two men were still outside. Their boots scuffed on the front-porch floorboards, and the shorter one spoke.

"Child, how much did you pay that woman for the chicken mash?"

"A quarter," I told him.

He put a quarter in my hand. "You take this here, and go home and tell your daddy something. Tell him not never to send his little girls to Wall's feed store. Tell him to send his boys if he has to, but not his little girls." His hat was off, and his hair lay back in wet orange strips. A clean line separated the white top of his forehead from the red-burned hide of his face. In this way, it was like my father's face.

"No, sir, I can't tell him, because all my daddy's got is girls."

"That's George Bowles's child, Bud," the tall man said. "He's just got the two girls."

"Then tell him to come for hisself," Bud said. His eyes had the sun in them, and looked like a pair of new pennies.

Aunt Minnie didn't see the man give me the quarter because she was looking at herself in the side-view mirror of the Dodge. Aunt Minnie was older than Mama, but everyone mistook her for the younger because of the way she fixed herself up. And, of course, Mama was married.

Mama said if Aunt Minnie ever found a man she would act her age.

When I climbed in the car she was pulling gray hairs out of her part. She said it was teaching school that caused them, but early gray ran in my mama's family.

She jumped when I slammed the car door. "All set?"

"Yes, ma'am," I said. She put her little purple hat back on her head and slowly pushed the long pin through it. I shuddered as she started up the car.

Aunt Minnie laughed. "Somebody walked over your grave."

"I don't have a grave," I said. "I'm not dead."

"No, you most certainly are not. That's just what they say when a person shivers like that." She smiled. I liked Aunt Minnie most of the time.

"I don't think they mean your real grave, with you in it," she said after a minute. "I think it means the place where your grave is going to be someday."

I thought about this for a while. I tried to picture the place, but could not. Then I thought about the two men outside Wall's store. I asked Aunt Minnie why it was all right for boys to do some things that girls couldn't.

"Oh, there's all kinds of reasons," she said. "Like what kinds of things, do you mean?"

"Like going into Wall's feed store."

"Who told you that?"

"Somebody."

Aunt Minnie didn't say anything.

Then I said, "It's because of Rose-Johnny, isn't it?"

Aunt Minnie raised her chin just a tiny bit. She might have been checking her lipstick in the mirror, or she might have been saying yes.

"Why?" I asked.

"Why what?"

"Why because of Rose-Johnny?"

"I can't tell you that, Georgeann."

"Why can't you tell me?" I whined. "Tell me."

The car rumbled over a cattle grate. When we came to the crossing, Aunt Minnie stepped on the brake so hard we both flopped forward. She looked at me. "Georgeann, Rose-Johnny is a Lebanese. That's all I'm going to tell you. You'll understand better when you're older."

When I got home I put the laying mash in the henhouse. The hens were already roosting high above my head, clucking softly into their feathers and shifting back and forth on their feet. I collected the eggs as I did every day, and took them into the house. I hadn't yet decided what to do about the quarter, and so I held on to it until dinnertime.

Mary Etta was late coming down, and even though she had washed and changed she looked pale as a haunt from helping with the haying all day. She didn't speak and she hardly ate.

"Here, girls, both of you, eat up these potatoes," Mama said after a while. "There's not but just a little bit left. Something to grow on."

"I don't need none then," Mary Etta said. "I've done growed all I'm going to grow."

"Don't talk back to your mama," Daddy said.

"I'm not talking back. It's the truth." Mary Etta looked at Mama. "Well, it is."

"Eat a little bite, Mary Etta. Just because you're in the same dresses for a year don't mean you're not going to grow no more."

"I'm as big as you are, Mama."

"All right then." Mama scraped the mashed potatoes onto my plate. "I expect now you'll be telling me you don't want to grow no more either," she said to me.

"No, ma'am, I won't," I said. But I was distressed, and looked sideways at the pink shirtwaist I had looked forward to inheriting along with the grown-up shape that would have to be worn inside it. Now it appeared that I was condemned to my present clothes and potato-shaped body;

keeping these forever seemed to me far more likely than the possibility of having clothes that, like the Wilcox automobile, had never before been owned. I ate my potatoes quietly. Dinner was almost over when Daddy asked if I had remembered to get the laying mash.

"Yes, sir. I put it in the henhouse." I hesitated. "And here's the quarter back. Mr. Wall gave me the mash for nothing."

"Why did he do that?" Mama asked.

Mary Etta was staring like the dead. Even her hair looked tired, slumped over the back of her chair like a long black shadow.

"I helped him out," I said. "Rose-Johnny wasn't there, she was sick, and Mr. Wall said if I would help him clean out the bins and dust the shelves and water the chicks, then it wouldn't cost me for the laying mash."

"And Aunt Minnie waited while you did all that?"

"She didn't mind," I said. "She had some magazines to look at."

It was the first important lie I had told in my life, and I was thrilled with its power. Every member of my family believed I had brought home the laying mash in exchange for honest work.

I was also astonished at how my story, once I had begun it, wouldn't finish. "He wants me to come back and help him again the next time we need something," I said.

"I don't reckon you let on like we couldn't pay for the mash?" Daddy asked sternly.

"No, sir. I put the quarter right up there on the counter. But he said he needed the help. Rose-Johnny's real sick."

He looked at me like he knew. Like he had found the hole in the coop where the black snake was getting in. But he just said, "All right. You can go, if Aunt Minnie don't mind waiting for you."

"You don't have to say a thing to her about it," I said.

"I can walk home the same as I do every day. Five pound of mash isn't nothing to carry."

"We'll see," Mama said.

That night I believed I would burst. For a long time after Mary Etta fell asleep I twisted in my blankets and told the story over to myself, both the true and false versions. I talked to my doll, Miss Regina. She was a big doll, a birthday present from my Grandma and Grandpa Bowles, with a tiny wire crown and lovely long blond curls.

"Rose-Johnny isn't really sick," I told Miss Regina. "She's a Lebanese."

I looked up the word in Aunt Minnie's Bible dictionary after school. I pretended to be looking up St. John the Baptist but then turned over in a hurry to the *L*'s while she was washing her chalkboards. My heart thumped when I found it, but I read the passage quickly, several times over, and found it empty. It said the Lebanese were a seafaring people who built great ships from cedar trees. I couldn't believe that even when I was older I would be able, as Aunt Minnie promised, to connect this with what I had seen of Rose-Johnny. Nevertheless, I resolved to understand. The following week I went back to the store, confident that my lie would continue to carry its own weight.

Rose-Johnny recognized me. "Five pounds of laying mash," she said, and this time I followed her to the feed bins. There were flecks of white dust in her hair.

"Is it true you come from over the sea?" I asked her quietly as she bent over with the scoop.

She laughed and rolled her eyes. "A lot of them says I come from the moon," she said, and I was afraid she was going to be struck dumb and animal-eyed as she was the time before. But, when she finished weighing the bag, she just said, "I was born in Slate Holler, and that's as far from here as I ever been or will be."

"Is that where you get the osters from?" I asked, looking into the mash and trying to pick out which of the colored flecks they might be.

Rose-Johnny looked at me for a long time, and then suddenly laughed her big laugh. "Why, honey child, don't you know? Osters comes from the sea."

She rang up twenty-five cents on the register, but I didn't look at her.

"That was all, wasn't it?"

I leaned over the counter and tried to put tears in my eyes, but they wouldn't come. "I can't pay," I said. "My daddy said to ask you if I could do some work for it. Clean up or something."

"Your daddy said to ask me that? Well, bless your heart," she said. "Let me see if we can't find something for you to do. Bless your little heart, child, what's your name?"

"Georgeann," I told her.

"I'm Rose-Johnny," she said, and I did not say that I knew it, that like every other child I had known it since the first time I saw her in town, when I was five or six, and had to ask Mama if it was a man or a lady.

"Pleased to meet you," I said.

We kept it between the two of us: I came in every week to help with the pullets and the feed, and took home my mash. We did not tell Mr. Wall, although it seemed it would not have mattered one whit to him. Mr. Wall was in the store so seldom that he might not have known I was there. He kept to himself in the apartment at the back where he and Rose-Johnny lived.

It was she who ran the store, kept the accounts, and did the orders. She showed me how to feed and water the pullets and ducklings and pull out the sick ones. Later I learned how to weigh out packages of seed and to mix the different kinds of mash. There were lists nailed to the wall telling how much cracked corn and oats and grit to put in. I followed the recipes with enormous care, adding tiny amounts at a time to the bag on the hanging scales until the needle touched the right number. Although she was patient with me, I felt slow next to Rose-Johnny, who never had to look at the lists and used the scales only to check herself. It seemed to me she knew how to do more things than anyone I had ever known, woman or man.

She also knew the names of all the customers, although she rarely spoke to them. Sometimes such a change came over her when the men were there that it wasn't clear to me whether she was pretending or had really lost the capacity to speak. But afterward she would tell me their names and everything about them. Once she told me about Ed Charney, Sr. and Bud Mattox, the two men I had seen the first day I was in the store. According to Rose-Johnny, Ed had an old red mule he was in the habit of mistreating. "But even so," she said, "Ed's mule don't have it as bad as Bud's wife." I never knew how she acquired this knowledge.

When she said "Bud Mattox," I remembered his penny-colored eyes and connected him then with all the Mattox boys at school. It had never occurred to me that eyes could run in families, like early gray.

Occasionally a group of black-skinned children came to the store, always after hours. Rose-Johnny opened up for them. She called each child by name, and asked after their families and the health of their mothers' laying hens.

The oldest one, whose name was Cleota, was shaped like Mary Etta. Her hair was straight and pointed, and smelled to me like citronella candles. The younger girls had plaits that curved out from their heads like so many handles. Several of them wore dresses made from the same bolt of cloth, but they were not sisters. Rose-Johnny filled a separate order for each child.

I watched, but didn't speak. The skin on their heels and palms was creased, and as light as my own. Once, after they had left, I asked Rose-Johnny why they only came into the store when it was closed.

"People's got their ways," she said, stoking up the wood stove for the night. Then she told me all their names again, starting with Cleota and working down. She looked me in the eye. "When you see them in town, you speak. Do you hear? By *name*. I don't care who is watching."

I was allowed to spend half an hour or more with Rose-Johnny nearly every day after school, so long as I did not neglect my chores at home. Sometimes on days that were rainy or cold Aunt Minnie would pick me up, but I preferred to walk. By myself, without Mary Etta to hurry me up.

As far as I know, my parents believed I was helping Mr. Wall because of Rose-Johnny's illness. They had no opportunity to learn otherwise, though I worried that someday Aunt Minnie would come inside the store to fetch me, instead of just honking, or that Daddy would have to go to Wall's for something and see for himself that Rose-Johnny was fit and well. Come springtime he would be needing to buy tobacco seed.

It was soon after Christmas when I became consumed with a desire to confess. I felt the lies down inside me like cold, dirty potatoes in a root cellar, beginning to sprout and crowd. At night I told Miss Regina of my dishonesty and the things that were likely to happen to me because of it. In so doing, there were several times I nearly confessed by accident to Mary Etta.

"Who's going to wring your neck?" she wanted to know, coming into the room one night when I thought she was downstairs washing the supper dishes.

"Nobody," I said, clutching Miss Regina to my pillow. I pretended to be asleep. I could hear Mary Etta starting to brush her hair. Every night before she went to bed she sat with her dress hiked up and her head hung over between her knees, brushing her hair all the way down to the floor.

This improved the circulation to the hair, she told me, and would prevent it turning. Mary Etta was already beginning to get white hairs.

"Is it because Mama let you watch Daddy kill the cockerels? Did it scare you to see them jump around like that with their necks broke?"

"I'm not scared," I murmured, but I wanted so badly to tell the truth that I started to cry. I knew, for certain, that something bad was going to happen. I believe I also knew it would happen to my sister, instead of me.

"Nobody's going to hurt you," Mary Etta said. She smoothed my bangs and laid my pigtails down flat on top of the quilt. "Give me Miss Regina and let me put her up for you now, so you won't get her hair all messed up."

I let her have the doll. "I'm not scared abcut the cockerels, Mary Etta. I promise." With my finger, under the covers, I traced a cross over my heart.

When Rose-Johnny fell ill I was sick with guilt. When I first saw Mr. Wall behind the counter instead of Rose-Johnny, so help me God, I prayed this would be the day Aunt Minnie would come inside to get me. Immediately after, I felt sure God would kill me for my wickedness. I pictured myself falling dead beside the oat bin. I begged Mr. Wall to let me see her.

"Go on back, littl'un. She told me you'd be coming in," he said.

I had never been in the apartment before. There was little in it beyond the necessary things and a few old photographs on the walls, all of the same woman. The rooms were cold and felt infused with sickness and an odor I incorrectly believed to be medicine. Because my father didn't drink, I had never before encountered the smell of whiskey.

Rose-Johnny was propped on the pillows in a lifeless flannel gown. Her face changed when she saw me, and I remembered the way her face was lit by the light bulb in the chick tub, the first time I saw her. With fresh guilt I threw myself on her bosom.

"I'm sorry. I could have paid for the mash. I didn't mean to make you sick." Through my sobs I heard accusing needly wheezing sounds in Rose-Johnny's chest. She breathed with a great pulling effort.

"Child, don't talk foolish."

As weeks passed and Rose-Johnny didn't improve, it became clear that my lie was prophetic. Without Rose-Johnny to run the store, Mr. Wall badly needed my help. He seemed mystified by his inventory and was rendered helpless by any unusual demand from a customer. It was March, the busiest time for the store. I had turned eleven, one week before Mary Etta turned sixteen. These seven days out of each year, during which she was only four years older, I considered to be God's greatest gifts to me.

The afternoon my father would come in to buy the vegetable garden and tobacco seed was an event I had rehearsed endlessly in my mind. When it finally did transpire, Mr. Wall's confusion gave such complete respectability to my long-standing lie that I didn't need to say a word myself in support of it. I waited on him with dignity, precisely weighing out his tobacco seed, and even recommended to him the white runner beans that Mr. Wall had accidentally overstocked, and which my father did not buy.

Later on that same afternoon, after the winter light had come slanting through the dusty windows and I was alone in the store cleaning up, Cleota and the other children came pecking at the glass. I let them in. When I had filled all the orders Cleota unwrapped their coins, knotted all together into a blue handkerchief. I counted, and counted again. It was not the right amount, not even half.

"That's what Miss Rose-Johnny ast us for it," Cleota

said. "Same as always." The smaller children—Venise, Anita, Little-Roy, James—shuffled and elbowed each other like fighting cocks, paying no attention. Cleota gazed at me calmly, steadily. Her eyebrows were two perfect arches.

"I thank you very much," I said, and put the coins in their proper places in the cash drawer.

During that week I also discovered an epidemic of chick droop in the pullets. I had to pull Mr. Wall over by the hand to make him look. There were more sick ones than well.

"It's because it's so cold in the store," I told him. "They can't keep warm. Can't we make it warmer in here?"

Mr. Wall shrugged at the wood stove, helpless. He could never keep a fire going for long, the way Rose-Johnny could.

"We have to try. The one light bulb isn't enough," I said. The chicks were huddled around the bulb just the way the men would collect around the stove in the mornings to say howdy-do to Mr. Wall and warm up their hands on the way to work. Except the chicks were more ruthless: they climbed and shoved, and the healthy ones pecked at the eyes and feet of the sick ones, making them bleed.

I had not noticed before what a very old man Mr. Wall was. As he stared down at the light, I saw that his eyes were covered with a film. "How do we fix them up?" he asked me.

"We can't. We've got to take the sick ones out so they won't all get it. Rose-Johnny puts them in that tub over there. We give them water and keep them warm, but it don't do any good. They've got to die."

He looked so sad I stood and patted his old freckled hand.

I spent much more time than before at the store, but no longer enjoyed it particularly. Working in the shadow of Rose-Johnny's expertise, I had been a secret witness to a wondrous ritual of counting, weighing, and tending. Together we created little packages that sailed out like ships to all parts of the county, giving rise to gardens and barnyard life in places I had never even seen. I felt superior to my schoolmates, knowing that I had had a hand in the creation of their families' poultry flocks and their mothers' kitchen gardens. By contrast, Mr. Wall's bewilderment was pathetic and only increased my guilt. But each day I was able to spend a little time in the back rooms with Rose-Johnny.

There were rumors about her illness, both before and after the fact. It did not occur to me that I might have been the source of some of the earlier rumors. But, if I didn't think of this, it was because Walnut Knobs was overrun with tales of Rose-Johnny, and not because I didn't take notice of the stories. I did.

The tales that troubled me most were those about Rose-Johnny's daddy. I had heard many adults say that he was responsible for her misfortune, which I presumed to mean her short hair. But it was also said that he was a colored man, and this I knew to be untrue. Aunt Minnie, when I pressed her, would offer nothing more than that if it were up to her I wouldn't go near either one of them, advice which I ignored. I was coming to understand that I would not hear the truth about Rose-Johnny from Aunt Minnie or anyone else. I knew, in a manner that went beyond the meanings of words I could not understand, that she was no more masculine than my mother or aunt, and no more lesbian than Lebanese. Rose-Johnny was simply herself, and alone.

And yet she was such a capable woman that I couldn't believe she would be sick for very long. But as the warm weather came she grew sluggish and pale. Her slow, difficult breathing frightened me. I brought my schoolbooks and read to her from the foot of the bed. Sometimes the rather ordinary adventures of the boy in my reader would make her laugh aloud until she choked. Other times she fell asleep while I read, but then would make me read those parts over again.

She worried about the store. Frequently she would ask about Mr. Wall and the customers, and how he was managing. "He does all right," I always said. But eventually my eagerness to avoid the burden of further lies, along with the considerable force of my pride, led me to confess that I had to tell him nearly everything. "He forgets something awful," I told her.

Rose-Johnny smiled. "He used to be as smart as anything, and taught me. Now I've done taught you, and you him again." She was lying back on the pillows with her eyes closed and her plump hands folded on her stomach.

"But he's a nice man," I said. I listened to her breathing. "He don't hurt you does he? Your pa?"

Nothing moved except her eyelids. They opened and let the blue eyes out at me. I looked down and traced my finger over the triangles of the flying-geese patch on the quilt. I whispered, "Does he make you cut off your hair?"

Rose-Johnny's eyes were so pale they were almost white, like ice with water running underneath. "He cuts it with a butcher knife. Sometimes he chases me all the way down to the river." She laughed a hissing laugh like a boy, and she had the same look the yearling calves get when they are cornered and jump the corral and run to the woods and won't be butchered. I understood then that Rose-Johnny, too, knew the power of a lie.

It was the youngest Mattox boy who started the fight at school on the Monday after Easter. He was older than me, and a boy, so nobody believed he would hit me, but when he started the name calling I called them right back, and he threw me down on the ground. The girls screamed and ran to get the teacher, but by the time she arrived I had a bloody nose and had bitten his arm wonderfully hard.

Miss Althea gave me her handkerchief for my nose and dragged Roy Mattox inside to see the principal. All the other children stood in a circle, looking at me.

"It isn't true, what he said," I told them. "And not about Rose-Johnny either. She isn't a pervert. I love her."

"Pervert," one of the boys said.

I marveled at the sight of my own blood soaking through the handkerchief. "I love her," I said.

I did not get to see Rose-Johnny that day. The door of Wall's store was locked. I could see Mr. Wall through the window, though, so I banged on the glass with the flats of my hands until he came. He had the strong medicine smell on his breath.

"Not today, littl'un." The skin under his eyes was dark blue.

"I need to see Rose-Johnny." I was irritated with Mr. Wall, and did not consider him important enough to prevent me from seeing her. But evidently he was.

"Not today," he said. "We're closed." He shut the door and locked it.

I shouted at him through the glass. "Tell her I hit a boy and bit his arm, that was calling her names. Tell her I fought with a boy, Mr. Wall."

The next day the door was open, but I didn't see him in the store. In the back, the apartment was dark except for the lamp by Rose-Johnny's bed. A small brown bottle and a glass stood just touching each other on the night table. Rose-Johnny looked asleep but made a snuffing sound when I climbed onto the bottom of the bed.

"Did your daddy tell you what I told him yesterday?"

She said nothing.

"Is your daddy sick?"

"My daddy's dead," she said suddenly, causing me to swallow a little gulp of air. She opened her eyes, then closed them again. "Pa's all right, honey, just stepped out, I imagine." She stopped to breathe between every few words. "I didn't mean to give you a fright. Pa's not my daddy, he's my mama's daddy."

I was confused. "And your real daddy's dead?"

She nodded. "Long time."

"And your mama, what about her? Is she dead too?"

"Mm-hmm," she said, in the same lazy sort of way Mama would say it when she wasn't really listening.

"That her?" I pointed to the picture over the bed. The woman's shoulders were bare except for a dark lace shawl. She was looking backward toward you, over her shoulder.

Rose-Johnny looked up at the picture, and said yes it was.

"She's pretty," I said.

"People used to say I looked just like her." Rose-Johnny laughed a wheezy laugh, and coughed.

"Why did she die?"

Rose-Johnny shook her head. "I can't tell you that."

"Can you when I'm older?"

She didn't answer.

"Well then, if Mr. Wall isn't your daddy, then the colored man is your daddy," I said, mostly to myself.

She looked at me. "Is that what they say?"

I shrugged.

"Does no harm to me. Every man is some color," she said.

"Oh," I said.

"My daddy was white. After he died my mama loved another man and he was brown."

"What happened then?"

"What happened then," she said. "Then they had a sweet little baby Johnny." Her voice was more like singing than talking, and her eyes were so peacefully closed I was afraid they might not open again. Every time she breathed there was the sound of a hundred tiny birds chirping inside her chest.

"Where's he?"

"Mama's Rose and sweet little baby Johnny," she sang it like an old song. "Not nothing bad going to happen to them, not nobody going to take her babies." A silvery moth flew into the lamp and clicked against the inside of the lampshade. Rose-Johnny stretched out her hand toward the night table. "I want you to pour me some of that bottle."

I lifted the bottle carefully and poured the glass half full. "That your medicine?" I asked. No answer. I feared this would be another story without an end, without meaning. "Did somebody take your mama's babies?" I persisted.

"Took her man, is what they did, and hung him up from a tree." She sat up slowly on her elbows, and looked straight at me. "Do you know what lynched is?"

"Yes, ma'am," I said, although until that moment I had not been sure.

"People will tell you there's never been no lynchings north of where the rivers don't freeze over. But they done it. Do you know where Jackson Crick is, up there by Floyd's Mill?" I nodded. "They lynched him up there, and drowned her baby Johnny in Jackson Crick, and it was as froze as you're ever going to see it. They had to break a hole in the ice to do it." She would not stop looking right into me. "In that river. Poor little baby in that cold river. Poor Mama, what they did to Mama. And said they would do to me, when I got old enough."

She didn't drink the medicine I poured for her, but let it sit. I was afraid to hear any more, and afraid to leave. I watched the moth crawl up the outside of the lampshade.

And then, out of the clear blue, she sat up and said, "But they didn't do a thing to me!" The way she said it, she sounded more like she ought to be weighing out bags of mash than sick in bed. "Do you want to know what Mama did?"

I didn't say.

"I'll tell you what she did. She took her scissors and cut my hair right off, every bit of it. She said, 'From now on,

I want you to be Rose and Johnny both.' And then she went down to the same hole in the crick where they put baby Johnny in."

I sat with Rose-Johnny for a long time. I patted the lump in the covers where her knees were, and wiped my nose on my sleeve. "You'd better drink your medicine, Rose-Johnny," I said. "Drink up and get better now," I told her. "It's all over now."

It was the last time I saw Rose-Johnny. The next time I saw the store, more than a month later, it was locked and boarded up. Later on, the Londroski brothers took it over. Some people said she had died. Others thought she and Mr. Wall had gone to live somewhere up in the Blue Ridge, and opened a store there. This is the story I believed. In the years since, when passing through that part of the country, I have never failed to notice the Plymouth Rocks and Rhode Islands scratching in the yards, and the tomato vines tied up around the back doors.

I would like to stop here and say no more, but there are enough half-true stories in my past. This one will have to be heard to the end.

Whatever became of Rose-Johnny and her grandfather, I am certain that their going away had something to do with what happened on that same evening to Mary Etta. And I knew this to be my fault.

It was late when I got home. As I walked I turned Rose-Johnny's story over and over, like Grandpa Bowles's Indian penny with the head on both sides. You never could stop turning it over.

When I caught sight of Mama standing like somebody's ghost in the front doorway I thought she was going to thrash me, but she didn't. Instead she ran out into the yard and picked me up like she used to when I was a little girl, and carried me into the house.

"Where's Daddy?" I asked. It was suppertime, but there was no supper.

"Daddy's gone looking for you in the truck. He'll be back directly, when he don't find you."

"Why's he looking for me? What did I do?"

"Georgeann, some men tried to hurt Mary Etta. We don't know why they done it, but we was afraid they might try to hurt you."

"No, ma'am, nobody hurt me," I said quietly. "Did they kill her?" I asked.

"Oh Lordy no," Mama said, and hugged me. "She's all right. You can go upstairs and see her, but don't bother her if she don't want to be bothered."

Our room was dark, and Mary Etta was in bed crying. "Can I turn on the little light?" I asked. I wanted to see Mary Etta. I was afraid that some part of her might be missing.

"If you want to."

She was all there: arms, legs, hair. Her face was swollen, and there were marks on her neck.

"Don't stare at me," she said.

"I'm sorry." I looked around the room. Her dress was hanging over the chair. It was her best dress, the solid green linen with covered buttons and attached petticoat that had taken her all winter to make. It was red with dirt and torn nearly in half at the bodice.

"I'll fix your dress, Mary Etta. I can't sew as good as you, but I can mend," I said.

"Can't be mended," she said, but then tried to smile with her swollen mouth. "You can help me make another one."

"Who was it that done it?" I asked.

"I don't know." She rolled over and faced the wallpaper. "Some men. Three or four of them. Some of them might have been boys, I couldn't tell for sure. They had things over their faces."

"What kind of things?"

"I don't know. Just bandanners and things." She spoke quietly to the wall. "You know how the Mattoxes have those funny-colored eyes? I think some of them might of been Mattoxes. Don't tell, Georgeann. Promise."

I remembered the feeling of Roy Mattox's muscle in my teeth. I did not promise.

"Did you hit them?"

"No. I screamed. Mr. Dorsey come along the road."

"What did they say, before you screamed?"

"Nothing. They just kept saying, 'Are you the Bowles girl, are you the Bowles girl?' And they said nasty things."

"It was me they was looking for," I said. And no matter what anyone said, I would not believe otherwise. I took to my bed and would not eat or speak to anyone. My convalescence was longer than Mary Etta's. It was during that time that I found my sister's sewing scissors and cut off all my hair and all of Miss Regina's. I said that my name was George-Etta, not Georgeann, and I called my doll Rose-Johnny.

For the most part, my family tolerated my distress. My mother retrimmed my hair as neatly as she could, but there was little that could be done. Every time I looked in the mirror I was startled and secretly pleased to see that I looked exactly like a little boy. Mama said that when I went back to school I would have to do the explaining for myself. Aunt Minnie said I was going through a stage and oughtn't to be pampered.

But there was only a month left of school, and my father let Mary Etta and me stay home to help set tobacco. By the end of the summer my hair had grown out sufficiently so that no explanations were needed. Miss Regina's hair, of course, never grew back.

WHY I AM A DANGER TO THE PUBLIC

Bueno, if I get backed into a corner I can just about raise up the dead. I'll fight, sure. But I am no lady wrestler. If you could see me you would know this thing is a *joke*—Tony, my oldest, is already taller than me, and he's only eleven. So why are they so scared of me I have to be in jail? I'll tell you.

Number one, this strike. There has never been one that turned so many old friends *chingándose*, not here in Bolton. And you can't get away from it because Ellington don't just run the mine, they own our houses, the water we drink and the dirt in our shoes and pretty much the state of New Mexico as I understand it. So if something is breathing, it's on one side or the other. And in a town like this that matters because everybody you know some way, you go to the same church or they used to babysit your kids, something. Nobody is a stranger.

My sister went down to Las Cruces New Mexico and got a job down there, but me, no. I stayed here and got married to Junior Morales. Junior was my one big mistake. But I like Bolton. From far away Bolton looks like some kind of all-colored junk that got swept up off the street after a big old party and stuffed down in the canyon. Our houses are all exactly alike, company houses, but people paint them yellow, purple, colors you wouldn't think a house could be.

If you go down to the Big Dipper and come walking home *loca* you still know which one is yours. The copper mine is at the top of the canyon and the streets run straight uphill; some of them you can't drive up, you got to walk. There's steps. Oliver P. Snapp, that used to be the mailman for the west side, died of a heart attack one time right out there in his blue shorts. So the new mailman refuses to deliver to those houses; they have to pick up their mail at the P.O.

Now, this business with me and Vonda Fangham, I can't even tell you what got it started. I never had one thing in the world against her, no more than anybody else did. But this was around the fourth or fifth week so everybody knew by then who was striking and who was crossing. It don't take long to tell rats from cheese, and every night there was a big old fight in the Big Dipper. Somebody punching out his brother or his best friend. All that and no paycheck, can you imagine?

So it was a Saturday and there was just me and Corvallis Smith up at the picket line, setting in front of the picket shack passing the time of day. Corvallis is *un tipo*, he is real tall and lifts weights and wears his hair in those corn rows that hang down in the back with little pieces of aluminum foil on the ends. But good-looking in a certain way. I went out with Corvallis one time just so people would have something to talk about, and sure enough, they had me getting ready to have brown and black polka-dotted babies. All you got to do to get pregnant around here is have two beers with somebody in the Dipper, so watch out.

"What do you hear from Junior," he says. That's a joke; everybody says it including my friends. See, when Manuela wasn't hardly even born one minute and Tony still in diapers, Junior says, "Vicki, I can't find a corner to piss in around this town." He said there was jobs in Tucson and he would send a whole lot of money. Ha ha. That's how I got started up at Ellington. I was not going to support my kids in no little short skirt down at the Frosty King. That was eight years ago. I got started on the track gang, laying down rails for the cars that go into the pit, and now I am a crane operator. See, when Junior left I went up the hill and made such a rackus they had to hire me up there, hire me or shoot me, one.

"Oh, I hear from him about the same as I hear from Oliver P. Snapp," I say to Corvallis. That's the rest of the joke.

It was a real slow morning. Cecil Smoot was supposed to be on the picket shift with us but he wasn't there yet. Cecil will show up late when the Angel Gabriel calls the Judgment, saying he had to give his Datsun a lube job.

"Well, looka here," says Corvallis. "Here come the ladies." There is this club called Wives of Working Men, just started since the strike. Meaning Wives of Scabs. About six of them was coming up the hill all cram-packed into Vonda Fangham's daddy's air-condition Lincoln. She pulls the car right up next to where mine is at. My car is a Buick older than both my two kids put together. It gets me where I have to go.

They set and look at us for one or two minutes. Out in that hot sun, sticking to our T-shirts, and me in my work boots—I can't see no point in treating it like a damn tea party—and Corvallis, he's an eyeful anyway. All of a sudden the windows on the Lincoln all slide down. It has those electric windows.

"Isn't this a ni-i-ice day," says one of them, Doreen Carter. Doreen visited her sister in Laurel, Mississippi, for three weeks one time and now she has an accent. "Bein' payday an' all," she says. Her husband is the minister of Saint's Grace, which is scab headquarters. I quit going. I was raised up to believe in God and the union, but listen, if it comes to pushing or shoving I know which one of the two is going to keep tires on the car.

"Well, yes, it is a real nice day," another one of them says. They're all fanning theirselves with something paper.

I look, and Corvallis looks. They're fanning theirselves with their husbands' paychecks.

I haven't had a paycheck since July. My son couldn't go to Morse with his baseball team Friday night because they had to have three dollars for supper at McDonald's. Three damn dollars.

The windows start to go back up and they're getting ready to drive off, and I say, "Vonda Fangham, *vete al infierno*."

The windows whoosh back down.

"What did you say?" Vonda wants to know.

"I said, I'm surprised to see you in there with the scab ladies. I didn't know you had went and got married to a yellow-spine scab just so somebody would let you in their club."

Well, Corvallis laughs at that. But Vonda just gives me this look. She has a little sharp nose and yellow hair and teeth too big to fit behind her lips. For some reason she was a big deal in high school, and it's not her personality either. She was the queen of everything. Cheerleaders, drama club, every school play they ever had, I think.

I stare at her right back, ready to make a day out of it if I have to. The heat is rising up off that big blue hood like it's a lake all set to boil over.

"What I said was, Vonda Fangham, you can go to hell."

"I can't hear a word you're saying," she says. "Trash can't talk."

"This trash can go to bed at night and know I haven't cheated nobody out of a living. You want to see trash, *chica*, you ought to come up here at the shift change and see what kind of shit rolls over that picket line."

Well, that shit I was talking about was their husbands, so up go the windows and off they fly. Vonda just about goes in the ditch trying to get that big car turned around.

To tell you the truth I knew Vonda was engaged to get married to Tommy Jones, a scab. People said, Well, at least now Vonda will be just Vonda Jones. That name Fangham is *feo*, and the family has this whole certain way of showing off. Her dad's store, Fangham Drugs, has the biggest sign in town, as if he has to advertise. As if somebody would forget it was there and drive fifty-one miles over the mountains to Morse to go to another drugstore.

I couldn't care less about Tommy and Vonda getting engaged, I was just hurt when he crossed the line. Tommy was a real good man, I used to think. He was not ashamed like most good-looking guys are to act decent every once in a while. Me and him started out on the same track crew and he saved my butt one time covering the extra weight for me when I sprang my wrist. And he never acted like I owed him for it. Some guys, they would try to put the moves on me out by the slag pile. Shit, that was hell. And then I would be downtown in the drugstore and Carol Finch or somebody would go *huh-hmm*, clear her throat and roll her eyes, like, "Over here is what you want," looking at the condoms. Just because I'm up there with their husbands all day I am supposed to be screwing around. In all that mud, just think about it, in our steel toe boots that weigh around ten pounds, and our hard hats. And then the guys gave me shit too when I started training as a crane operator, saying a woman don't have no business taking up the good-paying jobs. You figure it out.

Tommy was different. He was a lone ranger. He didn't grow up here or have family, and in Bolton you can move in here and live for about fifty years and people still call you that fellow from El Paso, or wherever it was you come from. They say that's why he went in, that he was afraid if he lost his job he would lose Vonda too. But we all had something to lose.

That same day I come home and found Manuela and Tony in the closet. Like poor little kitties in there setting on the shoes. Tony was okay pretty much but Manuela was crying, screaming. I thought she would dig her eyes out.

Tony kept going, "They was up here looking for you!"

"Who was?" I asked him.

"Scab men," he said. "Çlifford Owens and Mr. Alphonso and them police from out of town. The ones with the guns."

"The State Police?" I said. I couldn't believe it. "The State Police was up here? What did they want?"

"They wanted to know where you was at." Tony almost started to cry. "Mama, I didn't tell them."

"He didn't," Manuela said.

"Well, I was just up at the damn picket shack. Anybody could have found me if they wanted to." I could have swore I saw Owens's car go right by the picket shack, anyway.

"They kept on saying where was you at, and we didn't tell them. We said you hadn't done nothing."

"Well, you're right, I haven't done nothing. Why didn't you go over to Uncle Manny's? He's supposed to be watching you guys."

"We was scared to go outside!" Manuela screamed. She was jumping from one foot to the other and hugging herself. "They said they'd get us!"

"Tony, did they say that? Did they threaten you?"

"They said stay away from the picket rallies," Tony said. "The one with the gun said he seen us and took all our pitchers. He said, your mama's got too big a mouth for her own good."

At the last picket rally I was up on Lalo Ruiz's shoulders with a bull horn. I've had almost every office in my local, and sergeant-at-arms twice because the guys say I have no toleration for BS. They got one of those big old trophies down at the union hall that says on it "MEN OF COPPER," and one time Lalo says, "Vicki ain't no Man of Copper, she's a damn stick of *mesquite*. She might break but she sure as hell won't bend."

Well, I want my kids to know what this is about. When

school starts, if some kid makes fun of their last-year's blue jeans and calls them trash I want them to hold their heads up. I take them to picket rallies so they'll know that. No law says you can't set up on nobody with a bull horn. They might have took my picture, though. I wouldn't be surprised.

"All I ever done was defend my union," I told the kids. "Even cops have to follow the laws, and it isn't no crime to defend your union. Your grandpapa done it and his papa and now me."

Well, my grandpapa one time got put on a railroad car like a cow, for being a Wobbly and a Mexican. My kids have heard that story a million times. He got dumped out in the desert someplace with no water or even a cloth for his head, and it took him two months to get back. All that time my granny and Tía Sonia thought he was dead.

I hugged Tony and Manuela and then we went and locked the door. I had to pull up on it while they jimmied the latch because that damn door had not been locked one time in seven years.

What we thought about when we wanted to feel better was: What a God-awful mess they got up there in the mine. Most of those scabs was out-of-towners and didn't have no idea what end of the gun to shoot. I heard it took them about one month to figure out how to start the equipment. Before the walkout there was some parts switched around between my crane and a locomotive, but we didn't have to do that because the scabs tied up the cat's back legs all by theirselves. Laying pieces of track backwards, running the conveyors too fast, I hate to think what else.

We even heard that one foreman, Willie Bunford, quit because of all the jackasses on the machinery, that he feared for his life. Willie Bunford used to be my foreman. He made fun of how I said his name, "Wee-lee!" so I called him Mr.

Bunford. So I have an accent, so what. When I was first starting on the crane he said, "You aren't going to get PG now, are you, Miss Morales, after I wasted four weeks training you as an operator? I know how you Mexican gals love to have babies." I said, "Mr. Bunford, as far as this job goes you can consider me a man." So I had to stick to that. I couldn't call up and say I'm staying in bed today because of my monthly. Then what does he do but lay off two weeks with so-call whiplash from a car accident on Top Street when I saw the whole story: Winnie Hask backing into his car in front of the Big Dipper and him not in it. If a man can get whiplash from his car getting bashed in while he is drinking beer across the street, well, that's a new one.

So I didn't cry for no Willie Bunford. At least he had the sense to get out of there. None of those scabs knew how to run the oxygen machine, so we were waiting for the whole damn place to blow up. I said to the guys, Let's go sit on Bolt Mountain with some beer and watch the fireworks.

The first eviction I heard about was the Frank Mickliffs, up the street from me, and then Joe Gomez on Alameda. Ellington wanted to clear out some company houses for the new hires, but how they decided who to throw out we didn't know. Then Janie Marley found out from her friend that babysits for the sister-in-law of a scab that company men were driving scab wives around town letting them pick out whatever house they wanted. Like they're going shopping and we're the peaches getting squeezed.

Friday of that same week I was out on my front porch thinking about a cold beer, just thinking, though, because of no cash, and here come an Ellington car. They slowed way, way down when they went by, then on up Church Street going about fifteen and then they come back. It was Vonda in there. She nodded her head at my house and the guy put something down on paper. They made a damn picture show out of it.

Oh, I was furious. I have been living in that house almost the whole time I worked for Ellington and it's all the home my kids ever had. It's a real good house. It's yellow. I have a big front porch where you can see just about everything, all of Bolton, and a railing so the kids won't fall over in the gulch, and a big yard. I keep it up nice, and my brother Manny being right next door helps out. I have this mother duck with her babies all lined up that the kids bought me at Fangham's for Mother's Day, and I planted marigolds in a circle around them. No way on this earth was I turning my house over to a scab.

The first thing I did was march over to Manny's house and knock on the door and walk in. "Manny," I say to him, "I don't want you mowing my yard anymore unless you feel like doing a favor for Miss Vonda." Manny is just pulling the pop top off a Coke and his mouth goes open at the same time; he just stares.

"Oh, no," he says.

"Oh, yes."

I went back over to my yard and Manny come hopping out putting on his shoes, to see what I'm going to do, I guess. He's my little brother but Mama always says "*Madre Santa*, Manuel, keep an eye on Vicki!" Well, what I was going to do was my own damn business. I pulled up the ducks, they have those metal things that poke in the ground, and then I pulled up the marigolds and threw them out on the sidewalk. If I had to get the neighbor kids to help make my house the ugliest one, I was ready to do it.

Well. The next morning I was standing in the kitchen drinking coffee, and Manny come through the door with this funny look on his face and says, "The tooth fairy has been to see you."

What in the world. I ran outside and there was *pink* petunias planted right in the circle where I already pulled up the marigolds. To think Vonda could sneak into my yard like a common thief and do a thing like that.

"Get the kids," I said. I went out and started pulling out petunias. I hate pink. And I hate how they smelled, they had these sticky roots. Manny woke up the kids and they come out and helped.

"This is fun, Mom," Tony said. He wiped his cheek and a line of dirt ran across like a scar. They were in their pajamas.

"Son, we're doing it for the union," I said. We threw them out on the sidewalk with the marigolds, to dry up and die.

After that I was scared to look out the window in the morning. God knows what Vonda might put in my yard, more flowers or one of those ugly pink flamingos they sell at Fangham's yard and garden department. I wouldn't put nothing past Vonda.

Whatever happened, we thought when the strike was over we would have our jobs. You could put up with high water and heck, thinking of that. It's like having a baby, you just grit your teeth and keep your eyes on the prize. But then Ellington started sending out termination notices saying, You will have no job to come back to whatsoever. They would fire you for any excuse, mainly strike-related misconduct, which means nothing, you looked cross-eyed at a policeman or whatever. People got scared.

The national office of the union was no help; they said, To hell with it, boys, take the pay cut and go on back. I had a fit at the union meeting. I told them it's not the pay cut, it's what all else they would take if we give in. "Ellington would not have hired me in two million years if it wasn't for the union raising a rackus about all people are created equal," I said. "Or half of you either because they don't like cunts or coloreds." I'm not that big of a person but I was standing up in front, and when I cussed, they shut up. "If my papa had been a chickenshit like you guys, I would be down at the Frosty King tonight in a little short skirt," I said. "You bunch of no-goods would be on welfare and your kids pushing drugs to pay the rent." Some of the guys laughed, but some didn't.

Men get pissed off in this certain way, though, where they have to tear something up. Lalo said, "Well, hell, let's drive a truck over the plant gate and shut the damn mine down." And there they go, off and running, making plans to do it. Corvallis had a baseball cap on backwards and was sitting back with his arms crossed like, Honey, don't look at me. I could have killed him.

"Great, you guys, you do something cute like that and we're dead ducks," I said. "We don't have to do but one thing, wait it out."

"Till when?" Lalo wanted to know. "Till hell freezes?" He is kind of a short guy with about twelve tattoos on each arm.

"Till they get fed up with the scabs pissing around and want to get the mine running. If it comes down to busting heads, no way. Do you hear me? They'll have the National Guards in here."

I knew I was right. The Boots in this town, the cops, they're on Ellington payroll. I've seen strikes before. When I was ten years old I saw a cop get a Mexican man down on the ground and kick his face till blood ran out of his ear. You would think I was the only one in that room that was born and raised in Bolton.

Ellington was trying to get back up to full production. They had them working twelve-hour shifts and seven-day weeks like Abraham Lincoln had never freed the slaves. We started hearing about people getting hurt, but just rumors;

it wasn't going to run in the paper. Ellington owns the paper.

The first I knew about it really was when Vonda come right to my house. I was running the vacuum cleaner and had the radio turned up all the way so I didn't hear her drive up. I just heard a knock on the door, and when I opened it: Vonda. Her skin looked like a flour tortilla. "What in the world," I said.

Her bracelets were going clack-clack-clack, she was shaking so hard. "I never thought I'd be coming to you," she said, like I was Dear Abby. "But something's happened to Tommy."

"Oh," I said. I had heard some real awful things: that a guy was pulled into a smelter furnace, and another guy got his legs run over on the tracks. I could picture Tommy either way, no legs or burnt up. We stood there a long time. Vonda looked like she might pass out. "Okay, come in," I told her. "Set down there and I'll get you a drink of water. Water is all we got around here." I stepped over the vacuum cleaner on the way to the kitchen. I wasn't going to put it away.

When I come back she was looking around the room all nervous, breathing like a bird. I turned down the radio.

"How are the kids?" she wanted to know, of all things.

"The kids are fine. Tell me what happened to Tommy."

"Something serious to do with his foot, that's all I know. Either cut off or half cut off, they won't tell me." She pulled this little hanky out of her purse and blew her nose. "They sent him to Morse in the helicopter ambulance, but they won't say what hospital because I'm not next of kin. He doesn't have any next of kin here, I *told* them that. I informed them I was the fiancée." She blew her nose again. "All they'll tell me is they don't want him in the Bolton hospital. I can't understand why."

"Because they don't want nobody to know about it," I told her. "They're covering up all the accidents."

"Well, why would they want to do that?"

"Vonda, excuse me please, but don't be stupid. They want to do that so we won't know how close we are to winning the strike."

Vonda took a little sip of water. She had on a yellow sun dress and her arms looked so skinny, like just bones with freckles. "Well, I know what you think of me," she finally said, "but for Tommy's sake maybe you can get the union to do something. Have an investigation so he'll at least get his compensation pay. I know you have a lot of influence on the union."

"I don't know if I do or not," I told her. I puffed my breath out and leaned my head back on the sofa. I pulled the bandana off my head and rubbed my hair in a circle. It's so easy to know what's right and so hard to do it.

"Vonda," I said, "I thought a lot of Tommy before all this shit. He helped me one time when I needed it real bad." She looked at me. She probably hated thinking of me and him being friends. "I'm sure Tommy knows he done the wrong thing," I said. "But it gets me how you people treat us like kitchen trash and then come running to the union as soon as you need help."

She picked up her glass and brushed at the water on the coffee table. I forgot napkins. "Yes, I see that now, and I'll try to make up for my mistake," she said.

Give me a break, Vonda, was what I was thinking. "Well, we'll see," I said. "There is a meeting coming up and I'll see what I can do. If you show up on the picket line tomorrow."

Vonda looked like she swallowed one of her ice cubes. She went over to the TV and picked up the kids' pictures one at a time, Manuela then Tony. Put them back down. Went over to the *armario* built by my grandpapa.

"What a nice little statue," she said.

"That's St. Joseph. Saint of people that work with their hands."

She turned around and looked at me. "I'm sorry about the house. I won't take your house. It wouldn't be right."

"I'm glad you feel that way, because I wasn't moving."

"Oh," she said.

"Vonda, I can remember when me and you were little girls and your daddy was already running the drugstore. You used to set up on a stool behind the counter and run the soda-water machine. You had a charm bracelet with everything in the world on it, poodle dogs and hearts and a real little pill box that opened."

Vonda smiled. "I don't have the foggiest idea what ever happened to that bracelet. Would you like it for your girl?"

I stared at her. "But you don't remember me, do you?"

"Well, I remember a whole lot of people coming in the store. You in particular, I guess not."

"I guess not," I said. "People my color was not allowed to go in there and set at the soda fountain. We had to get paper cups and take our drinks outside. Remember that? I used to think and *think* about why that was. I thought our germs must be so nasty they wouldn't wash off the glasses."

"Well, things have changed, haven't they?" Vonda said.

"Yeah." I put my feet up on the coffee table. It's my damn table. "Things changed because the UTU and the Machinists and my papa's union the Boilermakers took this whole fucking company town to court in 1973, that's why. This house right here was for whites only. And if there wasn't no union forcing Ellington to abide by the law, it still would be."

She was kind of looking out the window. She probably was thinking about what she was going to cook for supper.

"You think it wouldn't? You think Ellington would build a nice house for everybody if they could still put half of us in those falling-down shacks down by the river like I grew up in?"

"Well, you've been very kind to hear me out," she said.

"I'll do what you want, tomorrow. Right now I'd better be on my way."

I went out on the porch and watched her go down the sidewalk—click click, on her little spike heels. Her ankles wobbled.

"Vonda," I yelled out after her, "don't wear high heels on the line tomorrow. For safety's sake."

She never turned around.

Next day the guys were making bets on Vonda showing up or not. The odds were not real good in her favor. I had to laugh, but myself I really thought she would. It was a huge picket line for the morning shift change. The Women's Auxiliary thought it would boost up the morale, which needed a kick in the butt or somebody would be busting down the plant gate. Corvallis told me that some guys had a meeting after the real meeting and planned it out. But I knew that if I kept showing up at the union meetings and standing on the table and jumping and hollering, they wouldn't do it. Sometimes guys will listen to a woman.

The sun was just coming up over the canyon and already it was a hot day. Cicada bugs buzzing in the *paloverdes* like damn rattlesnakes. Me and Janie Marley were talking about our kids; she has a boy one size down from Tony and we trade clothes around. All of a sudden Janie grabs my elbow and says, "Look who's here." It was Vonda getting out of the Lincoln. Not in high heels either. She had on a tennis outfit and plastic sunglasses and a baseball bat slung over her shoulder. She stopped a little ways from the line and was looking around, waiting for the Virgin Mary to come down, I guess, and save her. Nobody was collecting any bets.

"Come on, Vonda," I said. I took her by the arm and stood her between me and Janie. "I'm glad you made it." But she wasn't talking, just looking around a lot.

After a while I said, "We're not supposed to have bats up here. I know a guy that got his termination papers for carrying a crescent wrench in his back pocket. He had forgot it was even in there." I looked at Vonda to see if she was paying attention. "It was Rusty Cochran," I said, "you know him. He's up at your dad's every other day for a prescription. They had that baby with the hole in his heart."

But Vonda held on to the bat like it was the last man in the world and she got him. "I'm only doing this for Tommy," she says.

"Well, so what," I said. "I'm doing it for my kids. So they can eat."

She kept squinting her eyes down the highway.

A bunch of people started yelling, "Here come the ladies!" Some of the women from the Auxiliary were even saying it. And here come trouble. They were in Doreen's car, waving signs out the windows: "We Support Our Working Men" and other shit not worth repeating. Doreen was driving. She jerked right dead to a stop, right in front of us. She looked at Vonda and you would think she had broke both her hinges the way her mouth was hanging open, and Vonda looked back at Doreen, and the rest of us couldn't wait to see what was next.

Doreen took a U-turn and almost ran over Cecil Smoot, and they beat it back to town like bats out of hell. Ten minutes later here come her car back up the hill again. Only this time her husband Milton was driving, and three other men from Saint's Grace was all in there besides Doreen. Two of them are cops.

"I don't know what they're up to but we don't need you getting in trouble," I told Vonda. I took the bat away from her and put it over my shoulder. She looked real white, and I patted her arm and said, "Don't worry." I can't believe I did that, now. Looking back.

They pulled up in front of us again but they didn't get

out, just all five of them stared and then they drove off, like whatever they come for they got.

That was yesterday. Last night I was washing the dishes and somebody come to the house. The kids were watching TV. I heard Tony slide the dead bolt over and then he yelled, "Mom, it's the Boot."

Before I can even put down a plate and get into the living room Larry Trevizo has pushed right by him into the house. I come out wiping my hands and see him there holding up his badge.

"Chief of Police, ma'am," he says, just like that, like I don't know who the hell he is. Like we didn't go through every grade of school together and go see *Suddenly Last Summer* one time in high school.

He says, "Mrs. Morales, I'm serving you with injunction papers."

"Oh, is that a fact," I say. "And may I ask what for?"

Tony already turned off the TV and is standing by me with his arms crossed, the meanest-looking damn eleven-year-old you ever hope to see in your life. All I can think of is the guys in the meeting, how they get so they just want to bust something in.

"Yes you may ask what for," Larry says, and starts to read, not looking any of us in the eye: "For being a danger to the public. Inciting a riot. Strike-related misconduct." And then real low he says something about Vonda Fangham and a baseball bat.

"What was that last thing?"

He clears his throat. "And for kidnapping Vonda Fangham and threatening her with a baseball bat. We got the affidavits."

"*Pa'fuera!*" I tell Larry Trevizo. I ordered him out of my house right then, told him if he wanted to see somebody get hurt with a baseball bat he could hang around my living room and find out. I trusted myself but not Tony. Larry got out of there.

The injunction papers said I was not to be in any public gathering of more than five people or I would be arrested. And what do you know, a squad of Boots was already lined up by the picket shack at the crack of dawn this morning with their hands on their sticks, just waiting. They knew I would be up there, I see that. They knew I would do just exactly all the right things. Like the guys say, Vicki might break but she don't bend.

They cuffed me and took me up to the jailhouse, which is in back of the Ellington main office, and took off my belt and my earrings so I wouldn't kill myself or escape. "With an earring?" I said. I was laughing. I could see this old rotten building through the office window; it used to be something or other but now there's chickens living in it. You could dig out of there with an earring, for sure. I said, "What's that over there, the Mexican jail? You better put me in there!"

I thought they would just book me and let me go like they did some other ones, before this. But no, I have to stay put. Five hundred thousand bond. I don't think this whole town could come up with that, not if they signed over every pink, purple, and blue house in Bolton.

It didn't hit me till right then about the guys wanting to tear into the plant. What they might do.

"Look, I got to get out by tonight," I told the cops. I don't know their names, it was some State Police I have never seen, seem like they just come up out of nowhere. I was getting edgy. "I have a union meeting and it's real important. Believe me, you don't want me to miss it."

They smiled. And then I got that terrible feeling you get when you see somebody has been looking you in the eye and smiling and setting a trap, and there you are in it like a damn rat.

What is going to happen I don't know. I'm keeping my

ears open. I found out my kids are driving Manny to distraction—Tony told his social-studies class he would rather have a jailbird than a scab mom, and they sent him home with a note that he was causing a dangerous disturbance in class.

I also learned that Tommy Jones was not in any accident. He got called off his shift one day and was took to Morse in a helicopter with no explanation. They put him up at Howard Johnson's over there for five days, his meals and everything, just told him not to call nobody, and today he's back at work. They say he is all in one piece.

Well, I am too.